The Short Stories of Edith Wharton

Volume I – Madame de Treymes & Others

Edith Newbold Jones was born in New York on January 24, 1862. Born into wealth, this background of privilege gave her a wealth of experience to eventually, after several false starts, produce many works based on it culminating in her Pulitzer Prize winning novel 'The Age Of Innocence'

Marriage to Edward Robbins Wharton, who was 12 years older in 1885 seemed to offer much and for some years they travelled extensively. After some years it was apparent that her husband suffered from acute depression and so the travelling ceased and they retired to The Mount, their estate designed by Edith. By 1908 his condition was said to be incurable and prior to divorcing Edward in 1913 she began an affair, in 1908, with Morton Fullerton, a Times journalist, who was her intellectual equal and allowed her writing talents to push forward and write the novels for which she is so well known.

Acknowledged as one of the great American writers with novels such as Ethan Frome and the House of Mirth among many. Wharton also wrote many short stories, including ghost stories and poems which we are pleased to publish.

Edith Wharton died of a stroke in 1937 at the Domaine Le Pavillon Colombe, her 18th-century house on Rue de Montmorency in Saint-Brice-sous-Forêt.

Index of Contents

MADAME DE TREYMES

I

John Durham, while he waited for Madame de Malrive to draw on her gloves, stood in the hotel doorway looking out across the Rue de Rivoli at the afternoon brightness of the Tuileries gardens.

His European visits were infrequent enough to have kept unimpaired the freshness of his eye, and he was always struck anew by the vast and consummately ordered spectacle of Paris: by its look of having been boldly and deliberately planned as a background for the enjoyment of life, instead of being forced into grudging concessions to the festive instincts, or barricading itself against them in unenlightened ugliness, like his own lamentable New York.

But to-day, if the scene had never presented itself more alluringly, in that moist spring bloom between showers, when the horse-chestnuts dome themselves in unreal green against a gauzy sky, and the very dust of the pavement seems the fragrance of lilac made visible, to-day for the first time the sense of a personal stake in it all, of having to reckon individually with its effects and influences, kept Durham from an unrestrained yielding to the spell. Paris might still be, to the unimplicated it doubtless still was, the most beautiful city in the world; but whether it were the most lovable or the most detestable depended for him, in the last analysis, on the buttoning of the white glove over which Fanny de Malrive still lingered.

The mere fact of her having forgotten to draw on her gloves as they were descending in the hotel lift from his mother's drawing-room was, in this connection, charged with significance to Durham. She was the kind of woman who always presents herself to the mind's eye as completely equipped, as made up of exquisitely cared for and finely-related details; and that the heat of her parting with his family should have left her unconscious that she was emerging gloveless into Paris, seemed, on the whole, to speak hopefully for Durham's future opinion of the city.

Even now, he could detect a certain confusion, a desire to draw breath and catch up with life, in the way she dawdled over the last buttons in the dimness of the porte-cochere, while her footman, outside, hung on her retarded signal.

When at length they emerged, it was to learn from that functionary that Madame la Marquise's carriage had been obliged to yield its place at the door, but was at the moment in the act of regaining it. Madame de Malrive cut the explanation short. "I shall walk home. The carriage this evening at eight."

As the footman turned away, she raised her eyes for the first time to Durham's.

"Will you walk with me? Let us cross the Tuileries. I should like to sit a moment on the terrace."

She spoke quite easily and naturally, as if it were the most commonplace thing in the world for them to be straying afoot together over Paris; but even his vague knowledge of the world she lived in, a knowledge mainly acquired through the perusal of yellow-backed fiction, gave a thrilling significance to her naturalness. Durham, indeed, was beginning to find that one of the charms of a sophisticated society is that it lends point and perspective to the slightest contact between the sexes. If, in the old unrestricted New York days, Fanny Frisbee, from a brown stone door-step, had proposed that they should take a walk in the Park, the idea would have presented itself to her companion as agreeable but unimportant; whereas Fanny de Malrive's suggestion that they should stroll across the Tuileries was obviously fraught with unspecified possibilities.

He was so throbbing with the sense of these possibilities that he walked beside her without speaking down the length of the wide alley which follows the line of the Rue de Rivoli, suffering her even, when they reached its farthest end, to direct him in silence up the steps to the terrace of the Feuillants. For, after all, the possibilities were double-faced, and her bold departure from custom might simply mean that what she had to say was so dreadful that it needed all the tenderest mitigation of circumstance.

There was apparently nothing embarrassing to her in his silence: it was a part of her long European discipline that she had learned to manage pauses with ease. In her Frisbee days she might have packed this one with a random fluency; now she was content to let it widen slowly before them like the spacious prospect opening at their feet. The complicated beauty of this prospect, as they moved toward it between the symmetrically clipped limes of the lateral terrace, touched him anew through her nearness, as with the hint of some vast impersonal power, controlling and regulating her life in ways he could not guess, putting between himself and her the whole width of the civilization into which her marriage had absorbed her. And there was such fear in the thought, he read such derision of what he had to offer in the splendour of the great avenues tapering upward to the sunset glories of the Arch, that all he had meant to say when he finally spoke compressed itself at last into an abrupt unmitigated: "Well?"

She answered at once, as though she had only awaited the call of the national interrogation—"I don't know when I have been so happy."

"So happy?" The suddenness of his joy flushed up through his fair skin.

"As I was just now—taking tea with your mother and sisters."

Durham's "Oh!" of surprise betrayed also a note of disillusionment, which she met only by the reconciling murmur: "Shall we sit down?"

He found two of the springy yellow chairs indigenous to the spot, and placed them under the tree near which they had paused, saying reluctantly, as he did so: "Of course it was an immense pleasure to them to see you again."

"Oh, not in the same way. I mean—" she paused, sinking into the chair, and betraying, for the first time, a momentary inability to deal becomingly with the situation. "I mean," she resumed smiling, "that it was not an event for them, as it was for me."

"An event?" he caught her up again, eagerly; for what, in the language of any civilization, could that word mean but just the one thing he most wished it to?

"To be with dear, good, sweet, simple, real Americans again!" she burst out, heaping up her epithets with reckless prodigality.

Durham's smile once more faded to impersonality, as he rejoined, just a shade on the defensive: "If it's merely our Americanism you enjoyed, I've no doubt we can give you all you want in that line."

"Yes, it's just that! But if you knew what the word means to me! It means—it means—" she paused as if to assure herself that they were sufficiently isolated from the desultory groups beneath the other trees—"it means that I'm safe with them: as safe as in a bank!"

Durham felt a sudden warmth behind his eyes and in his throat. "I think I do know—"

"No, you don't, really; you can't know how dear and strange and familiar it all sounded: the old New York names that kept coming up in your mother's talk, and her charming quaint ideas about Europe, their all regarding it as a great big innocent pleasure ground and shop for Americans; and your mother's missing the home-made bread and preferring the American asparagus, I'm so tired of Americans who despise even their own asparagus! And then your married sister's spending her summers at, where is it?—the Kittawittany House on Lake Pohunk—"

A vision of earnest women in Shetland shawls, with spectacles and thin knobs of hair, eating blueberry pie at unwholesome hours in a shingled dining-room on a bare New England hill-top, rose pallidly between Durham and the verdant brightness of the Champs Elysees, and he protested with a slight smile: "Oh, but my married sister is the black sheep of the family, the rest of us never sank as low as that."

"Low? I think it's beautiful, fresh and innocent and simple. I remember going to such a place once. They have early dinner, rather late, and go off in buckboards over terrible roads, and bring back golden rod and autumn leaves, and read nature books aloud on the piazza; and there is always one shy young man in flannels, only one, who has come to see the prettiest girl (though how he can choose among so many!) and who takes her off in a buggy for hours and hours—" She paused and summed up with a long sigh: "It is fifteen years since I was in America."

"And you're still so good an American."

"Oh, a better and better one every day!"

He hesitated. "Then why did you never come back?"

Her face altered instantly, exchanging its retrospective light for the look of slightly shadowed watchfulness which he had known as most habitual to it.

"It was impossible, it has always been so. My husband would not go; and since, since our separation, there have been family reasons."

Durham sighed impatiently. "Why do you talk of reasons? The truth is, you have made your life here. You could never give all this up!" He made a discouraged gesture in the direction of the Place de la Concorde.

"Give it up! I would go tomorrow! But it could never, now, be for more than a visit. I must live in France on account of my boy."

Durham's heart gave a quick beat. At last the talk had neared the point toward which his whole mind was straining, and he began to feel a personal application in her words. But that made him all the more cautious about choosing his own.

"It is an agreement, about the boy?" he ventured.

"I gave my word. They knew that was enough," she said proudly; adding, as if to put him in full possession of her reasons: "It would have been much more difficult for me to obtain complete control of my son if it had not been understood that I was to live in France."

"That seems fair," Durham assented after a moment's reflection: it was his instinct, even in the heat of personal endeavour, to pause a moment on the question of "fairness." The personal claim reasserted itself as he added tentatively: "But when he is brought up, when he's grown up: then you would feel freer?"

She received this with a start, as a possibility too remote to have entered into her view of the future. "He is only eight years old!" she objected.

"Ah, of course it would be a long way off?"

"A long way off, thank heaven! French mothers part late with their sons, and in that one respect I mean to be a French mother."

"Of course, naturally, since he has only you," Durham again assented.

He was eager to show how fully he took her point of view, if only to dispose her to the reciprocal fairness of taking his when the time came to present it. And he began to think that the time had now come; that their walk would not have thus resolved itself, without excuse or pretext, into a tranquil session beneath the trees, for any purpose less important than that of giving him his opportunity.

He took it, characteristically, without seeking a transition. "When I spoke to you, the other day, about myself, about what I felt for you, I said nothing of the future, because, for the moment, my mind refused to travel beyond its immediate hope of happiness. But I felt, of course, even then, that the hope involved various difficulties, that we can't, as we might once have done, come together without any thought but for ourselves; and whatever your answer is to be, I want to tell you now that I am ready to accept my share of the difficulties." He paused, and then added explicitly: "If there's the least chance of your listening to me, I'm willing to live over here as long as you can keep your boy with you."

Whatever Madame de Malrive's answer was to be, there could be no doubt as to her readiness to listen. She received Durham's words without sign of resistance, and took time to ponder them gently before she answered in a voice touched by emotion: "You are very generous, very unselfish; but when you fix a limit, no matter how remote, to my remaining here, I see how wrong it is to let myself consider for a moment such possibilities as we have been talking of."

"Wrong? Why should it be wrong?"

"Because I shall want to keep my boy always! Not, of course, in the sense of living with him, or even forming an important part of his life; I am not deluded enough to think that possible. But I do believe it possible never to pass wholly out of his life; and while there is a hope of that, how can I leave him?" She paused, and turned on him a new face, a face in which the past of which he was still so ignorant showed itself like a shadow suddenly darkening a clear pane. "How can I make you understand?" she went on urgently. "It is not only because of my love for him, not only, I mean, because of my own happiness in being with him; that I can't, in imagination, surrender even the remotest hour of his future; it is because, the moment he passes out of my influence, he passes under that other, the influence I have been fighting against every hour since he was born! I don't mean, you know," she added, as Durham, with bent head, continued to offer the silent fixity of his attention, "I don't mean the special personal influence, except inasmuch as it represents something wider, more general, something that encloses and circulates through the whole world in which he belongs. That is what I meant when I said you could never understand! There is nothing in your experience, in any American experience, to correspond with that far-reaching family organization, which is itself a part of the larger system, and which encloses a young man of my son's position in a network of accepted prejudices and opinions. Everything is prepared in advance, his political and religious convictions, his judgments of people, his sense of honour, his ideas of women, his whole view of life. He is taught to see vileness and corruption in every one not of his own way of thinking, and in every idea that does not directly serve the religious and political purposes of his class. The truth isn't a fixed thing: it's not used to test actions by, it's tested by them, and made to fit in with them. And this forming of the mind begins with the child's first consciousness; it's in his nursery stories, his baby prayers, his very games with his playmates! Already he is only half mine, because the Church has the other half, and will be reaching out for my share as soon as his education begins. But that other half is still mine, and I mean to make it the strongest and most living half of the two, so that, when the inevitable conflict begins, the energy and the truth and the endurance shall be on my side and not on theirs!"

She paused, flushing with the repressed fervour of her utterance, though her voice had not been raised beyond its usual discreet modulations; and Durham felt himself tingling with the transmitted force of her resolve. Whatever shock her words brought to his personal hope, he was grateful to her for speaking them so clearly, for having so sure a grasp of her purpose.

Her decision strengthened his own, and after a pause of deliberation he said quietly: "There might be a good deal to urge on the other side, the ineffectualness of your sacrifice, the probability that when your son marries he will inevitably be absorbed back into the life of his class and his people; but I can't look at it in that way, because if I were in your place I believe I should feel just as you do about it. As long as there was a fighting chance I should want to keep hold of my half, no matter how much the struggle cost me. And one reason why I understand your feeling about your boy is that I have the same feeling about you: as long as there's a fighting chance of keeping my half of you, the half he is willing to spare me, I don't see how I can ever give it up." He waited again, and then brought out firmly: "If you'll marry me, I'll agree to live out here as long as you want, and we'll be two instead of one to keep hold of your half of him."

He raised his eyes as he ended, and saw that hers met them through a quick clouding of tears.

"Ah, I am glad to have had this said to me! But I could never accept such an offer."

He caught instantly at the distinction. "That doesn't mean that you could never accept me?"

"Under such conditions—"

"But if I am satisfied with the conditions? Don't think I am speaking rashly, under the influence of the moment. I have expected something of this sort, and I have thought out my side of the case. As far as material circumstances go, I have worked long enough and successfully enough to take my ease and take it where I choose. I mention that because the life I offer you is offered to your boy as well." He let this sink into her mind before summing up gravely: "The offer I make is made deliberately, and at least I have a right to a direct answer."

She was silent again, and then lifted a cleared gaze to his. "My direct answer then is: if I were still Fanny Frisbee I would marry you."

He bent toward her persuasively. "But you will be—when the divorce is pronounced."

"Ah, the divorce—" She flushed deeply, with an instinctive shrinking back of her whole person which made him straighten himself in his chair.

"Do you so dislike the idea?"

"The idea of divorce? No—not in my case. I should like anything that would do away with the past, obliterate it all, make everything new in my life!"

"Then what—?" he began again, waiting with the patience of a wooer on the uneasy circling of her tormented mind.

"Oh, don't ask me; I don't know; I am frightened."

Durham gave a deep sigh of discouragement. "I thought your coming here with me today, and above all your going with me just now to see my mother, was a sign that you were not frightened!"

"Well, I was not when I was with your mother. She made everything seem easy and natural. She took me back into that clear American air where there are no obscurities, no mysteries—"

"What obscurities, what mysteries, are you afraid of?"

She looked about her with a faint shiver. "I am afraid of everything!" she said.

"That's because you are alone; because you've no one to turn to. I'll clear the air for you fast enough if you'll let me."

He looked forth defiantly, as if flinging his challenge at the great city which had come to typify the powers contending with him for her possession.

"You say that so easily! But you don't know; none of you know."

"Know what?"

"The difficulties—"

"I told you I was ready to take my share of the difficulties—and my share naturally includes yours. You know Americans are great hands at getting over difficulties." He drew himself up confidently. "Just leave that to me, only tell me exactly what you're afraid of."

She paused again, and then said: "The divorce, to begin with—they will never consent to it."

He noticed that she spoke as though the interests of the whole clan, rather than her husband's individual claim, were to be considered; and the use of the plural pronoun shocked his free individualism like a glimpse of some dark feudal survival.

"But you are absolutely certain of your divorce! I've consulted—of course without mentioning names—"

She interrupted him, with a melancholy smile: "Ah, so have I. The divorce would be easy enough to get, if they ever let it come into the courts."

"How on earth can they prevent that?"

"I don't know; my never knowing how they will do things is one of the secrets of their power."

"Their power? What power?" he broke in with irrepressible contempt. "Who are these bogeys whose machinations are going to arrest the course of justice in a, comparatively, civilized country? You've told me yourself that Monsieur de Malrive is the least likely to give you trouble; and the others are his uncle the abbe, his mother and sister. That kind of a syndicate doesn't scare me much. A priest and two women contra mundum!"

She shook her head. "Not contra mundum, but with it, their whole world is behind them. It's that mysterious solidarity that you can't understand. One doesn't know how far they may reach, or in how many directions. I have never known. They have always cropped up where I least expected them."

Before this persistency of negation Durham's buoyancy began to flag, but his determination grew the more fixed.

"Well, then, supposing them to possess these supernatural powers; do you think it's to people of that kind that I'll ever consent to give you up?"

She raised a half-smiling glance of protest. "Oh, they're not wantonly wicked. They'll leave me alone as long as—"

"As I do?" he interrupted. "Do you want me to leave you alone? Was that what you brought me here to tell me?"

The directness of the challenge seemed to gather up the scattered strands of her hesitation, and lifting her head she turned on him a look in which, but for its underlying shadow, he might have recovered the full free beam of Fanny Frisbee's gaze.

"I don't know why I brought you here," she said gently, "except from the wish to prolong a little the illusion of being once more an American among Americans. Just now, sitting there with your mother and Katy and Nannie, the difficulties seemed to vanish; the problems grew as trivial to me as they are to you. And I wanted them to remain so a little longer; I wanted to put off going back to them. But it was of no use, they were waiting for me here. They are over there now in that house across the river." She indicated the grey sky-line of the Faubourg, shining in the splintered radiance of the sunset beyond the long sweep of the quays. "They are a part of me, I belong to them. I must go back to them!" she sighed.

She rose slowly to her feet, as though her metaphor had expressed an actual fact and she felt herself bodily drawn from his side by the influences of which she spoke.

Durham had risen too. "Then I go back with you!" he exclaimed energetically; and as she paused, wavering a little under the shock of his resolve: "I don't mean into your house, but into your life!" he said.

She suffered him, at any rate, to accompany her to the door of the house, and allowed their debate to prolong itself through the almost monastic quiet of the quarter which led thither. On the way, he succeeded in wresting from her the confession that, if it were possible to ascertain in advance that her husband's family would not oppose her action, she might decide to apply for a divorce. Short of a positive assurance on this point, she made it clear that she would never move in the matter; there must be no scandal, no retentissement, nothing which her boy, necessarily brought up in the French tradition of scrupulously preserved appearances, could afterward regard as the faintest blur on his much-quartered escutcheon. But even this partial concession again raised fresh obstacles; for there seemed to be no one to whom she could entrust so delicate an investigation, and to apply directly to the Marquis de Malrive or his relatives appeared, in the light of her past experience, the last way of learning their intentions.

"But," Durham objected, beginning to suspect a morbid fixity of idea in her perpetual attitude of distrust—"but surely you have told me that your husband's sister, what is her name? Madame de Treymes?—was the most powerful member of the group, and that she has always been on your side."

She hesitated. "Yes, Christiane has been on my side. She dislikes her brother. But it would not do to ask her."

"But could no one else ask her? Who are her friends?"

"She has a great many; and some, of course, are mine. But in a case like this they would be all hers; they wouldn't hesitate a moment between us."

"Why should it be necessary to hesitate between you? Suppose Madame de Treymes sees the reasonableness of what you ask; suppose, at any rate, she sees the hopelessness of opposing you? Why should she make a mystery of your opinion?"

"It's not that; it is that, if I went to her friends, I should never get her real opinion from them. At least I should never know if it is was her real opinion; and therefore I should be no farther advanced. Don't you see?"

Durham struggled between the sentimental impulse to soothe her, and the practical instinct that it was a moment for unmitigated frankness.

"I'm not sure that I do; but if you can't find out what Madame de Treymes thinks, I'll see what I can do myself."

"Oh—you!" broke from her in mingled terror and admiration; and pausing on her doorstep to lay her hand in his before she touched the bell, she added with a half-whimsical flash of regret: "Why didn't this happen to Fanny Frisbee?"

III

Why had it not happened to Fanny Frisbee?

Durham put the question to himself as he walked back along the quays, in a state of inner commotion which left him, for once, insensible to the ordered beauty of his surroundings. Propinquity had not been lacking: he had known Miss Frisbee since his college days. In unsophisticated circles, one family is apt to quote another; and the Durham ladies had always quoted the Frisbees. The Frisbees were bold, experienced, enterprising: they had what the novelists of the day called "dash." The beautiful Fanny was especially dashing; she had the showiest national attributes, tempered only by a native grace of softness, as the beam of her eyes was subdued by the length of their lashes. And yet young Durham, though not unsusceptible to such charms, had remained content to enjoy them from a safe distance of good fellowship. If he had been asked why, he could not have told; but the Durham of forty understood. It was because there were, with minor modifications, many other Fanny Frisbees; whereas never before, within his ken, had there been a Fanny de Malrive.

He had felt it in a flash, when, the autumn before, he had run across her one evening in the dining-room of the Beaurivage at Ouchy; when, after a furtive exchange of glances, they had simultaneously arrived at recognition, followed by an eager pressure of hands, and a long evening of reminiscence on the starlit terrace. She was the same, but so mysteriously changed! And it was the mystery, the sense of unprobed depths of initiation, which drew him to her as her freshness had never drawn him. He had not hitherto attempted to define the nature of the change: it remained for his sister Nannie to do that when, on his return to the Rue de Rivoli, where the family were still sitting in conclave upon their recent visitor, Miss Durham summed up their groping comments in the phrase: "I never saw anything so French!"

Durham, understanding what his sister's use of the epithet implied, recognized it instantly as the explanation of his own feelings. Yes, it was the finish, the modelling, which Madame de Malrive's experience had given her that set her apart from the fresh uncomplicated personalities of which she had once been simply the most charming type. The influences that had lowered her voice, regulated her gestures, toned her down to harmony with the warm dim background of a long social past, these influences had lent to her natural fineness of perception a command of expression adapted to complex conditions. She had moved in surroundings through which one could hardly bounce and bang on the genial American plan without knocking the angles off a number of sacred institutions; and her acquired dexterity of movement seemed to Durham a crowning grace. It was a shock, now that he knew at what cost the dexterity had been acquired, to acknowledge this even to himself; he hated to think that she could owe anything to such conditions as she had been placed in. And it gave him a sense of the tremendous strength of the organization into which she had been absorbed, that in spite of her horror, her moral revolt, she had not reacted against its external forms. She might abhor her husband, her marriage, and the world to which it had introduced her, but she had become a product of that world in its outward expression, and no better proof of the fact was needed than her exotic enjoyment of Americanism.

The sense of the distance to which her American past had been removed was never more present to him than when, a day or two later, he went with his mother and sisters to return her visit. The region beyond the river existed, for the Durham ladies, only as the unmapped environment of the Bon Marche; and Nannie Durham's exclamation on the pokiness of the streets and the dulness of the houses showed Durham, with a start, how far he had already travelled from the family point of view.

"Well, if this is all she got by marrying a Marquis!" the young lady summed up as they paused before the small sober hotel in its high-walled court; and Katy, following her mother through the stone-vaulted and stone-floored vestibule, murmured: "It must be simply freezing in winter."

In the softly-faded drawing-room, with its old pastels in old frames, its windows looking on the damp green twilight of a garden sunk deep in blackened walls, the American ladies might have been even more conscious of the insufficiency of their friend's compensations, had not the warmth of her welcome precluded all other reflections. It was not till she had gathered them about her in the corner beside the tea-table, that Durham identified the slender dark lady loitering negligently in the background, and introduced in a comprehensive murmur to the American group, as the redoubtable sister-in-law to whom he had declared himself ready to throw down his challenge.

There was nothing very redoubtable about Madame de Treymes, except perhaps the kindly yet critical observation which she bestowed on her sister-in-law's visitors: the unblinking attention of a civilized spectator observing an encampment of aborigines. He had heard of her as a beauty, and was surprised to find her, as Nannie afterward put it, a mere stick to hang clothes on (but they did hang!), with a small brown glancing face, like that of a charming little inquisitive animal. Yet before she had addressed ten words to him, nibbling at the hard English consonants like nuts, he owned the justice of the epithet. She was a beauty, if beauty, instead of being restricted to the cast of the face, is a pervasive attribute informing the hands, the voice, the gestures, the very fall of a flounce and tilt of a feather. In this impalpable aura of grace Madame de Treymes' dark meagre presence unmistakably moved, like a thin flame in a wide quiver of light. And as he realized that she looked much handsomer than she was, so while they talked, he felt that she understood a great deal more than she betrayed. It was not through the groping speech which formed their apparent medium of communication that she imbibed her information: she found it in the air, she extracted it from Durham's look and manner, she caught it in the turn of her sister-in-law's defenseless eyes, for in her presence Madame de Malrive became Fanny Frisbee again!—she put it together, in short, out of just such unconsidered indescribable trifles as differentiated the quiet felicity of her dress from Nannie and Katy's "handsome" haphazard clothes.

Her actual converse with Durham moved, meanwhile, strictly in the conventional ruts: had he been long in Paris, which of the new plays did he like best, was it true that American jeunes filles were sometimes taken to the Boulevard theatres? And she threw an interrogative glance at the young ladies beside the tea-table. To Durham's reply that it depended how much French they knew, she shrugged and smiled, replying that his compatriots all spoke French like Parisians, enquiring, after a moment's thought, if they learned it, la bas, des negres, and laughing heartily when Durham's astonishment revealed her blunder.

When at length she had taken leave, enveloping the Durham ladies in a last puzzled penetrating look, Madame de Malrive turned to Mrs. Durham with a faintly embarrassed smile.

"My sister-in-law was much interested; I believe you are the first Americans she has ever known."

"Good gracious!" ejaculated Nannie, as though such social darkness required immediate missionary action on some one's part.

"Well, she knows us," said Durham, catching in Madame de Malrive's rapid glance, a startled assent to his point.

"After all," reflected the accurate Katy, as though seeking an excuse for Madame de Treymes' unenlightenment, "we don't know many French people, either."

To which Nannie promptly if obscurely retorted: "Ah, but we couldn't and she could!"

IV

Madame de Treymes' friendly observation of her sister-in-law's visitors resulted in no expression on her part of a desire to renew her study of them. To all appearances, she passed out of their lives when Madame de Malrive's door closed on her; and Durham felt that the arduous task of making her acquaintance was still to be begun.

He felt also, more than ever, the necessity of attempting it; and in his determination to lose no time, and his perplexity how to set most speedily about the business, he bethought himself of applying to his cousin Mrs. Boykin.

Mrs. Elmer Boykin was a small plump woman, to whose vague prettiness the lines of middle-age had given no meaning: as though whatever had happened to her had merely added to the sum total of her inexperience. After a Parisian residence of twenty-five years, spent in a state of feverish servitude to the great artists of the rue de la Paix, her dress and hair still retained a certain rigidity in keeping with the directness of her gaze and the unmodulated candour of her voice. Her very drawing-room had the hard bright atmosphere of her native skies, and one felt that she was still true at heart to the national ideals in electric lighting and plumbing.

She and her husband had left America owing to the impossibility of living there with the finish and decorum which the Boykin standard demanded; but in the isolation of their exile they had created about them a kind of phantom America, where the national prejudices continued to flourish unchecked by the national progressiveness: a little world sparsely peopled by compatriots in the same attitude of chronic opposition toward a society chronically unaware of them. In this uncontaminated air Mr. and Mrs. Boykin had preserved the purity of simpler conditions, and Elmer Boykin, returning rakishly from a Sunday's racing at Chantilly, betrayed, under his "knowing" coat and the racing-glasses slung ostentatiously across his shoulder, the unmistakeable cut of the American business man coming "up town" after a long day in the office.

It was a part of the Boykins' uncomfortable but determined attitude, and perhaps a last expression of their latent patriotism, to live in active disapproval of the world about them, fixing in memory with little stabs of reprobation innumerable instances of what the abominable foreigner was doing; so that they reminded Durham of persons peacefully following the course of a horrible war by pricking red pins in a map. To Mrs. Durham, with her gentle tourist's view of the European continent, as a vast Museum in which the human multitudes simply furnished the element of costume, the Boykins seemed abysmally instructed, and darkly expert in forbidden things; and her son, without sharing her simple faith in their omniscience, credited them with an ample supply of the kind of information of which he was in search.

Mrs. Boykin, from the corner of an intensely modern Gobelin sofa, studied her cousin as he balanced himself insecurely on one of the small gilt chairs which always look surprised at being sat in.

"Fanny de Malrive? Oh, of course: I remember you were all very intimate with the Frisbees when they lived in West Thirty-third Street. But she has dropped all her American friends since her marriage. The excuse was that de Malrive didn't like them; but as she's been separated for five or six years, I can't see—. You say she's been very nice to your mother and the girls? Well, I daresay she is beginning to feel the need of friends she can really trust; for as for her French relations—! That Malrive set is the worst in the Faubourg. Of course you know what he is; even the family, for decency's sake, had to back her up, and urge her to get a separation. And Christiane de Treymes—"

Durham seized his opportunity. "Is she so very reprehensible too?"

Mrs. Boykin pursed up her small colourless mouth. "I can't speak from personal experience. I know Madame de Treymes slightly, I have met her at Fanny's, but she never remembers the fact except when she wants me to go to one of her ventes de charite. They all remember us then; and some American women are silly enough to ruin themselves at the smart bazaars, and fancy they will get invitations in return. They say Mrs. Addison G. Pack followed Madame d'Alglade around for a whole winter, and spent a hundred thousand francs at her stalls; and at the end of the season Madame d'Alglade asked her to tea, and when she got there she found that was for a charity too, and she had to pay a hundred francs to get in."

Mrs. Boykin paused with a smile of compassion. "That is not my way," she continued. "Personally I have no desire to thrust myself into French society, I can't see how any American woman can do so without loss of self-respect. But anyone can tell you about Madame de Treymes."

"I wish you would, then," Durham suggested.

"Well, I think Elmer had better," said his wife mysteriously, as Mr. Boykin, at this point, advanced across the wide expanse of Aubusson on which his wife and Durham were islanded in a state of propinquity without privacy.

"What's that, Bessy? Hah, Durham, how are you? Didn't see you at Auteuil this afternoon. You don't race? Busy sight-seeing, I suppose? What was that my wife was telling you? Oh, about Madame de Treymes."

He stroked his pepper-and-salt moustache with a gesture intended rather to indicate than conceal the smile of experience beneath it. "Well, Madame de Treymes has not been like a happy country, she's had a history: several of 'em. Someone said she constituted the feuilleton of the Faubourg daily news. La suite au prochain numero, you see the point? Not that I speak from personal knowledge. Bessy and I have never cared to force our way—" He paused, reflecting that his wife had probably anticipated him in the expression of this familiar sentiment, and added with a significant nod: "Of course you know the Prince d'Armillac by sight? No? I'm surprised at that. Well, he's one of the choicest ornaments of the Jockey Club: very fascinating to the ladies, I believe, but the deuce and all at baccara. Ruined his mother and a couple of maiden aunts already, and now Madame de Treymes has put the family pearls up the spout, and is wearing imitation for love of him."

"I had that straight from my maid's cousin, who is employed by Madame d'Armillac's jeweller," said Mrs. Boykin with conscious pride. "Oh, it's straight enough, more than she is!" retorted her husband, who was slightly jealous of having his facts reinforced by any information not of his own gleaning.

"Be careful of what you say, Elmer," Mrs. Boykin interposed with archness. "I suspect John of being seriously smitten by the lady."

Durham let this pass unchallenged, submitting with a good grace to his host's low whistle of amusement, and the sardonic enquiry: "Ever do anything with the foils? D'Armillac is what they call over here a fine lame."

"Oh, I don't mean to resort to bloodshed unless it's absolutely necessary; but I mean to make the lady's acquaintance," said Durham, falling into his key.

Mrs. Boykin's lips tightened to the vanishing point. "I am afraid you must apply for an introduction to more fashionable people than we are. Elmer and I so thoroughly disapprove of French society that we have always declined to take any part in it. But why should not Fanny de Malrive arrange a meeting for you?"

Durham hesitated. "I don't think she is on very intimate terms with her husband's family—"

"You mean that she's not allowed to introduce her friends to them," Mrs. Boykin interjected sarcastically; while her husband added, with an air of portentous initiation: "Ah, my dear fellow, the way they treat the Americans over here, that's another chapter, you know."

"How some people can stand it!" Mrs. Boykin chimed in; and as the footman, entering at that moment, tendered her a large coronetted envelope, she held it up as if in illustration of the indignities to which her countrymen were subjected.

"Look at that, my dear John," she exclaimed—"another card to one of their everlasting bazaars! Why, it's at Madame d'Armillac's, the Prince's mother. Madame de Treymes must have sent it, of course. The brazen way in which they combine religion and immorality! Fifty francs admission—rien que cela!—to see some of the most disreputable people in Europe. And if you're an American, you're expected to leave at least a thousand behind you. Their own people naturally get off cheaper." She tossed over the card to her cousin. "There's your opportunity to see Madame de Treymes."

"Make it two thousand, and she'll ask you to tea," Mr. Boykin scathingly added.

V

In the monumental drawing-room of the Hotel de Malrive—it had been a surprise to the American to read the name of the house emblazoned on black marble over its still more monumental gateway—Durham found himself surrounded by a buzz of feminine tea-sipping oddly out of keeping with the wigged and cuirassed portraits frowning high on the walls, the majestic attitude of the furniture, the rigidity of great gilt consoles drawn up like lords-in-waiting against the tarnished panels.

It was the old Marquise de Malrive's "day," and Madame de Treymes, who lived with her mother, had admitted Durham to the heart of the enemy's country by inviting him, after his prodigal disbursements at the charity bazaar, to come in to tea on a Thursday. Whether, in thus fulfilling Mr. Boykin's prediction, she had been aware of Durham's purpose, and had her own reasons for falling in with it; or whether she simply wished to reward his lavishness at the fair, and permit herself another glimpse of an American so picturesquely embodying the type familiar to French fiction, on these points Durham was still in doubt.

Meanwhile, Madame de Treymes being engaged with a venerable Duchess in a black shawl, all the older ladies present had the sloping shoulders of a generation of shawl-wearers, her American visitor, left in the isolation of his unimportance, was using it as a shelter for a rapid survey of the scene.

He had begun his study of Fanny de Malrive's situation without any real understanding of her fears. He knew the repugnance to divorce existing in the French Catholic world, but since the French laws sanctioned it, and in a case so flagrant as his injured friend's, would inevitably accord it with the least possible delay and exposure, he could not take seriously any risk of opposition on the part of the husband's family. Madame de Malrive had not become a Catholic, and since her religious scruples could not be played on, the only weapon remaining to the enemy, the threat of fighting the divorce, was one they could not wield without self-injury. Certainly, if the chief object were to avoid scandal, common sense must counsel Monsieur de Malrive and his friends not to give the courts an opportunity of exploring his past; and since the echo of such explorations, and their ultimate transmission to her son, were what Madame de Malrive most dreaded, the opposing parties seemed to have a common ground for agreement, and Durham could not but regard his friend's fears as the result of over-taxed sensibilities. All this had seemed evident enough to him as he entered the austere portals of the Hotel de Malrive and passed, between the faded liveries of old family servants, to the presence of the dreaded dowager above. But he had not been ten minutes in that presence before he had arrived at a faint intuition of what poor Fanny meant. It was not in the exquisite mildness of the old Marquise, a little gray-haired bunch of a woman in dowdy mourning, or in the small neat presence of the priestly uncle, the Abbe who had so obviously just stepped down from one of the picture-frames overhead: it was not in the aspect of these chief protagonists, so outwardly unformidable, that Durham read an occult danger to his friend. It was rather in their setting, their surroundings, the little company of elderly and dowdy persons, so uniformly clad in weeping blacks and purples that they might have been assembled for some mortuary anniversary, it was in the remoteness and the solidarity of this little group that Durham had his first glimpse of the social force of which Fanny de Malrive had spoken. All these amiably chatting visitors, who mostly bore the stamp of personal insignificance on their mildly sloping or aristocratically beaked faces, hung together in a visible closeness of tradition, dress, attitude and manner, as different as possible from the loose aggregation of a roomful of his own countrymen. Durham felt, as he observed them, that he had never before known what "society" meant; nor understood that, in an organized and inherited system, it exists full-fledged where two or three of its members are assembled.

Upon this state of bewilderment, this sense of having entered a room in which the lights had suddenly been turned out, even Madame de Treymes' intensely modern presence threw no illumination. He was conscious, as she smilingly rejoined him, not of her points of difference from the others, but of the myriad invisible threads by which she held to them; he even recognized the audacious slant of her little brown profile in the portrait of a powdered ancestress beneath which she had paused a moment in advancing. She was simply one particular facet of the solid, glittering impenetrable body which he had thought to turn in his hands and look through like a crystal; and when she said, in her clear staccato English, "Perhaps you will like to see the other rooms," he felt like crying out in his blindness: "If I could only be sure of seeing anything here!" Was she conscious of his blindness, and was he as remote and unintelligible to her as she was to him? This possibility, as he followed her through the nobly-unfolding rooms of the great house, gave him his first hope of recoverable advantage. For, after all, he had some vague traditional lights on her world and its antecedents; whereas to her he was a wholly new phenomenon, as unexplained as a fragment of meteorite dropped at her feet on the smooth gravel of the garden-path they were pacing.

She had led him down into the garden, in response to his admiring exclamation, and perhaps also because she was sure that, in the chill spring afternoon, they would have its embowered privacies to themselves. The garden was small, but intensely rich and deep, one of those wells of verdure and fragrance which everywhere sweeten the air of Paris by wafts blown above old walls on quiet streets; and as Madame de Treymes paused against the ivy bank masking its farther boundary, Durham felt more than ever removed from the normal bearings of life.

His sense of strangeness was increased by the surprise of his companion's next speech.

"You wish to marry my sister-in-law?" she asked abruptly; and Durham's start of wonder was followed by an immediate feeling of relief. He had expected the preliminaries of their interview to be as complicated as the bargaining in an Eastern bazaar, and had feared to lose himself at the first turn in a labyrinth of "foreign" intrigue.

"Yes, I do," he said with equal directness; and they smiled together at the sharp report of question and answer.

The smile put Durham more completely at his ease, and after waiting for her to speak, he added with deliberation: "So far, however, the wishing is entirely on my side." His scrupulous conscience felt itself justified in this reserve by the conditional nature of Madame de Malrive's consent.

"I understand; but you have been given reason to hope—"

"Every man in my position gives himself his own reasons for hoping," he interposed with a smile.

"I understand that too," Madame de Treymes assented. "But still—you spent a great deal of money the other day at our bazaar."

"Yes: I wanted to have a talk with you, and it was the readiest, if not the most distinguished—means of attracting your attention."

"I understand," she once more reiterated, with a gleam of amusement.

"It is because I suspect you of understanding everything that I have been so anxious for this opportunity."

She bowed her acknowledgement, and said: "Shall we sit a moment?" adding, as he drew their chairs under a tree: "You permit me, then, to say that I believe I understand also a little of our good Fanny's mind?"

"On that point I have no authority to speak. I am here only to listen."

"Listen, then: you have persuaded her that there would be no harm in divorcing my brother—since I believe your religion does not forbid divorce?"

"Madame de Malrive's religion sanctions divorce in such a case as—"

"As my brother has furnished? Yes, I have heard that your race is stricter in judging such ecarts. But you must not think," she added, "that I defend my brother. Fanny must have told you that we have always given her our sympathy."

"She has let me infer it from her way of speaking of you."

Madame de Treymes arched her dramatic eyebrows. "How cautious you are! I am so straightforward that I shall have no chance with you."

"You will be quite safe, unless you are so straightforward that you put me on my guard."

She met this with a low note of amusement.

"At this rate we shall never get any farther; and in two minutes I must go back to my mother's visitors. Why should we go on fencing? The situation is really quite simple. Tell me just what you wish to know. I have always been Fanny's friend, and that disposes me to be yours."

Durham, during this appeal, had had time to steady his thoughts; and the result of his deliberation was that he said, with a return to his former directness: "Well, then, what I wish to know is, what position your family would take if Madame de Malrive should sue for a divorce." He added, without giving her time to reply: "I naturally wish to be clear on this point before urging my cause with your sister-in-law."

Madame de Treymes seemed in no haste to answer; but after a pause of reflection she said, not unkindly: "My poor Fanny might have asked me that herself."

"I beg you to believe that I am not acting as her spokesman," Durham hastily interposed. "I merely wish to clear up the situation before speaking to her in my own behalf."

"You are the most delicate of suitors! But I understand your feeling. Fanny also is extremely delicate: it was a great surprise to us at first. Still, in this case—" Madame de Treymes paused—"since she has no religious scruples, and she had no difficulty in obtaining a separation, why should she fear any in demanding a divorce?"

"I don't know that she does: but the mere fact of possible opposition might be enough to alarm the delicacy you have observed in her."

"Ah, yes: on her boy's account."

"Partly, doubtless, on her boy's account."

"So that, if my brother objects to a divorce, all he has to do is to announce his objection? But, my dear sir, you are giving your case into my hands!" She flashed an amused smile on him.

"Since you say you are Madame de Malrive's friend, could there be a better place for it?"

As she turned her eyes on him he seemed to see, under the flitting lightness of her glance, the sudden concentrated expression of the ancestral will. "I am Fanny's friend, certainly. But with us family considerations are paramount. And our religion forbids divorce."

"So that, inevitably, your brother will oppose it?"

She rose from her seat, and stood fretting with her slender boot-tip the minute red pebbles of the path.

"I must really go in: my mother will never forgive me for deserting her."

"But surely you owe me an answer?" Durham protested, rising also.

"In return for your purchases at my stall?"

"No: in return for the trust I have placed in you."

She mused on this, moving slowly a step or two toward the house.

"Certainly I wish to see you again; you interest me," she said smiling. "But it is so difficult to arrange. If I were to ask you to come here again, my mother and uncle would be surprised. And at Fanny's—"

"Oh, not there!" he exclaimed.

"Where then? Is there any other house where we are likely to meet?"

Durham hesitated; but he was goaded by the flight of the precious minutes. "Not unless you'll come and dine with me," he said boldly.

"Dine with you? Au cabaret? Ah, that would be diverting, but impossible!"

"Well, dine with my cousin, then, I have a cousin, an American lady, who lives here," said Durham, with suddenly-soaring audacity.

She paused with puzzled brows. "An American lady whom I know?"

"By name, at any rate. You send her cards for all your charity bazaars."

She received the thrust with a laugh. "We do exploit your compatriots."

"Oh, I don't think she has ever gone to the bazaars."

"But she might if I dined with her?"

"Still less, I imagine."

She reflected on this, and then said with acuteness: "I like that, and I accept, but what is the lady's name?"

VI

On the way home, in the first drop of his exaltation, Durham had said to himself: "But why on earth should Bessy invite her?"

He had, naturally, no very cogent reasons to give Mrs. Boykin in support of his astonishing request, and could only, marvelling at his own growth in duplicity, suffer her to infer that he was really, shamelessly "smitten" with the lady he thus proposed to thrust upon her hospitality. But, to his surprise, Mrs. Boykin hardly gave herself time to pause upon his reasons. They were swallowed up in the fact that Madame de Treymes wished to dine with her, as the lesser luminaries vanish in the blaze of the sun.

"I am not surprised," she declared, with a faint smile intended to check her husband's unruly wonder. "I wonder you are, Elmer. Didn't you tell me that Armillac went out of his way to speak to you the other day at the races? And at Madame d'Alglade's sale, yes, I went there after all, just for a minute, because I found Katy and Nannie were so anxious to be taken, well, that day I noticed that Madame de Treymes was quite empressée when we went up to her stall. Oh, I didn't buy anything: I merely waited while the girls chose some lampshades. They thought it would be interesting to take home something painted by a real Marquise, and of course I didn't tell them that those women never make the things they sell at their stalls. But I repeat I'm not surprised: I suspected that Madame de Treymes had heard of our little dinners. You know they're really horribly bored in that poky old Faubourg. My poor John, I see now why she's been making up to you! But on one point I am quite determined, Elmer; whatever you say, I shall not invite the Prince d'Armillac."

Elmer, as far as Durham could observe, did not say much; but, like his wife, he continued in a state of pleasantly agitated activity till the momentous evening of the dinner.

The festivity in question was restricted in numbers, either owing to the difficulty of securing suitable guests, or from a desire not to have it appear that Madame de Treymes' hosts attached any special importance to her presence; but the smallness of the company was counterbalanced by the multiplicity of the courses.

The national determination not to be "downed" by the despised foreigner, to show a wealth of material resource obscurely felt to compensate for the possible lack of other distinctions, this resolve had taken, in Mrs. Boykin's case, the shape, or rather the multiple shapes, of a series of culinary feats, of gastronomic combinations, which would have commanded her deep respect had she seen them on any other table, and which she naturally relied on to produce the same effect on her guest. Whether or not the desired result was achieved, Madame de Treymes' manner did not specifically declare; but it showed a general complaisance, a charming willingness to be amused, which made Mr. Boykin, for months afterward, allude to her among his compatriots as "an old friend of my wife's—takes potluck with us, you know. Of course there's not a word of truth in any of those ridiculous stories."

It was only when, to Durham's intense surprise, Mr. Boykin hazarded to his neighbour the regret that they had not been so lucky as to "secure the Prince"—it was then only that the lady showed, not indeed anything so simple and unprepared as embarrassment, but a faint play of wonder, an under-flicker of amusement, as though recognizing that, by some odd law of social compensation, the crudity of the talk might account for the complexity of the dishes.

But Mr. Boykin was tremulously alive to hints, and the conversation at once slid to safer topics, easy generalizations which left Madame de Treymes ample time to explore the table, to use her narrowed gaze like a knife slitting open the unsuspicious personalities about her. Nannie and Katy

Durham, who, after much discussion (to which their hostess candidly admitted them), had been included in the feast, were the special objects of Madame de Treymes' observation. During dinner she ignored in their favour the other carefully-selected guests—the fashionable art-critic, the old Legitimist general, the beauty from the English Embassy, the whole impressive marshalling of Mrs. Boykin's social resources—and when the men returned to the drawing-room, Durham found her still fanning in his sisters the flame of an easily kindled enthusiasm. Since she could hardly have been held by the intrinsic interest of their converse, the sight gave him another swift intuition of the working of those hidden forces with which Fanny de Malrive felt herself encompassed. But when Madame de Treymes, at his approach, let him see that it was for him she had been reserving herself, he felt that so graceful an impulse needed no special explanation. She had the art of making it seem quite natural that they should move away together to the remotest of Mrs. Boykin's far-drawn salons, and that there, in a glaring privacy of brocade and ormolu, she should turn to him with a smile which avowed her intentional quest of seclusion.

"Confess that I have done a great deal for you!" she exclaimed, making room for him on a sofa judiciously screened from the observation of the other rooms.

"In coming to dine with my cousin?" he enquired, answering her smile.

"Let us say, in giving you this half hour."

"For that I am duly grateful, and shall be still more so when I know what it contains for me."

"Ah, I am not sure. You will not like what I am going to say."

"Shall I not?" he rejoined, changing colour.

She raised her eyes from the thoughtful contemplation of her painted fan. "You appear to have no idea of the difficulties."

"Should I have asked your help if I had not had an idea of them?"

"But you are still confident that with my help you can surmount them?"

"I can't believe you have come here to take that confidence from me?"

She leaned back, smiling at him through her lashes. "And all this I am to do for your beaux yeux?"

"No—for your own: that you may see with them what happiness you are conferring."

"You are extremely clever, and I like you." She paused, and then brought out with lingering emphasis: "But my family will not hear of a divorce."

She threw into her voice such an accent of finality that Durham, for the moment, felt himself brought up against an insurmountable barrier; but, almost at once, his fear was mitigated by the conviction that she would not have put herself out so much to say so little.

"When you speak of your family, do you include yourself?" he suggested.

She threw a surprised glance at him. "I thought you understood that I am simply their mouthpiece."

At this he rose quietly to his feet with a gesture of acceptance. "I have only to thank you, then, for not keeping me longer in suspense."

His air of wishing to put an immediate end to the conversation seemed to surprise her. "Sit down a moment longer," she commanded him kindly; and as he leaned against the back of his chair, without appearing to hear her request, she added in a low voice: "I am very sorry for you and Fanny—but you are not the only persons to be pitied."

She had dropped her light manner as she might have tossed aside her fan, and he was startled at the intimacy of misery to which her look and movement abruptly admitted him. Perhaps no Anglo-Saxon fully understands the fluency in self-revelation which centuries of the confessional have given to the Latin races, and to Durham, at any rate, Madame de Treymes' sudden avowal gave the shock of a physical abandonment.

"I am so sorry," he stammered—"is there any way in which I can be of use to you?"

She sat before him with her hands clasped, her eyes fixed on his in a terrible intensity of appeal. "If you would—if you would! Oh, there is nothing I would not do for you. I have still a great deal of influence with my mother, and what my mother commands we all do. I could help you, I am sure I could help you; but not if my own situation were known. And if nothing can be done it must be known in a few days."

Durham had reseated himself at her side. "Tell me what I can do," he said in a low tone, forgetting his own preoccupations in his genuine concern for her distress.

She looked up at him through tears. "How dare I? Your race is so cautious, so self-controlled, you have so little indulgence for the extravagances of the heart. And my folly has been incredible, and unrewarded." She paused, and as Durham waited in a silence which she guessed to be compassionate, she brought out below her breath: "I have lent money, my husband's, my brother's, money that was not mine, and now I have nothing to repay it with."

Durham gazed at her in genuine astonishment. The turn the conversation had taken led quite beyond his uncomplicated experiences with the other sex. She saw his surprise, and extended her hands in deprecation and entreaty. "Alas, what must you think of me? How can I explain my humiliating myself before a stranger? Only by telling you the whole truth, the fact that I am not alone in this disaster, that I could not confess my situation to my family without ruining myself, and involving in my ruin some one who, however undeservedly, has been as dear to me as, as you are to—"

Durham pushed his chair back with a sharp exclamation.

"Ah, even that does not move you!" she said.

The cry restored him to his senses by the long shaft of light it sent down the dark windings of the situation. He seemed suddenly to know Madame de Treymes as if he had been brought up with her in the inscrutable shades of the Hotel de Malrive.

She, on her side, appeared to have a startled but uncomprehending sense of the fact that his silence was no longer completely sympathetic, that her touch called forth no answering vibration; and she made a desperate clutch at the one chord she could be certain of sounding.

"You have asked a great deal of me—much more than you can guess. Do you mean to give me nothing, not even your sympathy, in return? Is it because you have heard horrors of me? When are they not said of a woman who is married unhappily? Perhaps not in your fortunate country, where she may seek liberation without dishonour. But here—! You who have seen the consequences of our disastrous marriages—you who may yet be the victim of our cruel and abominable system; have you no pity for one who has suffered in the same way, and without the possibility of release?" She paused, laying her hand on his arm with a smile of deprecating irony. "It is not because you are not rich. At such times the crudest way is the shortest, and I don't pretend to deny that I know I am asking you a trifle. You Americans, when you want a thing, always pay ten times what it is worth, and I am giving you the wonderful chance to get what you most want at a bargain."

Durham sat silent, her little gloved hand burning his coat-sleeve as if it had been a hot iron. His brain was tingling with the shock of her confession. She wanted money, a great deal of money: that was clear, but it was not the point. She was ready to sell her influence, and he fancied she could be counted on to fulfil her side of the bargain. The fact that he could so trust her seemed only to make her more terrible to him, more supernaturally dauntless and baleful. For what was it that she exacted of him? She had said she must have money to pay her debts; but he knew that was only a pre- text which she scarcely expected him to believe. She wanted the money for some one else; that was what her allusion to a fellow-victim meant. She wanted it to pay the Prince's gambling debts, it was at that price that Durham was to buy the right to marry Fanny de Malrive.

Once the situation had worked itself out in his mind, he found himself unexpectedly relieved of the necessity of weighing the arguments for and against it. All the traditional forces of his blood were in revolt, and he could only surrender himself to their pressure, without thought of compromise or parley.

He stood up in silence, and the abruptness of his movement caused Madame de Treymes' hand to slip from his arm.

"You refuse?" she exclaimed; and he answered with a bow: "Only because of the return you propose to make me."

She stood staring at him, in a perplexity so genuine and profound that he could almost have smiled at it through his disgust.

"Ah, you are all incredible," she murmured at last, stooping to repossess herself of her fan; and as she moved past him to rejoin the group in the farther room, she added in an incisive undertone: "You are quite at liberty to repeat our conversation to your friend!"

VII

Durham did not take advantage of the permission thus strangely flung at him: of his talk with her sister-in-law he gave to Madame de Malrive only that part which concerned her.

Presenting himself for this purpose, the day after Mrs. Boykin's dinner, he found his friend alone with her son; and the sight of the child had the effect of dispelling whatever illusive hopes had attended him to the threshold. Even after the governess's descent upon the scene had left Madame de Malrive and her visitor alone, the little boy's presence seemed to hover admonishingly between them, reducing to a bare statement of fact Durham's confession of the total failure of his errand.

Madame de Malrive heard the confession calmly; she had been too prepared for it not to have prepared a countenance to receive it. Her first comment was: "I have never known them to declare themselves so plainly—" and Durham's baffled hopes fastened themselves eagerly on the words. Had she not always warned him that there was nothing so misleading as their plainness? And might it not be that, in spite of his advisedness, he had suffered too easy a rebuff? But second thoughts reminded him that the refusal had not been as unconditional as his necessary reservations made it seem in the repetition; and that, furthermore, it was his own act, and not that of his opponents, which had determined it. The impossibility of revealing this to Madame de Malrive only made the difficulty shut in more darkly around him, and in the completeness of his discouragement he scarcely needed her reminder of his promise to regard the subject as closed when once the other side had defined its position.

He was secretly confirmed in this acceptance of his fate by the knowledge that it was really he who had defined the position. Even now that he was alone with Madame de Malrive, and subtly aware of the struggle under her composure, he felt no temptation to abate his stand by a jot. He had not yet formulated a reason for his resistance: he simply went on feeling, more and more strongly with every precious sign of her participation in his unhappiness, that he could neither owe his escape from it to such a transaction, nor suffer her, innocently, to owe hers.

The only mitigating effect of his determination was in an increase of helpless tenderness toward her; so that, when she exclaimed, in answer to his announcement that he meant to leave Paris the next night: "Oh, give me a day or two longer!" he at once resigned himself to saying: "If I can be of the least use, I'll give you a hundred."

She answered sadly that all he could do would be to let her feel that he was there, just for a day or two, till she had readjusted herself to the idea of going on in the old way; and on this note of renunciation they parted.

But Durham, however pledged to the passive part, could not long sustain it without rebellion. To "hang round" the shut door of his hopes seemed, after two long days, more than even his passion required of him; and on the third he despatched a note of goodbye to his friend. He was going off for a few weeks, he explained, his mother and sisters wished to be taken to the Italian lakes: but he would return to Paris, and say his real farewell to her, before sailing for America in July.

He had not intended his note to act as an ultimatum: he had no wish to surprise Madame de Malrive into unconsidered surrender. When, almost immediately, his own messenger returned with a reply from her, he even felt a pang of disappointment, a momentary fear lest she should have stooped a little from the high place where his passion had preferred to leave her; but her first words turned his fear into rejoicing.

"Let me see you before you go: something extraordinary has happened," she wrote.

What had happened, as he heard from her a few hours later, finding her in a tremor of frightened gladness, with her door boldly closed to all the world but himself, was nothing less extraordinary than a visit from Madame de Treymes, who had come, officially delegated by the family, to announce that Monsieur de Malrive had decided not to oppose his wife's suit for divorce. Durham, at the news, was almost afraid to show himself too amazed; but his small signs of alarm and wonder were swallowed up in the flush of Madame de Malrive's incredulous joy.

"It's the long habit, you know, of not believing them, of looking for the truth always in what they don't say. It took me hours and hours to convince myself that there's no trick under it, that there can't be any," she explained.

"Then you are convinced now?" escaped from Durham; but the shadow of his question lingered no more than the flit of a wing across her face.

"I am convinced because the facts are there to reassure me. Christiane tells me that Monsieur de Malrive has consulted his lawyers, and that they have advised him to free me. Maitre Enguerrand has been instructed to see my lawyer whenever I wish it. They quite understand that I never should have taken the step in face of any opposition on their part, I am so thankful to you for making that perfectly clear to them!—and I suppose this is the return their pride makes to mine. For they can be proud collectively—" She broke off and added, with happy hands outstretched: "And I owe it all to you, Christiane said it was your talk with her that had convinced them."

Durham, at this statement, had to repress a fresh sound of amazement; but with her hands in his, and, a moment after, her whole self drawn to him in the first yielding of her lips, doubt perforce gave way to the lover's happy conviction that such love was after all too strong for the powers of darkness.

It was only when they sat again in the blissful after-calm of their understanding, that he felt the pricking of an unappeased distrust.

"Did Madame de Treymes give you any reason for this change of front?" he risked asking, when he found the distrust was not otherwise to be quelled.

"Oh, yes: just what I've said. It was really her admiration of you, of your attitude, your delicacy. She said that at first she hadn't believed in it: they're always looking for a hidden motive. And when she found that yours was staring at her in the actual words you said: that you really respected my scruples, and would never, never try to coerce or entrap me, something in her, poor Christiane!—answered to it, she told me, and she wanted to prove to us that she was capable of understanding us too. If you knew her history you'd find it wonderful and pathetic that she can!"

Durham thought he knew enough of it to infer that Madame de Treymes had not been the object of many conscientious scruples on the part of the opposite sex; but this increased rather his sense of the strangeness than of the pathos of her action. Yet Madame de Malrive, whom he had once inwardly taxed with the morbid raising of obstacles, seemed to see none now; and he could only infer that her sister-in-law's actual words had carried more conviction than reached him in the repetition of them. The mere fact that he had so much to gain by leaving his friend's faith undisturbed was no doubt stirring his own suspicions to unnatural activity; and this sense gradually reasoned him back into acceptance of her view, as the most normal as well as the pleasantest he could take.

VIII

The uneasiness thus temporarily repressed slipped into the final disguise of hoping he should not again meet Madame de Treymes; and in this wish he was seconded by the decision, in which Madame de Malrive concurred, that it would be well for him to leave Paris while the preliminary negotiations were going on. He committed her interests to the best professional care, and his mother, resigning her dream of the lakes, remained to fortify Madame de Malrive by her mild unimaginative view of the transaction, as an uncomfortable but commonplace necessity, like house-cleaning or dentistry. Mrs. Durham would doubtless have preferred that her only son, even with his hair turning gray, should have chosen a Fanny Frisbee rather than a Fanny de Malrive; but it was a part of her acceptance of life on a general basis of innocence and kindliness, that she entered generously into his dream of rescue and renewal, and devoted herself without after-thought to keeping up Fanny's courage with so little to spare for herself.

The process, the lawyers declared, would not be a long one, since Monsieur de Malrive's acquiescence reduced it to a formality; and when, at the end of June, Durham returned from Italy with Katy and Nannie, there seemed no reason why he should not stop in Paris long enough to learn what progress had been made.

But before he could learn this he was to hear, on entering Madame de Malrive's presence, news more immediate if less personal. He found her, in spite of her gladness in his return, so evidently preoccupied and distressed that his first thought was one of fear for their own future. But she read and dispelled this by saying, before he could put his question: "Poor Christiane is here. She is very unhappy. You have seen in the papers—?"

"I have seen no papers since we left Turin. What has happened?"

"The Prince d'Armillac has come to grief. There has been some terrible scandal about money and he has been obliged to leave France to escape arrest."

"And Madame de Treymes has left her husband?"

"Ah, no, poor creature: they don't leave their husbands—they can't. But de Treymes has gone down to their place in Brittany, and as my mother-in-law is with another daughter in Auvergne, Christiane came here for a few days. With me, you see, she need not pretend—she can cry her eyes out."

"And that is what she is doing?"

It was so unlike his conception of the way in which, under the most adverse circumstances, Madame de Treymes would be likely to occupy her time, that Durham was conscious of a note of scepticism in his query.

"Poor thing, if you saw her you would feel nothing but pity. She is suffering so horribly that I reproach myself for being happy under the same roof."

Durham met this with a tender pressure of her hand; then he said, after a pause of reflection: "I should like to see her."

He hardly knew what prompted him to utter the wish, unless it were a sudden stir of compunction at the memory of his own dealings with Madame de Treymes. Had he not sacrificed the poor creature to a purely fantastic conception of conduct? She had said that she knew she was asking a trifle of him; and the fact that, materially, it would have been a trifle, had seemed at the moment only an added reason for steeling himself in his moral resistance to it. But now that he had gained his point, and through her own generosity, as it still appeared, the largeness of her attitude made his own seem cramped and petty. Since conduct, in the last resort, must be judged by its enlarging or diminishing effect on character, might it not be that the zealous weighing of the moral anise and cummin was less important than the unconsidered lavishing of the precious ointment? At any rate, he could enjoy no peace of mind under the burden of Madame de Treymes' magnanimity, and when he had assured himself that his own affairs were progressing favourably, he once more, at the risk of surprising his betrothed, brought up the possibility of seeing her relative.

Madame de Malrive evinced no surprise. "It is natural, knowing what she has done for us, that you should want to show her your sympathy. The difficulty is that it is just the one thing you can't show her. You can thank her, of course, for ourselves, but even that at the moment—"

"Would seem brutal? Yes, I recognize that I should have to choose my words," he admitted, guiltily conscious that his capability of dealing with Madame de Treymes extended far beyond her sister-in-law's conjecture.

Madame de Malrive still hesitated. "I can tell her; and when you come back tomorrow—"

It had been decided that, in the interests of discretion, the interests, in other words, of the poor little future Marquis de Malrive, Durham was to remain but two days in Paris, withdrawing then with his family till the conclusion of the divorce proceedings permitted him to return in the acknowledged character of Madame de Malrive's future husband. Even on this occasion, he had not come to her alone; Nannie Durham, in the adjoining room, was chatting conspicuously with the little Marquis, whom she could with difficulty be restrained from teaching to call her "Aunt Nannie." Durham thought her voice had risen unduly once or twice during his visit, and when, on taking leave, he went to summon her from the inner room, he found the higher note of ecstasy had been evoked by the appearance of Madame de Treymes, and that the little boy, himself absorbed in a new toy of Durham's bringing, was being bent over by an actual as well as a potential aunt.

Madame de Treymes raised herself with a slight start at Durham's approach: she had her hat on, and had evidently paused a moment on her way out to speak with Nannie, without expecting to be surprised by her sister-in-law's other visitor. But her surprises never wore the awkward form of embarrassment, and she smiled beautifully on Durham as he took her extended hand.

The smile was made the more appealing by the way in which it lit up the ruin of her small dark face, which looked seared and hollowed as by a flame that might have spread over it from her fevered eyes. Durham, accustomed to the pale inward grief of the inexpressive races, was positively startled by the way in which she seemed to have been openly stretched on the pyre; he almost felt an indelicacy in the ravages so tragically confessed.

The sight caused an involuntary readjustment of his whole view of the situation, and made him, as far as his own share in it went, more than ever inclined to extremities of self-disgust. With him such sensations required, for his own relief, some immediate penitential escape, and as Madame de Treymes turned toward the door he addressed a glance of entreaty to his betrothed.

Madame de Malrive, whose intelligence could be counted on at such moments, responded by laying a detaining hand on her sister-in-law's arm.

"Dear Christiane, may I leave Mr. Durham in your charge for two minutes? I have promised Nannie that she shall see the boy put to bed."

Madame de Treymes made no audible response to this request, but when the door had closed on the other ladies she said, looking quietly at Durham: "I don't think that, in this house, your time will hang so heavy that you need my help in supporting it."

Durham met her glance frankly. "It was not for that reason that Madame de Malrive asked you to remain with me."

"Why, then? Surely not in the interest of preserving appearances, since she is safely upstairs with your sister?"

"No; but simply because I asked her to. I told her I wanted to speak to you."

"How you arrange things! And what reason can you have for wanting to speak to me?"

He paused for a moment. "Can't you imagine? The desire to thank you for what you have done."

She stirred restlessly, turning to adjust her hat before the glass above the mantelpiece.

"Oh, as for what I have done—!"

"Don't speak as if you regretted it," he interposed.

She turned back to him with a flash of laughter lighting up the haggardness of her face. "Regret working for the happiness of two such excellent persons? Can't you fancy what a charming change it is for me to do something so innocent and beneficent?"

He moved across the room and went up to her, drawing down the hand which still flitted experimentally about her hat.

"Don't talk in that way, however much one of the persons of whom you speak may have deserved it."

"One of the persons? Do you mean me?"

He released her hand, but continued to face her resolutely. "I mean myself, as you know. You have been generous, extraordinarily generous."

"Ah, but I was doing good in a good cause. You have made me see that there is a distinction."

He flushed to the forehead. "I am here to let you say whatever you choose to me."

"Whatever I choose?" She made a slight gesture of deprecation. "Has it never occurred to you that I may conceivably choose to say nothing?"

Durham paused, conscious of the increasing difficulty of the advance. She met him, parried him, at every turn: he had to take his baffled purpose back to another point of attack.

"Quite conceivably," he said: "so much so that I am aware I must make the most of this opportunity, because I am not likely to get another."

"But what remains of your opportunity, if it isn't one to me?"

"It still remains, for me, an occasion to abase myself—" He broke off, conscious of a grossness of allusion that seemed, on a closer approach, the real obstacle to full expression. But the moments were flying, and for his self-esteem's sake he must find some way of making her share the burden of his repentance.

"There is only one thinkable pretext for detaining you: it is that I may still show my sense of what you have done for me."

Madame de Treymes, who had moved toward the door, paused at this and faced him, resting her thin brown hands on a slender sofa-back.

"How do you propose to show that sense?" she enquired.

Durham coloured still more deeply: he saw that she was determined to save her pride by making what he had to say of the utmost difficulty. Well! he would let his expiation take that form, then, it was as if her slender hands held out to him the fool's cap he was condemned to press down on his own ears.

"By offering in return, in any form, and to the utmost, any service you are forgiving enough to ask of me."

She received this with a low sound of laughter that scarcely rose to her lips. "You are princely. But, my dear sir, does it not occur to you that I may, meanwhile, have taken my own way of repaying myself for any service I have been fortunate enough to render you?"

Durham, at the question, or still more, perhaps, at the tone in which it was put, felt, through his compunction, a vague faint chill of apprehension. Was she threatening him or only mocking him? Or was this barbed swiftness of retort only the wounded creature's way of defending the privacy of her own pain? He looked at her again, and read his answer in the last conjecture.

"I don't know how you can have repaid yourself for anything so disinterested, but I am sure, at least, that you have given me no chance of recognizing, ever so slightly, what you have done."

She shook her head, with the flicker of a smile on her melancholy lips. "Don't be too sure! You have given me a chance and I have taken it, taken it to the full. So fully," she continued, keeping her eyes fixed on his, "that if I were to accept any farther service you might choose to offer, I should simply be robbing you, robbing you shamelessly." She paused, and added in an undefinable voice: "I was entitled, wasn't I, to take something in return for the service I had the happiness of doing you?"

Durham could not tell whether the irony of her tone was self-directed or addressed to himself, perhaps it comprehended them both. At any rate, he chose to overlook his own share in it in replying earnestly: "So much so, that I can't see how you can have left me nothing to add to what you say you have taken."

"Ah, but you don't know what that is!" She continued to smile, elusively, ambiguously. "And what's more, you wouldn't believe me if I told you."

"How do you know?" he rejoined.

"You didn't believe me once before; and this is so much more incredible."

He took the taunt full in the face. "I shall go away unhappy unless you tell me, but then perhaps I have deserved to," he confessed.

She shook her head again, advancing toward the door with the evident intention of bringing their conference to a close; but on the threshold she paused to launch her reply.

"I can't send you away unhappy, since it is in the contemplation of your happiness that I have found my reward."

IX

The next day Durham left with his family for England, with the intention of not returning till after the divorce should have been pronounced in September.

To say that he left with a quiet heart would be to overstate the case: the fact that he could not communicate to Madame de Malrive the substance of his talk with her sister-in-law still hung upon him uneasily. But of definite apprehensions the lapse of time gradually freed him, and Madame de Malrive's letters, addressed more frequently to his mother and sisters than to himself, reflected, in their reassuring serenity, the undisturbed course of events.

There was to Durham something peculiarly touching, as of an involuntary confession of almost unbearable loneliness, in the way she had regained, with her re-entry into the clear air of American associations, her own fresh trustfulness of view. Once she had accustomed herself to the surprise of finding her divorce unopposed, she had been, as it now seemed to Durham, in almost too great haste to renounce the habit of weighing motives and calculating chances. It was as though her coming liberation had already freed her from the garb of a mental slavery, as though she could not too soon or too conspicuously cast off the ugly badge of suspicion. The fact that Durham's cleverness had achieved so easy a victory over forces apparently impregnable, merely raised her estimate of that cleverness to the point of letting her feel that she could rest in it without farther demur. He had even noticed in her, during his few hours in Paris, a tendency to reproach herself for her lack of charity, and a desire, almost as fervent as his own, to expiate it by exaggerated recognition of the disinterestedness of her opponents, if opponents they could still be called. This sudden change in her attitude was peculiarly moving to Durham. He knew she would hazard herself lightly enough wherever her heart called her; but that, with the precious freight of her child's future weighing her down, she should commit herself so blindly to his hand stirred in him the depths of tenderness. Indeed, had the actual course of events been less auspiciously regular, Madame de Malrive's confidence would have gone far toward unsettling his own; but with the process of law going on unimpeded, and the other side making no sign of open or covert resistance, the fresh air of good faith gradually swept through the inmost recesses of his distrust.

It was expected that the decision in the suit would be reached by mid-September; and it was arranged that Durham and his family should remain in England till a decent interval after the conclusion of the proceedings. Early in the month, however, it became necessary for Durham to go to France to confer with a business associate who was in Paris for a few days, and on the point of sailing for Cherbourg. The most zealous observance of appearances could hardly forbid Durham's return for such a purpose; but it had been agreed between himself and Madame de Malrive, who had once more been left alone by Madame de Treymes' return to her family, that, so close to the fruition of their wishes, they would propitiate fate by a scrupulous adherence to usage, and communicate only, during his hasty visit, by a daily interchange of notes.

The ingenuity of Madame de Malrive's tenderness found, however, the day after his arrival, a means of tempering their privation. "Christiane," she wrote, "is passing through Paris on her way from

Trouville, and has promised to see you for me if you will call on her today. She thinks there is no reason why you should not go to the Hotel de Malrive, as you will find her there alone, the family having gone to Auvergne. She is really our friend and understands us."

In obedience to this request, though perhaps inwardly regretting that it should have been made, Durham that afternoon presented himself at the proud old house beyond the Seine. More than ever, in the semi-abandonment of the morte saison, with reduced service, and shutters closed to the silence of the high-walled court, did it strike the American as the incorruptible custodian of old prejudices and strange social survivals. The thought of what he must represent to the almost human consciousness which such old houses seem to possess, made him feel like a barbarian desecrating the silence of a temple of the earlier faith. Not that there was anything venerable in the attestations of the Hotel de Malrive, except in so far as, to a sensitive imagination, every concrete embodiment of a past order of things testifies to real convictions once suffered for. Durham, at any rate, always alive in practical issues to the view of the other side, had enough sympathy left over to spend it sometimes, whimsically, on such perceptions of difference. Today, especially, the assurance of success, the sense of entering like a victorious beleaguerer receiving the keys of the stronghold, disposed him to a sentimental perception of what the other side might have to say for itself, in the language of old portraits, old relics, old usages dumbly outraged by his mere presence.

On the appearance of Madame de Treymes, however, such considerations gave way to the immediate act of wondering how she meant to carry off her share of the adventure. Durham had not forgotten the note on which their last conversation had closed: the lapse of time serving only to give more precision and perspective to the impression he had then received.

Madame de Treymes' first words implied a recognition of what was in his thoughts.

"It is extraordinary, my receiving you here; but que voulez vous? There was no other place, and I would do more than this for our dear Fanny."

Durham bowed. "It seems to me that you are also doing a great deal for me."

"Perhaps you will see later that I have my reasons," she returned smiling. "But before speaking for myself I must speak for Fanny."

She signed to him to take a chair near the sofa-corner in which she had installed herself, and he listened in silence while she delivered Madame de Malrive's message, and her own report of the progress of affairs.

"You have put me still more deeply in your debt," he said, as she concluded; "I wish you would make the expression of this feeling a large part of the message I send back to Madame de Malrive."

She brushed this aside with one of her light gestures of deprecation. "Oh, I told you I had my reasons. And since you are here, and the mere sight of you assures me that you are as well as Fanny charged me to find you, with all these preliminaries disposed of, I am going to relieve you, in a small measure, of the weight of your obligation."

Durham raised his head quickly. "By letting me do something in return?"

She made an assenting motion. "By asking you to answer a question."

"That seems very little to do."

"Don't be so sure! It is never very little to your race." She leaned back, studying him through half-dropped lids.

"Well, try me," he protested.

She did not immediately respond; and when she spoke, her first words were explanatory rather than interrogative.

"I want to begin by saying that I believe I once did you an injustice, to the extent of misunderstanding your motive for a certain action."

Durham's uneasy flush confessed his recognition of her meaning. "Ah, if we must go back to that—"

"You withdraw your assent to my request?"

"By no means; but nothing consolatory you can find to say on that point can really make any difference."

"Will not the difference in my view of you perhaps make a difference in your own?"

She looked at him earnestly, without a trace of irony in her eyes or on her lips. "It is really I who have an amende to make, as I now understand the situation. I once turned to you for help in a painful extremity, and I have only now learned to understand your reasons for refusing to help me."

"Oh, my reasons—" groaned Durham.

"I have learned to understand them," she persisted, "by being so much, lately, with Fanny."

"But I never told her!" he broke in.

"Exactly. That was what told me. I understood you through her, and through your dealings with her. There she was, the woman you adored and longed to save; and you would not lift a finger to make her yours by means which would have seemed, I see it now, a desecration of your feeling for each other." She paused, as if to find the exact words for meanings she had never before had occasion to formulate. "It came to me first, a light on your attitude, when I found you had never breathed to her a word of our talk together. She had confidently commissioned you to find a way for her, as the mediaeval lady sent a prayer to her knight to deliver her from captivity, and you came back, confessing you had failed, but never justifying yourself by so much as a hint of the reason why. And when I had lived a little in Fanny's intimacy, at a moment when circumstances helped to bring us extraordinarily close, I understood why you had done this; why you had let her take what view she pleased of your failure, your passive acceptance of defeat, rather than let her suspect the alternative offered you. You couldn't, even with my permission, betray to any one a hint of my miserable secret, and you couldn't, for your life's happiness, pay the particular price that I asked." She leaned toward him in the intense, almost childlike, effort at full expression. "Oh, we are of different races, with a different point of honour; but I understand, I see, that you are good people, just simply, courageously good!"

She paused, and then said slowly: "Have I understood you? Have I put my hand on your motive?"

Durham sat speechless, subdued by the rush of emotion which her words set free.

"That, you understand, is my question," she concluded with a faint smile; and he answered hesitatingly: "What can it matter, when the upshot is something I infinitely regret?"

"Having refused me? Don't!" She spoke with deep seriousness, bending her eyes full on his: "Ah, I have suffered, suffered! But I have learned also, my life has been enlarged. You see how I have understood you both. And that is something I should have been incapable of a few months ago."

Durham returned her look. "I can't think that you can ever have been incapable of any generous interpretation."

She uttered a slight exclamation, which resolved itself into a laugh of self-directed irony.

"If you knew into what language I have always translated life! But that," she broke off, "is not what you are here to learn."

"I think," he returned gravely, "that I am here to learn the measure of Christian charity."

She threw him a new, odd look. "Ah, no, but to show it!" she exclaimed.

"To show it? And to whom?"

She paused for a moment, and then rejoined, instead of answering: "Do you remember that day I talked with you at Fanny's? The day after you came back from Italy?"

He made a motion of assent, and she went on: "You asked me then what return I expected for my service to you, as you called it; and I answered, the contemplation of your happiness. Well, do you know what that meant in my old language, the language I was still speaking then? It meant that I knew there was horrible misery in store for you, and that I was waiting to feast my eyes on it: that's all!"

She had flung out the words with one of her quick bursts of self-abandonment, like a fevered sufferer stripping the bandage from a wound. Durham received them with a face blanching to the pallour of her own.

"What misery do you mean?" he exclaimed.

She leaned forward, laying her hand on his with just such a gesture as she had used to enforce her appeal in Mrs. Boykin's boudoir. The remembrance made him shrink slightly from her touch, and she drew back with a smile.

"Have you never asked yourself," she enquired, "why our family consented so readily to a divorce?"

"Yes, often," he replied, all his unformed fears gathering in a dark throng about him. "But Fanny was so reassured, so convinced that we owed it to your good offices—"

She broke into a laugh. "My good offices! Will you never, you Americans, learn that we do not act individually in such cases? That we are all obedient to a common principle of authority?"

"Then it was not you—?"

She made an impatient shrugging motion. "Oh, you are too confiding—it is the other side of your beautiful good faith!"

"The side you have taken advantage of, it appears?"

"I—we—all of us. I especially!" she confessed.

X

There was another pause, during which Durham tried to steady himself against the shock of the impending revelation. It was an odd circumstance of the case that, though Madame de Treymes' avowal of duplicity was fresh in his ears, he did not for a moment believe that she would deceive him again. Whatever passed between them now would go to the root of the matter.

The first thing that passed was the long look they exchanged: searching on his part, tender, sad, undefinable on hers. As the result of it he said: "Why, then, did you consent to the divorce?"

"To get the boy back," she answered instantly; and while he sat stunned by the unexpectedness of the retort, she went on: "Is it possible you never suspected? It has been our whole thought from the first. Everything was planned with that object."

He drew a sharp breath of alarm. "But the divorce—how could that give him back to you?"

"It was the only thing that could. We trembled lest the idea should occur to you. But we were reasonably safe, for there has only been one other case of the same kind before the courts." She leaned back, the sight of his perplexity checking her quick rush of words. "You didn't know," she began again, "that in that case, on the remarriage of the mother, the courts instantly restored the child to the father, though he had—well, given as much cause for divorce as my unfortunate brother?"

Durham gave an ironic laugh. "Your French justice takes a grammar and dictionary to understand."

She smiled. " We understand it, and it isn't necessary that you should."

"So it would appear!" he exclaimed bitterly.

"Don't judge us too harshly, or not, at least, till you have taken the trouble to learn our point of view. You consider the individual, we think only of the family."

"Why don't you take care to preserve it, then?"

"Ah, that's what we do; in spite of every aberration of the individual. And so, when we saw it was impossible that my brother and his wife should live together, we simply transferred our allegiance to the child, we constituted him the family."

"A precious kindness you did him! If the result is to give him back to his father."

"That, I admit, is to be deplored; but his father is only a fraction of the whole. What we really do is to give him back to his race, his religion, his true place in the order of things."

"His mother never tried to deprive him of any of those inestimable advantages!"

Madame de Treymes unclasped her hands with a slight gesture of deprecation.

"Not consciously, perhaps; but silences and reserves can teach so much. His mother has another point of view—"

"Thank heaven!" Durham interjected.

"Thank heaven for her, yes, perhaps; but it would not have done for the boy."

Durham squared his shoulders with the sudden resolve of a man breaking through a throng of ugly phantoms.

"You haven't yet convinced me that it won't have to do for him. At the time of Madame de Malrive's separation, the court made no difficulty about giving her the custody of her son; and you must pardon me for reminding you that the father's unfitness was the reason alleged."

Madame de Treymes shrugged her shoulders. "And my poor brother, you would add, has not changed; but the circumstances have, and that proves precisely what I have been trying to show you: that, in such cases, the general course of events is considered, rather than the action of any one person."

"Then why is Madame de Malrive's action to be considered?"

"Because it breaks up the unity of the family."

" Unity—!" broke from Durham; and Madame de Treymes gently suffered his smile.

"Of the family tradition, I mean: it introduces new elements. You are a new element."

"Thank heaven!" said Durham again.

She looked at him singularly. "Yes, you may thank heaven. Why isn't it enough to satisfy Fanny?"

"Why isn't what enough?"

"Your being, as I say, a new element; taking her so completely into a better air. Why shouldn't she be content to begin a new life with you, without wanting to keep the boy too?"

Durham stared at her dumbly. "I don't know what you mean," he said at length.

"I mean that in her place—" she broke off, dropping her eyes. "She may have another son, the son of the man she adores."

Durham rose from his seat and took a quick turn through the room. She sat motionless, following his steps through her lowered lashes, which she raised again slowly as he stood before her.

"Your idea, then, is that I should tell her nothing?" he said.

"Tell her now? But, my poor friend, you would be ruined!"

"Exactly." He paused. "Then why have you told me?"

Under her dark skin he saw the faint colour stealing. "We see things so differently, but can't you conceive that, after all that has passed, I felt it a kind of loyalty not to leave you in ignorance?"

"And you feel no such loyalty to her?"

"Ah, I leave her to you," she murmured, looking down again.

Durham continued to stand before her, grappling slowly with his perplexity, which loomed larger and darker as it closed in on him.

"You don't leave her to me; you take her from me at a stroke! I suppose," he added painfully, "I ought to thank you for doing it before it's too late."

She stared. "I take her from you? I simply prevent your going to her unprepared. Knowing Fanny as I do, it seemed to me necessary that you should find a way in advance, a way of tiding over the first moment. That, of course, is what we had planned that you shouldn't have. We meant to let you marry, and then—. Oh, there is no question about the result: we are certain of our case, our measures have been taken de loin." She broke off, as if oppressed by his stricken silence. "You will think me stupid, but my warning you of this is the only return I know how to make for your generosity. I could not bear to have you say afterward that I had deceived you twice."

"Twice?" He looked at her perplexedly, and her colour rose.

"I deceived you once, that night at your cousin's, when I tried to get you to bribe me. Even then we meant to consent to the divorce, it was decided the first day that I saw you." He was silent, and she added, with one of her mocking gestures: "You see from what a milieu you are taking her!"

Durham groaned. "She will never give up her son!"

"How can she help it? After you are married there will be no choice."

"No, but there is one now."

" Now?" She sprang to her feet, clasping her hands in dismay. "Haven't I made it clear to you? Haven't I shown you your course?" She paused, and then brought out with emphasis: "I love Fanny, and I am ready to trust her happiness to you."

"I shall have nothing to do with her happiness," he repeated doggedly.

She stood close to him, with a look intently fixed on his face. "Are you afraid?" she asked with one of her mocking flashes.

"Afraid?"

"Of not being able to make it up to her—?"

Their eyes met, and he returned her look steadily.

"No; if I had the chance, I believe I could."

"I know you could!" she exclaimed.

"That's the worst of it," he said with a cheerless laugh.

"The worst—?"

"Don't you see that I can't deceive her? Can't trick her into marrying me now?"

Madame de Treymes continued to hold his eyes for a puzzled moment after he had spoken; then she broke out despairingly: "Is happiness never more to you, then, than this abstract standard of truth?"

Durham reflected. "I don't know, it's an instinct. There doesn't seem to be any choice."

"Then I am a miserable wretch for not holding my tongue!"

He shook his head sadly. "That would not have helped me; and it would have been a thousand times worse for her."

"Nothing can be as bad for her as losing you! Aren't you moved by seeing her need?"

"Horribly, are not you?" he said, lifting his eyes to hers suddenly.

She started under his look. "You mean, why don't I help you? Why don't I use my influence? Ah, if you knew how I have tried!"

"And you are sure that nothing can be done?"

"Nothing, nothing: what arguments can I use? We abhor divorce, we go against our religion in consenting to it, and nothing short of recovering the boy could possibly justify us."

Durham turned slowly away. "Then there is nothing to be done," he said, speaking more to himself than to her.

He felt her light touch on his arm. "Wait! There is one thing more—" She stood close to him, with entreaty written on her small passionate face. "There is one thing more," she repeated. "And that is, to believe that I am deceiving you again."

He stopped short with a bewildered stare. "That you are deceiving me—about the boy?"

"Yes, yes; why shouldn't I? You're so credulous, the temptation is irresistible."

"Ah, it would be too easy to find out—"

"Don't try, then! Go on as if nothing had happened. I have been lying to you," she declared with vehemence.

"Do you give me your word of honour?" he rejoined.

"A liar's? I haven't any! Take the logic of the facts instead. What reason have you to believe any good of me? And what reason have I to do any to you? Why on earth should I betray my family for your benefit? Ah, don't let yourself be deceived to the end!" She sparkled up at him, her eyes suffused with mockery; but on the lashes he saw a tear.

He shook his head sadly. "I should first have to find a reason for your deceiving me."

"Why, I gave it to you long ago. I wanted to punish you, and now I've punished you enough."

"Yes, you've punished me enough," he conceded.

The tear gathered and fell down her thin cheek. "It's you who are punishing me now. I tell you I'm false to the core. Look back and see what I've done to you!"

He stood silent, with his eyes fixed on the ground. Then he took one of her hands and raised it to his lips.

"You poor, good woman!" he said gravely.

Her hand trembled as she drew it away. "You're going to her, straight from here?"

"Yes, straight from here."

"To tell her everything, to renounce your hope?"

"That is what it amounts to, I suppose."

She watched him cross the room and lay his hand on the door.

"Ah, you poor, good man!" she said with a sob.

THE TRIUMPH OF NIGHT

I

It was clear that the sleigh from Weymore had not come; and the shivering young traveller from Boston, who had counted on jumping into it when he left the train at Northridge Junction, found himself standing alone on the open platform, exposed to the full assault of night-fall and winter.

The blast that swept him came off New Hampshire snow-fields and ice-hung forests. It seemed to have traversed interminable leagues of frozen silence, filling them with the same cold roar and sharpening its edge against the same bitter black-and-white landscape. Dark, searching and sword-like, it alternately muffled and harried its victim, like a bull-fighter now whirling his cloak and now planting his darts. This analogy brought home to the young man the fact that he himself had no cloak, and that the overcoat in which he had faced the relatively temperate air of Boston seemed no thicker than a sheet of paper on the bleak heights of Northridge. George Faxon said to himself that the place was uncommonly well-named. It clung to an exposed ledge over the valley from which the train had lifted him, and the wind combed it with teeth of steel that he seemed actually to hear scraping against the wooden sides of the station. Other building there was none: the village lay far down the road, and thither, since the Weymore sleigh had not come, Faxon saw himself under the necessity of plodding through several feet of snow.

He understood well enough what had happened: his hostess had forgotten that he was coming. Young as Faxon was, this sad lucidity of soul had been acquired as the result of long experience, and he knew that the visitors who can least afford to hire a carriage are almost always those whom their hosts forget to send for. Yet to say that Mrs. Culme had forgotten him was too crude a way of putting it Similar incidents led him to think that she had probably told her maid to tell the butler to telephone the coachman to tell one of the grooms (if no one else needed him) to drive over to Northridge to fetch the new secretary; but on a night like this, what groom who respected his rights would fail to forget the order?

Faxon's obvious course was to struggle through the drifts to the village, and there rout out a sleigh to convey him to Weymore; but what if, on his arrival at Mrs. Culme's, no one remembered to ask him what this devotion to duty had cost? That, again, was one of the contingencies he had expensively learned to look out for, and the perspicacity so acquired told him it would be cheaper to spend the night at the Northridge inn, and advise Mrs. Culme of his presence there by telephone. He had reached this decision, and was about to entrust his luggage to a vague man with a lantern, when his hopes were raised by the sound of bells.

Two sleighs were just dashing up to the station, and from the foremost there sprang a young man muffled in furs.

"Weymore? No, these are not the Weymore sleighs."

The voice was that of the youth who had jumped to the platform, a voice so agreeable that, in spite of the words, it fell consolingly on Faxon's ears. At the same moment the wandering station-lantern, casting a transient light on the speaker, showed his features to be in the pleasantest harmony with his voice. He was very fair and very young, hardly in the twenties, Faxon thought, but his face, though full of a morning freshness, was a trifle too thin and fine-drawn, as though a vivid spirit contended in him with a strain of physical weakness. Faxon was perhaps the quicker to notice such delicacies of balance because his own temperament hung on lightly quivering nerves, which yet, as he believed, would never quite swing him beyond a normal sensibility.

"You expected a sleigh from Weymore?" the newcomer continued, standing beside Faxon like a slender column of fur.

Mrs. Culme's secretary explained his difficulty, and the other brushed it aside with a contemptuous "Oh, Mrs. Culme!" that carried both speakers a long way toward reciprocal understanding.

"But then you must be—" The youth broke off with a smile of interrogation.

"The new secretary? Yes. But apparently there are no notes to be answered this evening." Faxon's laugh deepened the sense of solidarity which had so promptly established itself between the two.

His friend laughed also. "Mrs. Culme," he explained, "was lunching at my uncle's to-day, and she said you were due this evening. But seven hours is a long time for Mrs. Culme to remember anything."

"Well," said Faxon philosophically, "I suppose that's one of the reasons why she needs a secretary. And I've always the inn at Northridge," he concluded.

"Oh, but you haven't, though! It burned down last week."

"The deuce it did!" said Faxon; but the humour of the situation struck him before its inconvenience. His life, for years past, had been mainly a succession of resigned adaptations, and he had learned, before dealing practically with his embarrassments, to extract from most of them a small tribute of amusement.

"Oh, well, there's sure to be somebody in the place who can put me up."

"No one you could put up with. Besides, Northridge is three miles off, and our place, in the opposite direction, is a little nearer." Through the darkness, Faxon saw his friend sketch a gesture of self-introduction. "My name's Frank Rainer, and I'm staying with my uncle at Overdale. I've driven over to meet two friends of his, who are due in a few minutes from New York. If you don't mind waiting till they arrive I'm sure Overdale can do you better than Northridge. We're only down from town for a few days, but the house is always ready for a lot of people."

"But your uncle—?" Faxon could only object, with the odd sense, through his embarrassment, that it would be magically dispelled by his invisible friend's next words.

"Oh, my uncle, you'll see! I answer for him! I daresay you've heard of him, John Lavington?"

John Lavington! There was a certain irony in asking if one had heard of John Lavington! Even from a post of observation as obscure as that of Mrs. Culme's secretary the rumour of John Lavington's money, of his pictures, his politics, his charities and his hospitality, was as difficult to escape as the roar of a cataract in a mountain solitude. It might almost have been said that the one place in which one would not have expected to come upon him was in just such a solitude as now surrounded the speakers, at least in this deepest hour of its desertedness. But it was just like Lavington's brilliant ubiquity to put one in the wrong even there.

"Oh, yes, I've heard of your uncle."

"Then you will come, won't you? We've only five minutes to wait." young Rainer urged, in the tone that dispels scruples by ignoring them; and Faxon found himself accepting the invitation as simply as it was offered.

A delay in the arrival of the New York train lengthened their five minutes to fifteen; and as they paced the icy platform Faxon began to see why it had seemed the most natural thing in the world to accede to his new acquaintance's suggestion. It was because Frank Rainer was one of the privileged beings who simplify human intercourse by the atmosphere of confidence and good humour they diffuse. He produced this effect, Faxon noted, by the exercise of no gift but his youth, and of no art but his sincerity; and these qualities were revealed in a smile of such sweetness that Faxon felt, as never before, what Nature can achieve when she deigns to match the face with the mind.

He learned that the young man was the ward, and the only nephew, of John Lavington, with whom he had made his home since the death of his mother, the great man's sister. Mr. Lavington, Rainer said, had been "a regular brick" to him—"But then he is to every one, you know"—and the young fellow's situation seemed in fact to be perfectly in keeping with his person. Apparently the only shade that had ever rested on him was cast by the physical weakness which Faxon had already detected. Young Rainer had been threatened with tuberculosis, and the disease was so far advanced that, according to the highest authorities, banishment to Arizona or New Mexico was inevitable. "But luckily my uncle didn't pack me off, as most people would have done, without getting another opinion. Whose? Oh, an awfully clever chap, a young doctor with a lot of new ideas, who simply laughed at my being sent away, and said I'd do perfectly well in New York if I didn't dine out too much, and if I dashed off occasionally to Northridge for a little fresh air. So it's really my uncle's doing that I'm not in exile, and I feel no end better since the new chap told me I needn't bother." Young Rainer went on to confess that he was extremely fond of dining out, dancing and similar distractions; and Faxon, listening to him, was inclined to think that the physician who had refused to cut him off altogether from these pleasures was probably a better psychologist than his seniors.

"All the same you ought to be careful, you know." The sense of elder-brotherly concern that forced the words from Faxon made him, as he spoke, slip his arm through Frank Rainer 's.

The latter met the movement with a responsive pressure. "Oh, I am: awfully, awfully. And then my uncle has such an eye on me!"

"But if your uncle has such an eye on you, what does he say to your swallowing knives out here in this Siberian wild?"

Rainer raised his fur collar with a careless gesture. "It's not that that does it, the cold's good for me."

"And it's not the dinners and dances? What is it, then?" Faxon good-humouredly insisted; to which his companion answered with a laugh: "Well, my uncle says it's being bored; and I rather think he's right!"

His laugh ended in a spasm of coughing and a struggle for breath that made Faxon, still holding his arm, guide him hastily into the shelter of the fireless waitingroom.

Young Rainer had dropped down on the bench against the wall and pulled off one of his fur gloves to grope for a handkerchief. He tossed aside his cap and drew the handkerchief across his forehead, which was intensely white, and beaded with moisture, though his face retained a healthy glow. But Faxon's gaze remained fastened to the hand he had uncovered: it was so long, so colourless, so wasted, so much older than the brow he passed it over.

"It's queer, a healthy face but dying hands," the secretary mused: he somehow wished young Rainer had kept on his glove.

The whistle of the express drew the young men to their feet, and the next moment two heavily-furred gentlemen had descended to the platform and were breasting the rigour of the night. Frank Rainer introduced them as Mr. Grisben and Mr. Balch, and Faxon, while their luggage was being lifted into the second sleigh, discerned them, by the roving lantern-gleam, to be an elderly greyheaded pair, of the average prosperous business cut.

They saluted their host's nephew with friendly familiarity, and Mr. Grisben, who seemed the spokesman of the two, ended his greeting with a genial—"and many many more of them, dear boy!" which suggested to Faxon that their arrival coincided with an anniversary. But he could not press the enquiry, for the seat allotted him was at the coachman's side, while Frank Rainer joined his uncle's guests inside the sleigh.

A swift flight (behind such horses as one could be sure of John Lavington's having) brought them to tall gateposts, an illuminated lodge, and an avenue on which the snow had been levelled to the smoothness of marble. At the end of the avenue the long house loomed up, its principal bulk dark, but one wing sending out a ray of welcome; and the next moment Faxon was receiving a violent impression of warmth and light, of hot-house plants, hurrying servants, a vast spectacular oak hall like a stage-setting, and, in its unreal middle distance, a small figure, correctly dressed, conventionally featured, and utterly unlike his rather florid conception of the great John Lavington.

The surprise of the contrast remained with him through his hurried dressing in the large luxurious bedroom to which he had been shown. "I don't see where he comes in," was the only way he could put it, so difficult was it to fit the exuberance of Lavington's public personality into his host's contracted frame and manner. Mr. Laving ton, to whom Faxon's case had been rapidly explained by young Rainer, had welcomed him with a sort of dry and stilted cordiality that exactly matched his narrow face, his stiff hand, and the whiff of scent on his evening handkerchief. "Make yourself at home—at home!" he had repeated, in a tone that suggested, on his own part, a complete inability to perform the feat he urged on his visitor. "Any friend of Frank's... delighted... make yourself thoroughly at home!"

II

In spite of the balmy temperature and complicated conveniences of Faxon's bedroom, the injunction was not easy to obey. It was wonderful luck to have found a night's shelter under the opulent roof of Overdale, and he tasted the physical satisfaction to the full. But the place, for all its ingenuities of comfort, was oddly cold and unwelcoming. He couldn't have said why, and could only suppose that Mr. Lavington's intense personality, intensely negative, but intense all the same, must, in some occult way, have penetrated every corner of his dwelling. Perhaps, though, it was merely that Faxon himself was tired and hungry, more deeply chilled than he had known till he came in from the cold, and unutterably sick of all strange houses, and of the prospect of perpetually treading other people's stairs.

"I hope you're not famished?" Rainer's slim figure was in the doorway. "My uncle has a little business to attend to with Mr. Grisben, and we don't dine for half an hour. Shall I fetch you, or can you find your way down? Come straight to the dining-room, the second door on the left of the long gallery."

He disappeared, leaving a ray of warmth behind him, and Faxon, relieved, lit a cigarette and sat down by the fire.

Looking about with less haste, he was struck by a detail that had escaped him. The room was full of flowers, a mere "bachelor's room," in the wing of a house opened only for a few days, in the dead middle of a New Hampshire winter! Flowers were everywhere, not in senseless profusion, but placed with the same conscious art that he had remarked in the grouping of the blossoming shrubs in the hall. A vase of arums stood on the writing-table, a cluster of strange-hued carnations on the stand at his elbow, and from bowls of glass and porcelain clumps of freesia-bulbs diffused their melting fragrance. The fact implied acres of glass, but that was the least interesting part of it. The flowers themselves, their quality, selection and arrangement, attested on some one's part, and on whose but John Lavington's?—a solicitous and sensitive passion for that particular form of beauty. Well, it simply made the man, as he had appeared to Faxon, all the harder to understand!

The half-hour elapsed, and Faxon, rejoicing at the prospect of food, set out to make his way to the dining-room. He had not noticed the direction he had followed in going to his room, and was puzzled, when he left it, to find that two staircases, of apparently equal importance, invited him. He chose the one to his right, and reached, at its foot, a long gallery such as Rainer had described. The gallery was empty, the doors down its length were closed; but Rainer had said: "The second to the left," and Faxon, after pausing for some chance enlightenment which did not come, laid his hand on the second knob to the left.

The room he entered was square, with dusky picture-hung walls. In its centre, about a table lit by veiled lamps, he fancied Mr. Lavington and his guests to be already seated at dinner; then he perceived that the table was covered not with viands but with papers, and that he had blundered into what seemed to be his host's study. As he paused Frank Rainer looked up.

"Oh, here's Mr. Faxon. Why not ask him—?"

Mr. Lavington, from the end of the table, reflected his nephew's smile in a glance of impartial benevolence.

"Certainly. Come in, Mr. Faxon. If you won't think it a liberty—"

Mr. Grisben, who sat opposite his host, turned his head toward the door. "Of course Mr. Faxon's an American citizen?"

Frank Rainer laughed. "That's all right!... Oh, no, not one of your pin-pointed pens, Uncle Jack! Haven't you got a quill somewhere?"

Mr. Balch, who spoke slowly and as if reluctantly, in a muffled voice of which there seemed to be very little left, raised his hand to say: "One moment: you acknowledge this to be—?"

"My last will and testament?" Rainer's laugh redoubled. "Well, I won't answer for the 'last.' It's the first, anyway."

"It's a mere formula," Mr. Balch explained.

"Well, here goes." Rainer dipped his quill in the inkstand his uncle had pushed in his direction, and dashed a gallant signature across the document.

Faxon, understanding what was expected of him, and conjecturing that the young man was signing his will on the attainment of his majority, had placed himself behind Mr. Grisben, and stood awaiting his turn to affix his name to the instrument. Rainer, having signed, was about to push the paper across the table to Mr. Balch; but the latter, again raising his hand, said in his sad imprisoned voice: "The seal—?"

"Oh, does there have to be a seal?"

Faxon, looking over Mr. Grisben at John Lavington, saw a faint frown between his impassive eyes. "Really, Frank!" He seemed, Faxon thought, slightly irritated by his nephew's frivolity.

"Who's got a seal?" Frank Rainer continued, glancing about the table. "There doesn't seem to be one here."

Mr. Grisben interposed. "A wafer will do. Lavington, you have a wafer?"

Mr. Lavington had recovered his serenity. "There must be some in one of the drawers. But I'm ashamed to say I don't know where my secretary keeps these things. He ought to have seen to it that a wafer was sent with the document."

"Oh, hang it—" Frank Rainer pushed the paper aside: "It's the hand of God—and I'm as hungry as a wolf. Let's dine first, Uncle Jack."

"I think I've a seal upstairs," said Faxon.

Mr. Lavington sent him a barely perceptible smile. "So sorry to give you the trouble—"

"Oh, I say, don't send him after it now. Let's wait till after dinner!"

Mr. Lavington continued to smile on his guest, and the latter, as if under the faint coercion of the smile, turned from the room and ran upstairs. Having taken the seal from his writing-case he came down again, and once more opened the door of the study. No one was speaking when he entered— they were evidently awaiting his return with the mute impatience of hunger, and he put the seal in Rainer's reach, and stood watching while Mr. Grisben struck a match and held it to one of the candles flanking the inkstand. As the wax descended on the paper Faxon remarked again the strange emaciation, the premature physical weariness, of the hand that held it: he wondered if Mr. Lavington had ever noticed his nephew's hand, and if it were not poignantly visible to him now.

With this thought in his mind, Faxon raised his eyes to look at Mr. Lavington. The great man's gaze rested on Frank Rainer with an expression of untroubled benevolence; and at the same instant Faxon's attention was attracted by the presence in the room of another person, who must have joined the group while he was upstairs searching for the seal. The new-comer was a man of about Mr. Lavington's age and figure, who stood just behind his chair, and who, at the moment when Faxon first saw him, was gazing at young Rainer with an equal intensity of attention. The likeness between the two men, perhaps increased by the fact that the hooded lamps on the table left the figure behind the chair in shadow, struck Faxon the more because of the contrast in their expression. John Lavington, during his nephew's clumsy attempt to drop the wax and apply the seal, continued to fasten on him a look of half-amused affection; while the man behind the chair, so oddly reduplicating the lines of his features and figure, turned on the boy a face of pale hostility.

The impression was so startling that Faxon forgot what was going on about him. He was just dimly aware of young Reiner's exclaiming; "Your turn, Mr. Grisben!" of Mr. Grisben's protesting: "No, no; Mr. Faxon first," and of the pen's being thereupon transferred to his own hand. He received it with a deadly sense of being unable to move, or even to understand what was expected of him, till he became conscious of Mr. Grisben's paternally pointing out the precise spot on which he was to leave his autograph. The effort to fix his attention and steady his hand prolonged the process of signing, and when he stood up, a strange weight of fatigue on all his limbs, the figure behind Mr. Lavington's chair was gone.

Faxon felt an immediate sense of relief. It was puzzling that the man's exit should have been so rapid and noiseless, but the door behind Mr. Lavington was screened by a tapestry hanging, and Faxon concluded that the unknown looker-on had merely had to raise it to pass out. At any rate he was gone, and with his withdrawal the strange weight was lifted. Young Rainer was lighting a cigarette, Mr. Balch inscribing his name at the foot of the document, Mr. Lavington, his eyes no longer on his nephew, examining a strange white-winged orchid in the vase at his elbow. Every thing suddenly seemed to have grown natural and simple again, and Faxon found himself responding with a smile to the affable gesture with which his host declared: "And now, Mr. Faxon, we'll dine."

III

"I wonder how I blundered into the wrong room just now; I thought you told me to take the second door to the left," Faxon said to Frank Rainer as they followed the older men down the gallery.

"So I did; but I probably forgot to tell you which staircase to take. Coming from your bedroom, I ought to have said the fourth door to the right. It's a puzzling house, because my uncle keeps adding to it from year to year. He built this room last summer for his modern pictures."

Young Rainer, pausing to open another door, touched an electric button which sent a circle of light about the walls of a long room hung with canvases of the French impressionist school.

Faxon advanced, attracted by a shimmering Monet, but Rainer laid a hand on his arm.

"He bought that last week. But come along, I'll show you all this after dinner. Or he will, rather—he loves it."

"Does he really love things?"

Rainer stared, clearly perplexed at the question. "Rather! Flowers and pictures especially! Haven't you noticed the flowers? I suppose you think his manner's cold; it seems so at first; but he's really awfully keen about things."

Faxon looked quickly at the speaker. "Has your uncle a brother?"

"Brother? No—never had. He and my mother were the only ones."

"Or any relation who—who looks like him? Who might be mistaken for him?"

"Not that I ever heard of. Does he remind you of some one?"

"Yes."

"That's queer. We'll ask him if he's got a double. Come on!"

But another picture had arrested Faxon, and some minutes elapsed before he and his young host reached the dining-room. It was a large room, with the same conventionally handsome furniture and delicately grouped flowers; and Faxon's first glance showed him that only three men were seated about the dining-table. The man who had stood behind Mr. Lavington's chair was not present, and no seat awaited him.

When the young men entered, Mr. Grisben was speaking, and his host, who faced the door, sat looking down at his untouched soup-plate and turning the spoon about in his small dry hand.

"It's pretty late to call them rumours, they were devilish close to facts when we left town this morning," Mr. Grisben was saying, with an unexpected incisiveness of tone.

Mr. Lavington laid down his spoon and smiled interrogatively. "Oh, facts, what are facts? Just the way a thing happens to look at a given minute...."

"You haven't heard anything from town?" Mr. Grisben persisted.

"Not a syllable. So you see.... Balch, a little more of that petite marmite. Mr. Faxon... between Frank and Mr. Grisben, please."

The dinner progressed through a series of complicated courses, ceremoniously dispensed by a prelatical butler attended by three tall footmen, and it was evident that Mr. Lavington took a certain satisfaction in the pageant. That, Faxon reflected, was probably the joint in his armour, that and the flowers. He had changed the subject, not abruptly but firmly, when the young men entered, but Faxon perceived that it still possessed the thoughts of the two elderly visitors, and Mr. Balch presently observed, in a voice that seemed to come from the last survivor down a mine-shaft: "If it does come, it will be the biggest crash since '93."

Mr. Lavington looked bored but polite. "Wall Street can stand crashes better than it could then. It's got a robuster constitution."

"Yes; but—"

"Speaking of constitutions," Mr. Grisben intervened: "Frank, are you taking care of yourself?"

A flush rose to young Rainer's cheeks.

"Why, of course! Isn't that what I'm here for?"

"You're here about three days in the month, aren't you? And the rest of the time it's crowded restaurants and hot ballrooms in town. I thought you were to be shipped off to New Mexico?"

"Oh, I've got a new man who says that's rot."

"Well, you don't look as if your new man were right," said Mr. Grisben bluntly.

Faxon saw the lad's colour fade, and the rings of shadow deepen under his gay eyes. At the same moment his uncle turned to him with a renewed intensity of attention. There was such solicitude in Mr. Lavington's gaze that it seemed almost to fling a shield between his nephew and Mr. Grisben's tactless scrutiny.

"We think Frank's a good deal better," he began; "this new doctor—"

The butler, coming up, bent to whisper a word in his ear, and the communication caused a sudden change in Mr. Lavington's expression. His face was naturally so colourless that it seemed not so much to pale as to fade, to dwindle and recede into something blurred and blotted-out. He half rose, sat down again and sent a rigid smile about the table.

"Will you excuse me? The telephone. Peters, go on with the dinner." With small precise steps he walked out of the door which one of the footmen had thrown open.

A momentary silence fell on the group; then Mr. Grisben once more addressed himself to Rainer. "You ought to have gone, my boy; you ought to have gone."

The anxious look returned to the youth's eyes. "My uncle doesn't think so, really."

"You're not a baby, to be always governed by your uncle's opinion. You came of age to-day, didn't you? Your uncle spoils you.... that's what's the matter...."

The thrust evidently went home, for Rainer laughed and looked down with a slight accession of colour.

"But the doctor—"

"Use your common sense, Frank! You had to try twenty doctors to find one to tell you what you wanted to be told."

A look of apprehension overshadowed Rainer', gaiety. "Oh, come—I say!... What would you do?" he stammered.

"Pack up and jump on the first train." Mr. Grisben leaned forward and laid his hand kindly on the young man's arm. "Look here: my nephew Jim Grisben is out there ranching on a big scale. He'll take you in and be glad to have you. You say your new doctor thinks it won't do you any good; but he doesn't pretend to say it will do you harm, does he? Well, then—give it a trial. It'll take you out of hot theatres and night restaurants, anyhow.... And all the rest of it.... Eh, Balch?"

"Go!" said Mr. Balch hollowly. "Go at once," he added, as if a closer look at the youth's face had impressed on him the need of backing up his friend.

Young Rainer had turned ashy-pale. He tried to stiffen his mouth into a smile. "Do I look as bad as all that?"

Mr. Grisben was helping himself to terrapin. "You look like the day after an earthquake," he said.

The terrapin had encircled the table, and been deliberately enjoyed by Mr. Lavington's three visitors (Rainer, Faxon noticed, left his plate untouched) before the door was thrown open to re-admit their host. Mr. Lavington advanced with an air of recovered composure. He seated himself, picked up his napkin and consulted the gold-monogrammed menu. "No, don't bring back the filet.... Some terrapin; yes...." He looked affably about the table. "Sorry to have deserted you, but the storm has played the deuce with the wires, and I had to wait a long time before I could get a good connection. It must be blowing up for a blizzard."

"Uncle Jack," young Rainer broke out, "Mr. Grisben's been lecturing me."

Mr. Lavington was helping himself to terrapin. "Ah—what about?"

"He thinks I ought to have given New Mexico a show."

"I want him to go straight out to my nephew at Santa Paz and stay there till his next birthday." Mr. Lavington signed to the butler to hand the terrapin to Mr. Grisben, who, as he took a second helping, addressed himself again to Rainer. "Jim's in New York now, and going back the day after tomorrow in Olyphant's private car. I'll ask Olyphant to squeeze you in if you'll go. And when you've been out there a week or two, in the saddle all day and sleeping nine hours a night, I suspect you won't think much of the doctor who prescribed New York."

Faxon spoke up, he knew not why. "I was out there once: it's a splendid life. I saw a fellow, oh, a really bad case, who'd been simply made over by it."

"It does sound jolly," Rainer laughed, a sudden eagerness in his tone.

His uncle looked at him gently. "Perhaps Grisben's right. It's an opportunity—"

Faxon glanced up with a start: the figure dimly perceived in the study was now more visibly and tangibly planted behind Mr. Lavington's chair.

"That's right, Frank: you see your uncle approves. And the trip out there with Olyphant isn't a thing to be missed. So drop a few dozen dinners and be at the Grand Central the day after tomorrow at five."

Mr. Grisben's pleasant grey eye sought corroboration of his host, and Faxon, in a cold anguish of suspense, continued to watch him as he turned his glance on Mr. Lavington. One could not look at Lavington without seeing the presence at his back, and it was clear that, the next minute, some change in Mr. Grisben's expression must give his watcher a clue.

But Mr. Grisben's expression did not change: the gaze he fixed on his host remained unperturbed, and the clue he gave was the startling one of not seeming to see the other figure.

Faxon's first impulse was to look away, to look anywhere else, to resort again to the champagne glass the watchful butler had already brimmed; but some fatal attraction, at war in him with an overwhelming physical resistance, held his eyes upon the spot they feared.

The figure was still standing, more distinctly, and therefore more resemblingly, at Mr. Lavington's back; and while the latter continued to gaze affectionately at his nephew, his counterpart, as before, fixed young Rainer with eyes of deadly menace.

Faxon, with what felt like an actual wrench of the muscles, dragged his own eyes from the sight to scan the other countenances about the table; but not one revealed the least consciousness of what he saw, and a sense of mortal isolation sank upon him.

"It's worth considering, certainly—" he heard Mr. Lavington continue; and as Rainer's face lit up, the face behind his uncle's chair seemed to gather into its look all the fierce weariness of old unsatisfied hates. That was the thing that, as the minutes laboured by, Faxon was becoming most conscious of. The watcher behind the chair was no longer merely malevolent: he had grown suddenly, unutterably tired. His hatred seemed to well up out of the very depths of balked effort and thwarted hopes, and the fact made him more pitiable, and yet more dire.

Faxon's look reverted to Mr. Lavington, as if to surprise in him a corresponding change. At first none was visible: his pinched smile was screwed to his blank face like a gas-light to a white-washed wall. Then the fixity of the smile became ominous: Faxon saw that its wearer was afraid to let it go. It was evident that Mr. Lavington was unutterably tired too, and the discovery sent a colder current through Faxon's veins. Looking down at his untouched plate, he caught the soliciting twinkle of the champagne glass; but the sight of the wine turned him sick.

"Well, we'll go into the details presently," he heard Mr. Lavington say, still on the question of his nephew's future. "Let's have a cigar first. No, not here, Peters." He turned his smile on Faxon. "When we've had coffee I want to show you my pictures."

"Oh, by the way, Uncle Jack, Mr. Faxon wants to know if you've got a double?"

"A double?" Mr. Lavington, still smiling, continued to address himself to his guest. "Not that I know of. Have you seen one, Mr. Faxon?"

Faxon thought: "My God, if I look up now they'll both be looking at me!" To avoid raising his eyes he made as though to lift the glass to his lips; but his hand sank inert, and he looked up. Mr. Lavington's glance was politely bent on him, but with a loosening of the strain about his heart he saw that the figure behind the chair still kept its gaze on Rainer.

"Do you think you've seen my double, Mr. Faxon?"

Would the other face turn if he said yes? Faxon felt a dryness in his throat. "No," he answered.

"Ah? It's possible I've a dozen. I believe I'm extremely usual-looking," Mr. Lavington went on conversationally; and still the other face watched Rainer.

"It was... a mistake... a confusion of memory...." Faxon heard himself stammer. Mr. Lavington pushed back his chair, and as he did so Mr. Grisben suddenly leaned forward.

"Lavington! What have, we been thinking of? We haven't drunk Frank's health!"

Mr. Lavington reseated himself. "My dear boy!... Peters, another bottle...." He turned to his nephew. "After such a sin of omission I don't presume to propose the toast myself... but Frank knows.... Go ahead, Grisben!"

The boy shone on his uncle. "No, no, Uncle Jack! Mr. Grisben won't mind. Nobody but you—today!"

The butler was replenishing the glasses. He filled Mr. Lavington's last, and Mr. Lavington put out his small hand to raise it.... As he did so, Faxon looked away.

"Well, then—All the good I've wished you in all the past years.... I put it into the prayer that the coming ones may be healthy and happy and many... and many, dear boy!"

Faxon saw the hands about him reach out for their glasses. Automatically, he reached for his. His eyes were still on the table, and he repeated to himself with a trembling vehemence: "I won't look up! I won't.... I won't...."

His finders clasped the glass and raised it to the level of his lips. He saw the other hands making the same motion. He heard Mr. Grisben's genial "Hear! Hear!" and Mr. Batch's hollow echo. He said to himself, as the rim of the glass touched his lips: "I won't look up! I swear I won't!—" and he looked.

The glass was so full that it required an extraordinary effort to hold it there, brimming and suspended, during the awful interval before he could trust his hand to lower it again, untouched, to the table. It was this merciful preoccupation which saved him, kept him from crying out, from losing his hold, from slipping down into the bottomless blackness that gaped for him. As long as the problem of the glass engaged him he felt able to keep his seat, manage his muscles, fit unnoticeably into the group; but as the glass touched the table his last link with safety snapped. He stood up and dashed out of the room.

IV

In the gallery, the instinct of self-preservation helped him to turn back and sign to young Rainer not to follow. He stammered out something about a touch of dizziness, and joining them presently; and the boy nodded sympathetically and drew back.

At the foot of the stairs Faxon ran against a servant. "I should like to telephone to Weymore," he said with dry lips.

"Sorry, sir; wires all down. We've been trying the last hour to get New York again for Mr. Lavington."

Faxon shot on to his room, burst into it, and bolted the door. The lamplight lay on furniture, flowers, books; in the ashes a log still glimmered. He dropped down on the sofa and hid his face. The room was profoundly silent, the whole house was still: nothing about him gave a hint of what was going on, darkly and dumbly, in the room he had flown from, and with the covering of his eyes oblivion and reassurance seemed to fall on him. But they fell for a moment only; then his lids opened again to the monstrous vision. There it was, stamped on his pupils, a part of him forever, an indelible horror burnt into his body and brain. But why into his—just his? Why had he alone been chosen to see what he had seen? What business was it of his, in God's name? Any one of the others, thus enlightened, might have exposed the horror and defeated it; but he, the one weaponless and defenceless spectator, the one whom none of the others would believe or understand if he attempted to reveal what he knew, he alone had been singled out as the victim of this dreadful initiation!

Suddenly he sat up, listening: he had heard a step on the stairs. Some one, no doubt, was coming to see how he was, to urge him, if he felt better, to go down and join the smokers. Cautiously he opened his door; yes, it was young Rainer's step. Faxon looked down the passage, remembered the other stairway and darted to it. All he wanted was to get out of the house. Not another instant would he breathe its abominable air! What business was it of his, in God's name?

He reached the opposite end of the lower gallery, and beyond it saw the hall by which he had entered. It was empty, and on a long table he recognized his coat and cap. He got into his coat, unbolted the door, and plunged into the purifying night.

The darkness was deep, and the cold so intense that for an instant it stopped his breathing. Then he perceived that only a thin snow was falling, and resolutely he set his face for flight. The trees along the avenue marked his way as he hastened with long strides over the beaten snow. Gradually, while he walked, the tumult in his brain subsided. The impulse to fly still drove him forward, but he began feel that he was flying from a terror of his own creating, and that the most urgent reason for escape was the need of hiding his state, of shunning other eyes till he should regain his balance.

He had spent the long hours in the train in fruitless broodings on a discouraging situation, and he remembered how his bitterness had turned to exasperation when he found that the Weymore sleigh was not awaiting him. It was absurd, of course; but, though he had joked with Rainer over Mrs. Culme's forgetfulness, to confess it had cost a pang. That was what his rootless life had brought him to: for lack of a personal stake in things his sensibility was at the mercy of such trifles.... Yes; that, and the cold and fatigue, the absence of hope and the haunting sense of starved aptitudes, all these had brought him to the perilous verge over which, once or twice before, his terrified brain had hung.

Why else, in the name of any imaginable logic, human or devilish, should he, a stranger, be singled out for this experience? What could it mean to him, how was he related to it, what bearing had it on his case?... Unless, indeed, it was just because he was a stranger, a stranger everywhere, because he had no personal life, no warm screen of private egotisms to shield him from exposure, that he had developed this abnormal sensitiveness to the vicissitudes of others. The thought pulled him up with a shudder. No! Such a fate was too abominable; all that was strong and sound in him rejected it. A thousand times better regard himself as ill, disorganized, deluded, than as the predestined victim of such warnings!

He reached the gates and paused before the darkened lodge. The wind had risen and was sweeping the snow into his race. The cold had him in its grasp again, and he stood uncertain. Should he put his sanity to the test and go back? He turned and looked down the dark drive to the house. A single ray shone through the trees, evoking a picture of the lights, the flowers, the faces grouped about that fatal room. He turned and plunged out into the road....

He remembered that, about a mile from Overdale, the coachman had pointed out the road to Northridge; and he began to walk in that direction. Once in the road he had the gale in his face, and the wet snow on his moustache and eye-lashes instantly hardened to ice. The same ice seemed to be driving a million blades into his throat and lungs, but he pushed on, the vision of the warm room pursuing him.

The snow in the road was deep and uneven. He stumbled across ruts and sank into drifts, and the wind drove against him like a granite cliff. Now and then he stopped, gasping, as if an invisible hand had tightened an iron band about his body; then he started again, stiffening himself against the stealthy penetration of the cold. The snow continued to descend out of a pall of inscrutable darkness, and once or twice he paused, fearing he had missed the road to Northridge; but, seeing no sign of a turn, he ploughed on.

At last, feeling sure that he had walked for more than a mile, he halted and looked back. The act of turning brought immediate relief, first because it put his back to the wind, and then because, far down the road, it showed him the gleam of a lantern. A sleigh was coming, a sleigh that might perhaps give him a lift to the village! Fortified by the hope, he began to walk back toward the light. It came forward very slowly, with unaccountable sigsags and waverings; and even when he was within a few yards of it he could catch no sound of sleigh-bells. Then it paused and became stationary by the roadside, as though carried by a pedestrian who had stopped, exhausted by the cold. The thought made Faxon hasten on, and a moment later he was stooping over a motionless figure huddled against the snow-bank. The lantern had dropped from its bearer's hand, and Faxon, fearfully raising it, threw its light into the face of Frank Rainer.

"Rainer! What on earth are you doing here?"

The boy smiled back through his pallour. "What are you, I'd like to know?" he retorted; and, scrambling to his feet with a clutch oh Faxon's arm, he added gaily: "Well, I've run you down!"

Faxon stood confounded, his heart sinking. The lad's face was grey.

"What madness—" he began.

"Yes, it is. What on earth did you do it for?"

"I? Do what?... Why I.... I was just taking a walk.... I often walk at night...."

Frank Rainer burst into a laugh. "On such nights? Then you hadn't bolted?"

"Bolted?"

"Because I'd done something to offend you? My uncle thought you had."

Faxon grasped his arm. "Did your uncle send you after me?"

"Well, he gave me an awful rowing for not going up to your room with you when you said you were ill. And when we found you'd gone we were frightened, and he was awfully upset, so I said I'd catch you.... You're not ill, are you?"

"Ill? No. Never better." Faxon picked up the lantern. "Come; let's go back. It was awfully hot in that diningroom."

"Yes; I hoped it was only that."

They trudged on in silence for a few minutes; then Faxon questioned: "You're not too done up?"

"Oh, no. It's a lot easier with the wind behind us."

"All right Don't talk any more."

They pushed ahead, walking, in spite of the light that guided them, more slowly than Faxon had walked alone into the gale. The fact of his companion's stumbling against a drift gave Faxon a pretext for saying: "Take hold of my arm," and Rainer obeying, gasped out: "I'm blown!"

"So am I. Who wouldn't be?"

"What a dance you led me! If it hadn't been for one of the servants happening to see you—"

"Yes; all right. And now, won't you kindly shut up?"

Rainer laughed and hung on him. "Oh, the cold doesn't hurt me...."

For the first few minutes after Rainer had overtaken him, anxiety for the lad had been Faxon's only thought. But as each labouring step carried them nearer to the spot he had been fleeing, the reasons for his flight grew more ominous and more insistent. No, he was not ill, he was not distraught and deluded, he was the instrument singled out to warn and save; and here he was, irresistibly driven, dragging the victim back to his doom!

The intensity of the conviction had almost checked his steps. But what could he do or say? At all costs he must get Rainer out of the cold, into the house and into his bed. After that he would act.

The snow-fall was thickening, and as they reached a stretch of the road between open fields the wind took them at an angle, lashing their faces with barbed thongs. Rainer stopped to take breath, and Faxon felt the heavier pressure of his arm.

"When we get to the lodge, can't we telephone to the stable for a sleigh?" "If they're not all asleep at the lodge."

"Oh, I'll manage. Don't talk!" Faxon ordered; and they plodded on....

At length the lantern ray showed ruts that curved away from the road under tree-darkness.

Faxon's spirits rose. "There's the gate! We'll be there in five minutes."

As he spoke he caught, above the boundary hedge, the gleam of a light at the farther end of the dark avenue. It was the same light that had shone on the scene of which every detail was burnt into his brain; and he felt again its overpowering reality. No, he couldn't let the boy go back!

They were at the lodge at last, and Faxon was hammering on the door. He said to himself: "I'll get him inside first, and make them give him a hot drink. Then I'll see, I'll find an argument...."

There was no answer to his knocking, and after an interval Rainer said: "Look here, we'd better go on."

"No!"

"I can, perfectly—"

"You sha'n't go to the house, I say!" Faxon redoubled his blows, and at length steps sounded on the stairs. Rainer was leaning against the lintel, and as the door opened the light from the hall flashed on his pale face and fixed eyes. Faxon caught him by the arm and drew him in.

"It was cold out there." he sighed; and then, abruptly, as if invisible shears at a single stroke had cut every muscle in his body, he swerved, drooped on Faxon's arm, and seemed to sink into nothing at his feet.

The lodge-keeper and Faxon bent over him, and somehow, between them, lifted him into the kitchen and laid him on a sofa by the stove.

The lodge-keeper, stammering: "I'll ring up the house," dashed out of the room. But Faxon heard the words without heeding them: omens mattered nothing now, beside this woe fulfilled. He knelt down to undo the fur collar about Rainer's throat, and as he did so he felt a warm moisture on his hands. He held them up, and they were red....

V

The palms threaded their endless line along the yellow river. The little steamer lay at the wharf, and George Faxon, sitting in the verandah of the wooden hotel, idly watched the coolies carrying the freight across the gang-plank.

He had been looking at such scenes for two months. Nearly five had elapsed since he had descended from the train at Northridge and strained his eyes for the sleigh that was to take him to Weymore: Weymore, which he was never to behold!... Part of the interval, the first part, was still a great grey blur. Even now he could not be quite sure how he had got back to Boston, reached the house of a cousin, and been thence transferred to a quiet room looking out on snow under bare trees. He looked out a long time at the same scene, and finally one day a man he had known at Harvard came to see him and invited him to go out on a business trip to the Malay Peninsula.

"You've had a bad shake-up, and it'll do you no end of good to get away from things."

When the doctor came the next day it turned out that he knew of the plan and approved it. "You ought to be quiet for a year. Just loaf and look at the landscape," he advised.

Paxon felt the first faint stirrings of curiosity.

"What's been the matter with me, anyway?"

"Well, over-work, I suppose. You must have been bottling up for a bad breakdown before you started for New Hampshire last December. And the shock of that poor boy's death did the rest."

Ah, yes, Rainer had died. He remembered....

He started for the East, and gradually, by imperceptible degrees, life crept back into his weary bones and leaden brain. His friend was patient and considerate, and they travelled slowly and talked little. At first Faxon had felt a great shrinking from whatever touched on familiar things. He seldom looked at a newspaper and he never opened a letter without a contraction of the heart. It was not that he had any special cause for apprehension, but merely that a great trail of darkness lay on everything. He had looked too deep down into the abyss.... But little by little health and energy returned to him, and with them the common promptings of curiosity. He was beginning to wonder how the world was going, and when, presently, the hotel-keeper told him there were no letters for him in the steamer's mail-bag, he felt a distinct sense of disappointment. His friend had gone into the jungle on a long excursion, and he was lonely, unoccupied and wholesomely bored. He got up and strolled into the stuffy reading-room.

There he found a game of dominoes, a mutilated picture-puzzle, some copies of Zion's Herald and a pile of New York and London newspapers.

He began to glance through the papers, and was disappointed to find that they were less recent than he had hoped. Evidently the last numbers had been carried off by luckier travellers. He continued to turn them over, picking out the American ones first. These, as it happened, were the oldest: they dated back to December and January. To Faxon, however, they had all the flavour of novelty, since they covered the precise period during which he had virtually ceased to exist. It had never before occurred to him to wonder what had happened in the world during that interval of obliteration; but now he felt a sudden desire to know.

To prolong the pleasure, he began by sorting the papers chronologically, and as he found and spread out the earliest number, the date at the top of the page entered into his consciousness like a key slipping into a lock. It was the seventeenth of December: the date of the day after his arrival at Northridge. He glanced at the first page and read in blazing characters: "Reported Failure of Opal Cement Company. Lavington's name involved. Gigantic Exposure of Corruption Shakes Wall Street to Its Foundations."

He read on, and when he had finished the first paper he turned to the next. There was a gap of three days, but the Opal Cement "Investigation" still held the centre of the stage. From its complex revelations of greed and ruin his eye wandered to the death notices, and he read: "Rainer. Suddenly, at Northridge, New Hampshire, Francis John, only son of the late...."

His eyes clouded, and he dropped the newspaper and sat for a long time with his face in his hands. When he looked up again he noticed that his gesture had pushed the other papers from the table and scattered them at his feet. The uppermost lay spread out before him, and heavily his eyes began their search again. "John Lavington comes forward with plan for reconstructing Company. Offers to put in ten millions of his own—The proposal under consideration by the District Attorney."

Ten millions... ten millions of his own. But if John Lavington was ruined?... Pazon stood up with a cry. That was it, then—that was what the warning meant! And if he had not fled from it, dashed wildly away from it into the night, he might have broken the spell of iniquity, the powers of darkness might not have prevailed! He caught up the pile of newspapers and began to glance through each in turn for the head-line: "Wills Admitted to Probate." In the last of all he found the paragraph he sought, and it stared up at him as if with Rainer's dying eyes.

That—that was what he had done! The powers of pity had singled him out to warn and save, and he had closed his ears to their call, and washed his hands of it, and fled. Washed his hands of it! That was the word. It caught him back to the dreadful moment in the lodge when, raising himself up from Rainer's side, he had looked at his hands and seen that they were red....

AUTRES TEMPS...

I

Mrs. Lidcote, as the huge menacing mass of New York defined itself far off across the waters, shrank back into her corner of the deck and sat listening with a kind of unreasoning terror to the steady onward drive of the screws.

She had set out on the voyage quietly enough, in what she called her "reasonable" mood, but the week at sea had given her too much time to think of things and had left her too long alone with the past.

When she was alone, it was always the past that occupied her. She couldn't get away from it, and she didn't any longer care to. During her long years of exile she had made her terms with it, had learned to accept the fact that it would always be there, huge, obstructing, encumbering, bigger and more dominant than anything the future could ever conjure up. And, at any rate, she was sure of it, she understood it, knew how to reckon with it; she had learned to screen and manage and protect it as one does an afflicted member of one's family.

There had never been any danger of her being allowed to forget the past. It looked out at her from the face of every acquaintance, it appeared suddenly in the eyes of strangers when a word enlightened them: "Yes, the Mrs. Lidcote, don't you know?" It had sprung at her the first day out, when, across the dining-room, from the captain's table, she had seen Mrs. Lorin Boulger's revolving eye-glass pause and the eye behind it grow as blank as a dropped blind. The next day, of course, the captain had asked: "You know your ambassadress, Mrs. Boulger?" and she had replied that, No, she seldom left Florence, and hadn't been to Rome for more than a day since the Boulgers had been sent to Italy. She was so used to these phrases that it cost her no effort to repeat them. And the captain had promptly changed the subject.

No, she didn't, as a rule, mind the past, because she was used to it and understood it. It was a great concrete fact in her path that she had to walk around every time she moved in any direction. But now, in the light of the unhappy event that had summoned her from Italy, the sudden unanticipated news of her daughter's divorce from Horace Pursh and remarriage with Wilbour Barkley, the past, her own poor miserable past, started up at her with eyes of accusation, became, to her disordered fancy, like the afflicted relative suddenly breaking away from nurses and keepers and publicly parading the horror and misery she had, all the long years, so patiently screened and secluded.

Yes, there it had stood before her through the agitated weeks since the news had come, during her interminable journey from India, where Leila's letter had overtaken her, and the feverish halt in her apartment in Florence, where she had had to stop and gather up her possessions for a fresh start, there it had stood grinning at her with a new balefillness which seemed to say: "Oh, but you've got to look at me now, because I'm not only your own past but Leila's present."

Certainly it was a master-stroke of those arch-ironists of the shears and spindle to duplicate her own story in her daughter's. Mrs. Lidcote had always somewhat grimly fancied that, having so signally failed to be of use to Leila in other ways, she would at least serve her as a warning. She had even abstained from defending herself, from making the best of her case, had stoically refused to plead extenuating circumstances, lest Leila's impulsive sympathy should lead to deductions that might react disastrously on her own life. And now that very thing had happened, and Mrs. Lidcote could hear the whole of New York saying with one voice: "Yes, Leila's done just what her mother did. With such an example what could you expect?"

Yet if she had been an example, poor woman, she had been an awful one; she had been, she would have supposed, of more use as a deterrent than a hundred blameless mothers as incentives. For how could any one who had seen anything of her life in the last eighteen years have had the courage to repeat so disastrous an experiment?

Well, logic in such cases didn't count, example didn't count, nothing probably counted but having the same impulses in the blood; and that was the dark inheritance she had bestowed upon her daughter. Leila hadn't consciously copied her; she had simply "taken after" her, had been a projection of her own long-past rebellion.

Mrs. Lidcote had deplored, when she started, that the Utopia was a slow steamer, and would take eight full days to bring her to her unhappy daughter; but now, as the moment of reunion approached, she would willingly have turned the boat about and fled back to the high seas. It was not only because she felt still so unprepared to face what New York had in store for her, but because she needed more time to dispose of what the Utopia had already given her. The past was bad enough, but the present and future were worse, because they were less comprehensible, and because, as she grew older, surprises and inconsequences troubled her more than the worst certainties.

There was Mrs. Boulger, for instance. In the light, or rather the darkness, of new developments, it might really be that Mrs. Boulger had not meant to cut her, but had simply failed to recognize her. Mrs. Lidcote had arrived at this hypothesis simply by listening to the conversation of the persons sitting next to her on deck, two lively young women with the latest Paris hats on their heads and the latest New York ideas in them. These ladies, as to whom it would have been impossible for a person with Mrs. Lidcote's old-fashioned categories to determine whether they were married or unmarried, "nice" or "horrid," or any one or other of the definite things which young women, in her youth and her society, were conveniently assumed to be, had revealed a familiarity with the world of New York that, again according to Mrs. Lidcote's traditions, should have implied a recognized place in it. But in the present fluid state of manners what did anything imply except what their hats implied, that no one could tell what was coming next?

They seemed, at any rate, to frequent a group of idle and opulent people who executed the same gestures and revolved on the same pivots as Mrs. Lidcote's daughter and her friends: their Coras, Matties and Mabels seemed at any moment likely to reveal familiar patronymics, and once one of the speakers, summing up a discussion of which Mrs. Lidcote had missed the beginning, had affirmed with headlong confidence: "Leila? Oh, Leila's all right."

Could it be her Leila, the mother had wondered, with a sharp thrill of apprehension? If only they would mention surnames! But their talk leaped elliptically from allusion to allusion, their unfinished sentences dangled over bottomless pits of conjecture, and they gave their bewildered hearer the impression not so much of talking only of their intimates, as of being intimate with every one alive.

Her old friend Franklin Ide could have told her, perhaps; but here was the last day of the voyage, and she hadn't yet found courage to ask him. Great as had been the joy of discovering his name on the passenger-list and seeing his friendly bearded face in the throng against the taffrail at Cherbourg, she had as yet said nothing to him except, when they had met: "Of course I'm going out to Leila."

She had said nothing to Franklin Ide because she had always instinctively shrunk from taking him into her confidence. She was sure he felt sorry for her, sorrier perhaps than any one had ever felt; but he had always paid her the supreme tribute of not showing it. His attitude allowed her to imagine that compassion was not the basis of his feeling for her, and it was part of her joy in his friendship that it was the one relation seemingly unconditioned by her state, the only one in which she could think and feel and behave like any other woman.

Now, however, as the problem of New York loomed nearer, she began to regret that she had not spoken, had not at least questioned him about the hints she had gathered on the way. He did not know the two ladies next to her, he did not even, as it chanced, know Mrs. Lorin Boulger; but he knew New York, and New York was the sphinx whose riddle she must read or perish.

Almost as the thought passed through her mind his stooping shoulders and grizzled head detached themselves against the blaze of light in the west, and he sauntered down the empty deck and dropped into the chair at her side.

"You're expecting the Barkleys to meet you, I suppose?" he asked.

It was the first time she had heard any one pronounce her daughter's new name, and it occurred to her that her friend, who was shy and inarticulate, had been trying to say it all the way over and had at last shot it out at her only because he felt it must be now or never.

"I don't know. I cabled, of course. But I believe she's at—they're at—his place somewhere."

"Oh, Barkley's; yes, near Lenox, isn't it? But she's sure to come to town to meet you."

He said it so easily and naturally that her own constraint was relieved, and suddenly, before she knew what she meant to do, she had burst out: "She may dislike the idea of seeing people."

Ide, whose absent short-sighted gaze had been fixed on the slowly gliding water, turned in his seat to stare at his companion.

"Who? Leila?" he said with an incredulous laugh.

Mrs. Lidcote flushed to her faded hair and grew pale again. "It took me a long time—to get used to it," she said.

His look grew gently commiserating. "I think you'll find—" he paused for a word—"that things are different now, altogether easier."

"That's what I've been wondering, ever since we started." She was determined now to speak. She moved nearer, so that their arms touched, and she could drop her voice to a murmur. "You see, it all came on me in a flash. My going off to India and Siam on that long trip kept me away from letters for weeks at a time; and she didn't want to tell me beforehand, oh, I understand that, poor child! You know how good she's always been to me; how she's tried to spare me. And she knew, of course, what a state of horror I'd be in. She knew I'd rush off to her at once and try to stop it. So she never gave me a hint of anything, and she even managed to muzzle Susy Suffern, you know Susy is the one of the family who keeps me informed about things at home. I don't yet see how she prevented Susy's telling me; but she did. And her first letter, the one I got up at Bangkok, simply said the thing was over, the divorce, I mean, and that the very next day she'd, well, I suppose there was no use waiting; and he seems to have behaved as well as possible, to have wanted to marry her as much as—"

"Who? Barkley?" he helped her out. "I should say so! Why what do you suppose—" He interrupted himself. "He'll be devoted to her, I assure you."

"Oh, of course; I'm sure he will. He's written me, really beautifully. But it's a terrible strain on a man's devotion. I'm not sure that Leila realizes—"

Ide sounded again his little reassuring laugh. "I'm not sure that you realize. They're all right."

It was the very phrase that the young lady in the next seat had applied to the unknown "Leila," and its recurrence on Ide's lips flushed Mrs. Lidcote with fresh courage.

"I wish I knew just what you mean. The two young women next to me, the ones with the wonderful hats, have been talking in the same way."

"What? About Leila?"

"About a Leila; I fancied it might be mine. And about society in general. All their friends seem to be divorced; some of them seem to announce their engagements before they get their decree. One of them, her name was Mabel, as far as I could make out, her husband found out that she meant to divorce him by noticing that she wore a new engagement-ring."

"Well, you see Leila did everything 'regularly,' as the French say," Ide rejoined.

"Yes; but are these people in society? The people my neighbours talk about?"

He shrugged his shoulders. "It would take an arbitration commission a good many sittings to define the boundaries of society nowadays. But at any rate they're in New York; and I assure you you're not; you're farther and farther from it."

"But I've been back there several times to see Leila." She hesitated and looked away from him. Then she brought out slowly: "And I've never noticed, the least change—in—in my own case—"

"Oh," he sounded deprecatingly, and she trembled with the fear of having gone too far. But the hour was past when such scruples could restrain her. She must know where she was and where Leila was. "Mrs. Boulger still cuts me," she brought out with an embarrassed laugh.

"Are you sure? You've probably cut her; if not now, at least in the past. And in a cut if you're not first you're nowhere. That's what keeps up so many quarrels."

The word roused Mrs. Lidcote to a renewed sense of realities. "But the Pursues," she said—"the Pursues are so strong! There are so many of them, and they all back each other up, just as my husband's family did. I know what it means to have a clan against one. They're stronger than any number of separate friends. The Pursues will never forgive Leila for leaving Horace. Why, his mother opposed his marrying her because of—of me. She tried to get Leila to promise that she wouldn't see me when they went to Europe on their honeymoon. And now she'll say it was my example."

Her companion, vaguely stroking his beard, mused a moment upon this; then he asked, with seeming irrelevance, "What did Leila say when you wrote that you were coming?"

"She said it wasn't the least necessary, but that I'd better come, because it was the only way to convince me that it wasn't."

"Well, then, that proves she's not afraid of the Purshes."

She breathed a long sigh of remembrance. "Oh, just at first, you know—one never is."

He laid his hand on hers with a gesture of intelligence and pity. "You'll see, you'll see," he said.

A shadow lengthened down the deck before them, and a steward stood there, proffering a Marconigram.

"Oh, now I shall know!" she exclaimed.

She tore the message open, and then let it fall on her knees, dropping her hands on it in silence.

Ide's enquiry roused her: "It's all right?"

"Oh, quite right. Perfectly. She can't come; but she's sending Susy Suffern. She says Susy will explain." After another silence she added, with a sudden gush of bitterness: "As if I needed any explanation!"

She felt Ide's hesitating glance upon her. "She's in the country?"

"Yes. 'Prevented last moment. Longing for you, expecting you. Love from both.' Don't you see, the poor darling, that she couldn't face it?"

"No, I don't." He waited. "Do you mean to go to her immediately?" "It will be too late to catch a train this evening; but I shall take the first to-morrow morning." She considered a moment. "'Perhaps it's better. I need a talk with Susy first. She's to meet me at the dock, and I'll take her straight back to the hotel with me."

As she developed this plan, she had the sense that Ide was still thoughtfully, even gravely, considering her. When she ceased, he remained silent a moment; then he said almost ceremoniously: "If your talk with Miss Suffern doesn't last too late, may I come and see you when it's over? I shall be dining at my club, and I'll call you up at about ten, if I may. I'm off to Chicago on business to-morrow morning, and it would be a satisfaction to know, before I start, that your cousin's been able to reassure you, as I know she will."

He spoke with a shy deliberateness that, even to Mrs. Lidcote's troubled perceptions, sounded a long-silenced note of feeling. Perhaps the breaking down of the barrier of reticence between them had released unsuspected emotions in both. The tone of his appeal moved her curiously and loosened the tight strain of her fears.

"Oh, yes, come, do come," she said, rising. The huge threat of New York was imminent now, dwarfing, under long reaches of embattled masonry, the great deck she stood on and all the little specks of life it carried. One of them, drifting nearer, took the shape of her maid, followed by luggage-laden stewards, and signing to her that it was time to go below. As they descended to the main deck, the throng swept her against Mrs. Lorin Boulger's shoulder, and she heard the ambassadress call out to someone, over the vexed sea of hats: "So sorry! I should have been delighted, but I've promised to spend Sunday with some friends at Lenox."

II

Susy Suffern's explanation did not end till after ten o'clock, and she had just gone when Franklin Ide, who, complying with an old New York tradition, had caused himself to be preceded by a long white box of roses, was shown into Mrs. Lidcote's sitting-room.

He came forward with his shy half-humorous smile and, taking her hand, looked at her for a moment without speaking.

"It's all right," he then pronounced.

Mrs. Lidcote returned his smile. "It's extraordinary. Everything's changed. Even Susy has changed; and you know the extent to which Susy used to represent the old New York. There's no old New York left, it seems. She talked in the most amazing way. She snaps her fingers at the Pursues. She told me, me, that every woman had a right to happiness and that self-expression was the highest duty. She accused me of misunderstanding Leila; she said my point of view was conventional! She was bursting with pride at having been in the secret, and wearing a brooch that Wilbour Barkley'd given her!" Franklin Ide had seated himself in the arm-chair she had pushed forward for him under the electric chandelier. He threw back his head and laughed. "What did I tell you?"

"Yes; but I can't believe that Susy's not mistaken. Poor dear, she has the habit of lost causes; and she may feel that, having stuck to me, she can do no less than stick to Leila."

"But she didn't—did she?—openly defy the world for you? She didn't snap her fingers at the Lidcotes?"

Mrs. Lidcote shook her head, still smiling. "No. It was enough to defy my family. It was doubtful at one time if they would tolerate her seeing me, and she almost had to disinfect herself after each visit. I believe that at first my sister-in-law wouldn't let the girls come down when Susy dined with her."

"Well, isn't your cousin's present attitude the best possible proof that times have changed?"

"Yes, yes; I know." She leaned forward from her sofa-corner, fixing her eyes on his thin kindly face, which gleamed on her indistinctly through her tears. "If it's true, it's—it's dazzling. She says Leila's perfectly happy. It's as if an angel had gone about lifting gravestones, and the buried people walked again, and the living didn't shrink from them."

"That's about it," he assented.

She drew a deep breath, and sat looking away from him down the long perspective of lamp-fringed streets over which her windows hung.

"I can understand how happy you must be," he began at length.

She turned to him impetuously. "Yes, yes; I'm happy. But I'm lonely, too—lonelier than ever. I didn't take up much room in the world before; but now, where is there a corner for me? Oh. since I've begun to confess myself, why shouldn't I go on? Telling you this lifts a gravestone from me! You see, before this, Leila needed me. She was unhappy, and I knew it, and though we hardly ever talked of it I felt that, in a way, the thought that I'd been through the same thing, and down to the dregs of it, helped her. And her needing me helped me. And when the news of her marriage came my first thought was that now she'd need me more than ever, that she'd have no one but me to turn to. Yes, under all my distress there was a fierce joy in that. It was so new and wonderful to feel again that there was one person who wouldn't be able to get on without me! And now what you and Susy tell me seems to have taken my child from me; and just at first that's all I can feel."

"Of course it's all you feel." He looked at her musingly. "Why didn't Leila come to meet you?"

"That was really my fault. You see, I'd cabled that I was not sure of being able to get off on the Utopia, and apparently my second cable was delayed, and when she received it she'd already asked some people over Sunday, one or two of her old friends, Susy says. I'm so glad they should have wanted to go to her at once; but naturally I'd rather have been alone with her."

"You still mean to go, then?"

"Oh, I must. Susy wanted to drag me off to Ridgefield with her over Sunday, and Leila sent me word that of course I might go if I wanted to, and that I was not to think of her; but I know how disappointed she would be. Susy said she was afraid I might be upset at her having people to stay, and that, if I minded, she wouldn't urge me to come. But if they don't mind, why should I? And of course, if they're willing to go to Leila it must mean—"

"Of course. I'm glad you recognize that," Franklin Ide exclaimed abruptly. He stood up and went over to her, taking her hand with one of his quick gestures. "There's something I want to say to you," he began—

The next morning, in the train, through all the other contending thoughts in Mrs. Lidcote's mind there ran the warm undercurrent of what Franklin Ide had wanted to say to her.

He had wanted, she knew, to say it once before, when, nearly eight years earlier, the hazard of meeting at the end of a rainy autumn in a deserted Swiss hotel had thrown them for a fortnight into unwonted propinquity. They had walked and talked together, borrowed each other's books and newspapers, spent the long chill evenings over the fire in the dim lamplight of her little pitch-pine sitting-room; and she had been wonderfully comforted by his presence, and hard frozen places in her had melted, and she had known that she would be desperately sorry when he went. And then, just at the end, in his odd indirect way, he had let her see that it rested with her to have him stay. She could still relive the sleepless night she had given to that discovery. It was preposterous, of course, to think of repaying his devotion by accepting such a sacrifice; but how find reasons to convince him? She could not bear to let him think her less touched, less inclined to him than she was: the generosity of his love deserved that she should repay it with the truth. Yet how let him see what she felt, and yet refuse what he offered? How confess to him what had been on her lips when he made the offer: "I've seen what it did to one man; and there must never, never be another"? The tacit ignoring of her past had been the element in which their friendship lived, and she could not suddenly, to him of all men, begin to talk of herself like a guilty woman in a play. Somehow, in the end, she had managed it, had averted a direct explanation, had made him understand that her life was over, that she existed only for her daughter, and that a more definite word from him would have been almost a breach of delicacy. She was so used to be having as if her life were over! And, at any rate, he had taken her hint, and she had been able to spare her sensitiveness and his. The next year, when he came to Florence to see her, they met again in the old friendly way; and that till now had continued to be the tenor of their intimacy.

And now, suddenly and unexpectedly, he had brought up the question again, directly this time, and in such a form that she could not evade it: putting the renewal of his plea, after so long an interval, on the ground that, on her own showing, her chief argument against it no longer existed.

"You tell me Leila's happy. If she's happy, she doesn't need you, need you, that is, in the same way as before. You wanted, I know, to be always in reach, always free and available if she should suddenly call you to her or take refuge with you. I understood that, I respected it. I didn't urge my case because I saw it was useless. You couldn't, I understood well enough, have felt free to take such happiness as life with me might give you while she was unhappy, and, as you imagined, with no hope of release. Even then I didn't feel as you did about it; I understood better the trend of things here. But ten years ago the change hadn't really come; and I had no way of convincing you that it was coming. Still, I always fancied that Leila might not think her case was closed, and so I chose to think that ours wasn't either. Let me go on thinking so, at any rate, till you've seen her, and confirmed with your own eyes what Susy Suffern tells you."

III

All through what Susy Suffern told and retold her during their four-hours' flight to the hills this plea of Ide's kept coming back to Mrs. Lidcote. She did not yet know what she felt as to its bearing on her own fate, but it was something on which her confused thoughts could stay themselves amid the welter of new impressions, and she was inexpressibly glad that he had said what he had, and said it at that particular moment. It helped her to hold fast to her identity in the rush of strange names and new categories that her cousin's talk poured out on her.

With the progress of the journey Miss Suffern's communications grew more and more amazing. She was like a cicerone preparing the mind of an inexperienced traveller for the marvels about to burst on it.

"You won't know Leila. She's had her pearls reset. Sargent's to paint her. Oh, and I was to tell you that she hopes you won't mind being the least bit squeezed over Sunday. The house was built by Wilbour's father, you know, and it's rather old-fashioned, only ten spare bedrooms. Of course that's small for what they mean to do, and she'll show you the new plans they've had made. Their idea is to keep the present house as a wing. She told me to explain, she's so dreadfully sorry not to be able to give you a sitting-room just at first. They're thinking of Egypt for next winter, unless, of course, Wilbour gets his appointment. Oh, didn't she write you about that? Why, he wants Borne, you know, the second secretaryship. Or, rather, he wanted England; but Leila insisted that if they went abroad she must be near you. And of course what she says is law. Oh, they quite hope they'll get it. You see Horace's uncle is in the Cabinet, one of the assistant secretaries, and I believe he has a good deal of pull—"

"Horace's uncle? You mean Wilbour's, I suppose," Mrs. Lidcote interjected, with a gasp of which a fraction was given to Miss Suffern's flippant use of the language.

"Wilbour's? No, I don't. I mean Horace's. There's no bad feeling between them, I assure you. Since Horace's engagement was announced, you didn't know Horace was engaged? Why, he's marrying one of Bishop Thorbury's girls: the red-haired one who wrote the novel that every one's talking about, 'This Flesh of Mine.' They're to be married in the cathedral. Of course Horace can, because it was Leila who, but, as I say, there's not the least feeling, and Horace wrote himself to his uncle about Wilbour."

Mrs. Lidcote's thoughts fled back to what she had said to Ide the day before on the deck of the Utopia. "I didn't take up much room before, but now where is there a corner for me?" Where indeed in this crowded, topsy-turvey world, with its headlong changes and helter-skelter readjustments, its new tolerances and indifferences and accommodations, was there room for a character fashioned by slower sterner processes and a life broken under their inexorable pressure? And then, in a flash, she viewed the chaos from a new angle, and order seemed to move upon the void. If the old processes were changed, her case was changed with them; she, too, was a part of the general readjustment, a tiny fragment of the new pattern worked out in bolder freer harmonies. Since her daughter had no penalty to pay, was not she herself released by the same stroke? The rich arrears of youth and joy were gone; but was there not time enough left to accumulate new stores of happiness? That, of course, was what Franklin Ide had felt and had meant her to feel. He had seen at once what the change in her daughter's situation would make in her view of her own. It was almost—wondrously enough!—as if Leila's folly had been the means of vindicating hers.

Everything else for the moment faded for Mrs. Lidcote in the glow of her daughter's embrace. It was unnatural, it was almost terrifying, to find herself standing on a strange threshold, under an unknown roof, in a big hall full of pictures, flowers, firelight, and hurrying servants, and in this spacious unfamiliar confusion to discover Leila, bareheaded, laughing, authoritative, with a strange young man jovially echoing her welcome and transmitting her orders; but once Mrs. Lidcote had her child on her breast, and her child's "It's all right, you old darling!" in her ears, every other feeling was lost in the deep sense of well-being that only Leila's hug could give.

The sense was still with her, warming her veins and pleasantly fluttering her heart, as she went up to her room after luncheon. A little constrained by the presence of visitors, and not altogether sorry to defer for a few hours the "long talk" with her daughter for which she somehow felt herself tremulously unready, she had withdrawn, on the plea of fatigue, to the bright luxurious bedroom into which Leila had again and again apologized for having been obliged to squeeze her. The room was bigger and finer than any in her small apartment in Florence; but it was not the standard of affluence implied in her daughter's tone about it that chiefly struck her, nor yet the finish and complexity of its appointments. It was the look it shared with the rest of the house, and with the perspective of the gardens beneath its windows, of being part of an "establishment"—of something solid, avowed, founded on sacraments and precedents and principles. There was nothing about the place, or about Leila and Wilbour, that suggested either passion or peril: their relation seemed as comfortable as their furniture and as respectable as their balance at the bank.

This was, in the whole confusing experience, the thing that confused Mrs. Lidcote most, that gave her at once the deepest feeling of security for Leila and the strongest sense of apprehension for herself. Yes, there was something oppressive in the completeness and compactness of Leila's well-being. Ide had been right: her daughter did not need her. Leila, with her first embrace, had unconsciously attested the fact in the same phrase as Ide himself and as the two young women with the hats. "It's all right, you old darling!" she had said; and her mother sat alone, trying to fit herself into the new scheme of things which such a certainty betokened.

Her first distinct feeling was one of irrational resentment. If such a change was to come, why had it not come sooner? Here was she, a woman not yet old, who had paid with the best years of her life for the theft of the happiness that her daughter's contemporaries were taking as their due. There was no sense, no sequence, in it. She had had what she wanted, but she had had to pay too much for it. She had had to pay the last bitterest price of learning that love has a price: that it is worth so much and no more. She had known the anguish of watching the man she loved discover this first, and of reading the discovery in his eyes. It was a part of her history that she had not trusted herself to think of for a long time past: she always took a big turn about that haunted corner. But now, at the sight of the young man downstairs, so openly and jovially Leila's, she was overwhelmed at the senseless waste of her own adventure, and wrung with the irony of perceiving that the success or failure of the deepest human experiences may hang on a matter of chronology.

Then gradually the thought of Ide returned to her. "I chose to think that our case wasn't closed," he had said. She had been deeply touched by that. To every one else her case had been closed so long! Finis was scrawled all over her. But here was one man who had believed and waited, and what if what he believed in and waited for were coming true? If Leila's "all right" should really foreshadow hers?

As yet, of course, it was impossible to tell. She had fancied, indeed, when she entered the drawing-room before luncheon, that a too-sudden hush had fallen on the assembled group of Leila's friends, on the slender vociferous young women and the lounging golf-stockinged young men. They had all received her politely, with the kind of petrified politeness that may be either a tribute to age or a protest at laxity; but to them, of course, she must be an old woman because she was Leila's mother, and in a society so dominated by youth the mere presence of maturity was a constraint.

One of the young girls, however, had presently emerged from the group, and, attaching herself to Mrs. Lidcote, had listened to her with a blue gaze of admiration which gave the older woman a sudden happy consciousness of her long-forgotten social graces. It was agreeable to find herself attracting this young Charlotte Wynn, whose mother had been among her closest friends, and in whom something of the soberness and softness of the earlier manners had survived. But the little colloquy, broken up by the announcement of luncheon, could of course result in nothing more definite than this reminiscent emotion.

No, she could not yet tell how her own case was to be fitted into the new order of things; but there were more people—"older people" Leila had put it—arriving by the afternoon train, and that evening at dinner she would doubtless be able to judge. She began to wonder nervously who the new-comers might be. Probably she would be spared the embarrassment of finding old acquaintances among them; but it was odd that her daughter had mentioned no names.

Leila had proposed that, later in the afternoon, Wilbour should take her mother for a drive: she said she wanted them to have a "nice, quiet talk." But Mrs. Lidcote wished her talk with Leila to come first, and had, moreover, at luncheon, caught stray allusions to an impending tennis-match in which her son-in-law was engaged. Her fatigue had been a sufficient pretext for declining the drive, and she had begged Leila to think of her as peacefully resting in her room till such time as they could snatch their quiet moment.

"Before tea, then, you duck!" Leila with a last kiss had decided; and presently Mrs. Lidcote, through her open window, had heard the fresh loud voices of her daughter's visitors chiming across the gardens from the tennis-court.

IV

Leila had come and gone, and they had had their talk. It had not lasted as long as Mrs. Lidcote wished, for in the middle of it Leila had been summoned to the telephone to receive an important message from town, and had sent word to her mother that she couldn't come back just then, as one of the young ladies had been called away unexpectedly and arrangements had to be made for her departure. But the mother and daughter had had almost an hour together, and Mrs. Lidcote was happy. She had never seen Leila so tender, so solicitous. The only thing that troubled her was the very excess of this solicitude, the exaggerated expression of her daughter's annoyance that their first moments together should have been marred by the presence of strangers.

"Not strangers to me, darling, since they're friends of yours," her mother had assured her.

"Yes; but I know your feeling, you queer wild mother. I know how you've always hated people." (Hated people! Had Leila forgotten why?) "And that's why I told Susy that if you preferred to go with her to Ridgefield on Sunday I should perfectly understand, and patiently wait for our good hug. But you didn't really mind them at luncheon, did you, dearest?"

Mrs. Lidcote, at that, had suddenly thrown a startled look at her daughter. "I don't mind things of that kind any longer," she had simply answered.

"But that doesn't console me for having exposed you to the bother of it, for having let you come here when I ought to have ordered you off to Ridgefield with Susy. If Susy hadn't been stupid she'd have made you go there with her. I hate to think of you up here all alone."

Again Mrs. Lidcote tried to read something more than a rather obtuse devotion in her daughter's radiant gaze. "I'm glad to have had a rest this afternoon, dear; and later—"

"Oh, yes, later, when all this fuss is over, we'll more than make up for it, sha'n't we, you precious darling?" And at this point Leila had been summoned to the telephone, leaving Mrs. Lidcote to her conjectures.

These were still floating before her in cloudy uncertainty when Miss Suffern tapped at the door.

"You've come to take me down to tea? I'd forgotten how late it was," Mrs. Lidcote exclaimed.

Miss Suffern, a plump peering little woman, with prim hair and a conciliatory smile, nervously adjusted the pendent bugles of her elaborate black dress. Miss Suffern was always in mourning, and always commemorating the demise of distant relatives by wearing the discarded wardrobe of their next of kin. "It isn't exactly mourning," she would say; "but it's the only stitch of black poor Julia had, and of course George was only my mother's step-cousin."

As she came forward Mrs. Lidcote found herself humorously wondering whether she were mourning Horace Pursh's divorce in one of his mother's old black satins.

"Oh, did you mean to go down for tea?" Susy Suffern peered at her, a little fluttered. "Leila sent me up to keep you company. She thought it would be cozier for you to stay here. She was afraid you were feeling rather tired."

"I was; but I've had the whole afternoon to rest in. And this wonderful sofa to help me."

"Leila told me to tell you that she'd rush up for a minute before dinner, after everybody had arrived; but the train is always dreadfully late. She's in despair at not giving you a sitting-room; she wanted to know if I thought you really minded."

"Of course I don't mind. It's not like Leila to think I should." Mrs. Lidcote drew aside to make way for the housemaid, who appeared in the doorway bearing a table spread with a bewildering variety of tea-cakes.

"Leila saw to it herself," Miss Suffern murmured as the door closed. "Her one idea is that you should feel happy here."

It struck Mrs. Lidcote as one more mark of the subverted state of things that her daughter's solicitude should find expression in the multiplicity of sandwiches and the piping-hotness of muffins; but then everything that had happened since her arrival seemed to increase her confusion.

The note of a motor-horn down the drive gave another turn to her thoughts. "Are those the new arrivals already?" she asked.

"Oh, dear, no; they won't be here till after seven." Miss Suffern craned her head from the window to catch a glimpse of the motor. "It must be Charlotte leaving."

"Was it the little Wynn girl who was called away in a hurry? I hope it's not on account of illness."

"Oh, no; I believe there was some mistake about dates. Her mother telephoned her that she was expected at the Stepleys, at Fishkill, and she had to be rushed over to Albany to catch a train."

Mrs. Lidcote meditated. "I'm sorry. She's a charming young thing. I hoped I should have another talk with her this evening after dinner."

"Yes; it's too bad." Miss Suffern's gaze grew vague.

"You do look tired, you know," she continued, seating herself at the tea-table and preparing to dispense its delicacies. "You must go straight back to your sofa and let me wait on you. The excitement has told on you more than you think, and you mustn't fight against it any longer. Just stay quietly up here and let yourself go. You'll have Leila to yourself on Monday."

Mrs. Lidcote received the tea-cup which her cousin proffered, but showed no other disposition to obey her injunctions. For a moment she stirred her tea in silence; then she asked: "Is it your idea that I should stay quietly up here till Monday?"

Miss Suffern set down her cup with a gesture so sudden that it endangered an adjacent plate of scones. When she had assured herself of the safety of the scones she looked up with a fluttered laugh. "Perhaps, dear, by to-morrow you'll be feeling differently. The air here, you know—"

"Yes, I know." Mrs. Lidcote bent forward to help herself to a scone. "Who's arriving this evening?" she asked.

Miss Suffern frowned and peered. "You know my wretched head for names. Leila told me, but there are so many—"

"So many? She didn't tell me she expected a big party."

"Oh, not big: but rather outside of her little group. And of course, as it's the first time, she's a little excited at having the older set."

"The older set? Our contemporaries, you mean?"

"Why, yes." Miss Suffern paused as if to gather herself up for a leap. "The Ashton Gileses," she brought out.

"The Ashton Gileses? Really? I shall be glad to see Mary Giles again. It must be eighteen years," said Mrs. Lidcote steadily.

"Yes," Miss Suffern gasped, precipitately refilling her cup.

"The Ashton Gileses; and who else?"

"Well, the Sam Fresbies. But the most important person, of course, is Mrs. Lorin Boulger."

"Mrs. Boulger? Leila didn't tell me she was coming."

"Didn't she? I suppose she forgot everything when she saw you. But the party was got up for Mrs. Boulger. You see, it's very important that she should, well, take a fancy to Leila and Wilbour; his being appointed to Rome virtually depends on it. And you know Leila insists on Rome in order to be near you. So she asked Mary Giles, who's intimate with the Boulgers, if the visit couldn't possibly be arranged; and Mary's cable caught Mrs. Boulger at Cherbourg. She's to be only a fortnight in America; and getting her to come directly here was rather a triumph."

"Yes; I see it was," said Mrs. Lidcote.

"You know, she's rather, rather fussy; and Mary was a little doubtful if—"

"If she would, on account of Leila?" Mrs. Lidcote murmured.

"Well, yes. In her official position. But luckily she's a friend of the Barkleys. And finding the Gileses and Fresbies here will make it all right. The times have changed!" Susy Suffern indulgently summed up.

Mrs. Lidcote smiled. "Yes; a few years ago it would have seemed improbable that I should ever again be dining with Mary Giles and Harriet Fresbie and Mrs. Lorin Boulger."

Miss Suffern did not at the moment seem disposed to enlarge upon this theme; and after an interval of silence Mrs. Lidcote suddenly resumed: "Do they know I'm here, by the way?"

The effect of her question was to produce in Miss Suffern an exaggerated access of peering and frowning. She twitched the tea-things about, fingered her bugles, and, looking at the clock, exclaimed amazedly: "Mercy! Is it seven already?"

"Not that it can make any difference, I suppose," Mrs. Lidcote continued. "But did Leila tell them I was coming?"

Miss Suffern looked at her with pain. "Why, you don't suppose, dearest, that Leila would do anything—"

Mrs. Lidcote went on: "For, of course, it's of the first importance, as you say, that Mrs. Lorin Boulger should be favorably impressed, in order that Wilbour may have the best possible chance of getting Borne."

"I told Leila you'd feel that, dear. You see, it's actually on your account, so that they may get a post near you—that Leila invited Mrs. Boulger."

"Yes, I see that." Mrs. Lidcote, abruptly rising from her seat, turned her eyes to the clock. "But, as you say, it's getting late. Oughtn't we to dress for dinner?"

Miss Suffern, at the suggestion, stood up also, an agitated hand among her bugles. "I do wish I could persuade you to stay up here this evening. I'm sure Leila'd be happier if you would. Really, you're much too tired to come down."

"What nonsense, Susy!" Mrs. Lidcote spoke with a sudden sharpness, her hand stretched to the bell. "When do we dine? At half-past eight? Then I must really send you packing. At my age it takes time to dress."

Miss Suffern, thus projected toward the threshold, lingered there to repeat: "Leila'll never forgive herself if you make an effort you're not up to." But Mrs. Lidcote smiled on her without answering, and the icy lightwave propelled her through the door.

V

Mrs. Lidcote, though she had made the gesture of ringing for her maid, had not done so.

When the door closed, she continued to stand motionless in the middle of her soft spacious room. The fire which had been kindled at twilight danced on the brightness of silver and mirrors and sober gilding; and the sofa toward which she had been urged by Miss Suffern heaped up its cushions in inviting proximity to a table laden with new books and papers. She could not recall having ever been more luxuriously housed, or having ever had so strange a sense of being out alone, under the night, in a windbeaten plain. She sat down by the fire and thought.

A knock on the door made her lift her head, and she saw her daughter on the threshold. The intricate ordering of Leila's fair hair and the flying folds of her dressinggown showed that she had interrupted her dressing to hasten to her mother; but once in the room she paused a moment, smiling uncertainly, as though she had forgotten the object of her haste.

Mrs. Lidcote rose to her feet. "Time to dress, dearest? Don't scold! I shan't be late."

"To dress?" Leila stood before her with a puzzled look. "Why, I thought, dear, I mean, I hoped you'd decided just to stay here quietly and rest."

Her mother smiled. "But I've been resting all the afternoon!"

"Yes, but—you know you do look tired. And when Susy told me just now that you meant to make the effort—"

"You came to stop me?"

"I came to tell you that you needn't feel in the least obliged—"

"Of course. I understand that."

There was a pause during which Leila, vaguely averting herself from her mother's scrutiny, drifted toward the dressing-table and began to disturb the symmetry of the brushes and bottles laid out on it.

"Do your visitors know that I'm here?" Mrs. Lidcote suddenly went on.

"Do they—Of course—why, naturally," Leila rejoined, absorbed in trying to turn the stopper of a salts-bottle.

"Then won't they think it odd if I don't appear?"

"Oh, not in the least, dearest. I assure you they'll all understand." Leila laid down the bottle and turned back to her mother, her face alight with reassurance.

Mrs. Lidcote stood motionless, her head erect, her smiling eyes on her daughter's. "Will they think it odd if I do?"

Leila stopped short, her lips half parted to reply. As she paused, the colour stole over her bare neck, swept up to her throat, and burst into flame in her cheeks. Thence it sent its devastating crimson up to her very temples, to the lobes of her ears, to the edges of her eyelids, beating all over her in fiery waves, as if fanned by some imperceptible wind.

Mrs. Lidcote silently watched the conflagration; then she turned away her eyes with a slight laugh. "I only meant that I was afraid it might upset the arrangement of your dinner-table if I didn't come down. If you can assure me that it won't, I believe I'll take you at your word and go back to this irresistible sofa." She paused, as if waiting for her daughter to speak; then she held out her arms. "Run off and dress, dearest; and don't have me on your mind." She clasped Leila close, pressing a long kiss on the last afterglow of her subsiding blush. "I do feel the least bit overdone, and if it won't inconvenience you to have me drop out of things, I believe I'll basely take to my bed and stay there till your party scatters. And now run off, or you'll be late; and make my excuses to them all."

VI

The Barkleys' visitors had dispersed, and Mrs. Lidcote, completely restored by her two days' rest, found herself, on the following Monday alone with her children and Miss Suffern.

There was a note of jubilation in the air, for the party had "gone off" so extraordinarily well, and so completely, as it appeared, to the satisfaction of Mrs. Lorin Boulger, that Wilbour's early appointment to Rome was almost to be counted on. So certain did this seem that the prospect of a prompt reunion mitigated the distress with which Leila learned of her mother's decision to return almost immediately to Italy. No one understood this decision; it seemed to Leila absolutely unintelligible that Mrs. Lidcote should not stay on with them till their own fate was fixed, and Wilbour echoed her astonishment.

"Why shouldn't you, as Leila says, wait here till we can all pack up and go together?"

Mrs. Lidcote smiled her gratitude with her refusal. "After all, it's not yet sure that you'll be packing up."

"Oh, you ought to have seen Wilbour with Mrs. Boulger," Leila triumphed.

"No, you ought to have seen Leila with her," Leila's husband exulted.

Miss Suffern enthusiastically appended: "I do think inviting Harriet Fresbie was a stroke of genius!"

"Oh, we'll be with you soon," Leila laughed. "So soon that it's really foolish to separate."

But Mrs. Lidcote held out with the quiet firmness which her daughter knew it was useless to oppose. After her long months in India, it was really imperative, she declared, that she should get back to Florence and see what was happening to her little place there; and she had been so comfortable on the Utopia that she had a fancy to return by the same ship. There was nothing for it, therefore, but to acquiesce in her decision and keep her with them till the afternoon before the day of the Utopia's sailing. This arrangement fitted in with certain projects which, during her two days' seclusion, Mrs. Lidcote had silently matured. It had become to her of the first importance to get away as soon as she could, and the little place in Florence, which held her past in every fold of its curtains and between every page of its books, seemed now to her the one spot where that past would be endurable to look upon.

She was not unhappy during the intervening days. The sight of Leila's well-being, the sense of Leila's tenderness, were, after all, what she had come for; and of these she had had full measure. Leila had never been happier or more tender; and the contemplation of her bliss, and the enjoyment of her affection, were an absorbing occupation for her mother. But they were also a sharp strain on certain overtightened chords, and Mrs. Lidcote, when at last she found herself alone in the New York hotel to which she had returned the night before embarking, had the feeling that she had just escaped with her life from the clutch of a giant hand.

She had refused to let her daughter come to town with her; she had even rejected Susy Suffern's company. She wanted no viaticum but that of her own thoughts; and she let these come to her without shrinking from them as she sat in the same high-hung sitting-room in which, just a week before, she and Franklin Ide had had their memorable talk.

She had promised her friend to let him hear from her, but she had not kept her promise. She knew that he had probably come back from Chicago, and that if he learned of her sudden decision to return to Italy it would be impossible for her not to see him before sailing; and as she wished above all things not to see him she had kept silent, intending to send him a letter from the steamer.

There was no reason why she should wait till then to write it. The actual moment was more favorable, and the task, though not agreeable, would at least bridge over an hour of her lonely evening. She went up to the writing-table, drew out a sheet of paper and began to write his name. And as she did so, the door opened and he came in.

The words she met him with were the last she could have imagined herself saying when they had parted. "How in the world did you know that I was here?"

He caught her meaning in a flash. "You didn't want me to, then?" He stood looking at her. "I suppose I ought to have taken your silence as meaning that. But I happened to meet Mrs. Wynn, who is stopping here, and she asked me to dine with her and Charlotte, and Charlotte's young man. They told me they'd seen you arriving this afternoon, and I couldn't help coming up."

There was a pause between them, which Mrs. Lidcote at last surprisingly broke with the exclamation: "Ah, she did recognize me, then!"

"Recognize you?" He stared. "Why—"

"Oh, I saw she did, though she never moved an eyelid. I saw it by Charlotte's blush. The child has the prettiest blush. I saw that her mother wouldn't let her speak to me."

Ide put down his hat with an impatient laugh. "Hasn't Leila cured you of your delusions?"

She looked at him intently. "Then you don't think Margaret Wynn meant to cut me?"

"I think your ideas are absurd."

She paused for a perceptible moment without taking this up; then she said, at a tangent: "I'm sailing tomorrow early. I meant to write to you, there's the letter I'd begun."

Ide followed her gesture, and then turned his eyes back to her face. "You didn't mean to see me, then, or even to let me know that you were going till you'd left?"

"I felt it would be easier to explain to you in a letter—"

"What in God's name is there to explain?" She made no reply, and he pressed on: "It can't be that you're worried about Leila, for Charlotte Wynn told me she'd been there last week, and there was a big party arriving when she left: Fresbies and Gileses, and Mrs. Lorin Boulger, all the board of examiners! If Leila has passed that, she's got her degree."

Mrs. Lidcote had dropped down into a corner of the sofa where she had sat during their talk of the week before. "I was stupid," she began abruptly. "I ought to have gone to Ridgefield with Susy. I didn't see till afterward that I was expected to."

"You were expected to?"

"Yes. Oh, it wasn't Leila's fault. She suffered—poor darling; she was distracted. But she'd asked her party before she knew I was arriving."

"Oh, as to that—" Ide drew a deep breath of relief. "I can understand that it must have been a disappointment not to have you to herself just at first. But, after all, you were among old friends or their children: the Gileses and Fresbies—and little Charlotte Wynn." He paused a moment before the last name, and scrutinized her hesitatingly. "Even if they came at the wrong time, you must have been glad to see them all at Leila's."

She gave him back his look with a faint smile. "I didn't see them."

"You didn't see them?"

"No. That is, excepting little Charlotte Wynn. That child is exquisite. We had a talk before luncheon the day I arrived. But when her mother found out that I was staying in the house she telephoned her to leave immediately, and so I didn't see her again."

The colour rushed to Ide's sallow face. "I don't know where you get such ideas!"

She pursued, as if she had not heard him: "Oh, and I saw Mary Giles for a minute too. Susy Suffern brought her up to my room the last evening, after dinner, when all the others were at bridge. She meant it kindly—but it wasn't much use."

"But what were you doing in your room in the evening after dinner?"

"Why, you see, when I found out my mistake in coming, how embarrassing it was for Leila, I mean, I simply told her I was very tired, and preferred to stay upstairs till the party was over."

Ide, with a groan, struck his hand against the arm of his chair. "I wonder how much of all this you simply imagined!"

"I didn't imagine the fact of Harriet Fresbie's not even asking if she might see me when she knew I was in the house. Nor of Mary Giles's getting Susy, at the eleventh hour, to smuggle her up to my room when the others wouldn't know where she'd gone; nor poor Leila's ghastly fear lest Mrs. Lorin Boulger, for whom the party was given, should guess I was in the house, and prevent her husband's giving Wilbour the second secretaryship because she'd been obliged to spend a night under the same roof with his mother-in-law!"

Ide continued to drum on his chair-arm with exasperated fingers. "You don't know that any of the acts you describe are due to the causes you suppose."

Mrs. Lidcote paused before replying, as if honestly trying to measure the weight of this argument. Then she said in a low tone: "I know that Leila was in an agony lest I should come down to dinner the first night. And it was for me she was afraid, not for herself. Leila is never afraid for herself."

"But the conclusions you draw are simply preposterous. There are narrow-minded women everywhere, but the women who were at Leila's knew perfectly well that their going there would give her a sort of social sanction, and if they were willing that she should have it, why on earth should they want to withhold it from you?"

"That's what I told myself a week ago, in this very room, after my first talk with Susy Suffern." She lifted a misty smile to his anxious eyes. "That's why I listened to what you said to me the same evening, and why your arguments half convinced me, and made me think that what had been possible for Leila might not be impossible for me. If the new dispensation had come, why not for me as well as for the others? I can't tell you the flight my imagination took!"

Franklin Ide rose from his seat and crossed the room to a chair near her sofa-corner. "All I cared about was that it seemed, for the moment, to be carrying you toward me," he said.

"I cared about that, too. That's why I meant to go away without seeing you." They gave each other grave look for look. "Because, you see, I was mistaken," she went on. "We were both mistaken. You say it's preposterous that the women who didn't object to accepting Leila's hospitality should have objected to meeting me under her roof. And so it is; but I begin to understand why. It's simply that society is much too busy to revise its own judgments. Probably no one in the house with me stopped to consider that my case and Leila's were identical. They only remembered that I'd done something which, at the time I did it, was condemned by society. My case has been passed on and classified: I'm the woman who has been cut for nearly twenty years. The older people have half forgotten why, and the younger ones have never really known: it's simply become a tradition to cut me. And traditions that have lost their meaning are the hardest of all to destroy."

Ide sat motionless while she spoke. As she ended, he stood up with a short laugh and walked across the room to the window. Outside, the immense black prospect of New York, strung with its myriad lines of light, stretched away into the smoky edges of the night. He showed it to her with a gesture.

"What do you suppose such words as you've been using, 'society,' 'tradition,' and the rest—mean to all the life out there?"

She came and stood by him in the window. "Less than nothing, of course. But you and I are not out there. We're shut up in a little tight round of habit and association, just as we're shut up in this room. Remember, I thought I'd got out of it once; but what really happened was that the other people went out, and left me in the same little room. The only difference was that I was there alone. Oh, I've made it habitable now, I'm used to it; but I've lost any illusions I may have had as to an angel's opening the door."

Ide again laughed impatiently. "Well, if the door won't open, why not let another prisoner in? At least it would be less of a solitude—"

She turned from the dark window back into the vividly lighted room.

"It would be more of a prison. You forget that I know all about that. We're all imprisoned, of course, all of us middling people, who don't carry our freedom in our brains. But we've accommodated ourselves to our different cells, and if we're moved suddenly into new ones we're likely to find a stone wall where we thought there was thin air, and to knock ourselves senseless against it. I saw a man do that once."

Ide, leaning with folded arms against the windowframe, watched her in silence as she moved restlessly about the room, gathering together some scattered books and tossing a handful of torn letters into the paperbasket. When she ceased, he rejoined: "All you say is based on preconceived theories. Why didn't you put them to the test by coming down to meet your old friends? Don't you see the inference they would naturally draw from your hiding yourself when they arrived? It looked as though you were afraid of them, or as though you hadn't forgiven them. Either way, you put them in the wrong instead of waiting to let them put you in the right. If Leila had buried herself in a desert do you suppose society would have gone to fetch her out? You say you were afraid for Leila and that she was afraid for you. Don't you see what all these complications of feeling mean? Simply that you were too nervous at the moment to let things happen naturally, just as you're too nervous now to judge them rationally." He paused and turned his eyes to her face. "Don't try to just yet. Give yourself a little more time. Give me a little more time. I've always known it would take time."

He moved nearer, and she let him have her hand.

With the grave kindness of his face so close above her she felt like a child roused out of frightened dreams and finding a light in the room.

"Perhaps you're right—" she heard herself begin; then something within her clutched her back, and her hand fell away from him.

"I know I'm right: trust me," he urged. "We'll talk of this in Florence soon."

She stood before him, feeling with despair his kindness, his patience and his unreality. Everything he said seemed like a painted gauze let down between herself and the real facts of life; and a sudden desire seized her to tear the gauze into shreds.

She drew back and looked at him with a smile of superficial reassurance. "You are right—about not talking any longer now. I'm nervous and tired, and it would do no good. I brood over things too much. As you say, I must try not to shrink from people." She turned away and glanced at the clock. "Why, it's only ten! If I send you off I shall begin to brood again; and if you stay we shall go on talking about the same thing. Why shouldn't we go down and see Margaret Wynn for half an hour?"

She spoke lightly and rapidly, her brilliant eyes on his face. As she watched him, she saw it change, as if her smile had thrown a too vivid light upon it.

"Oh, no, not to-night!" he exclaimed.

"Not to-night? Why, what other night have I, when I'm off at dawn? Besides, I want to show you at once that I mean to be more sensible, that I'm not going to be afraid of people any more. And I should really like another glimpse of little Charlotte." He stood before her, his hand in his beard, with the gesture he had in moments of perplexity. "Come!" she ordered him gaily, turning to the door.

He followed her and laid his hand on her arm. "Don't you think, hadn't you better let me go first and see? They told me they'd had a tiring day at the dressmaker's* I daresay they have gone to bed."

"But you said they'd a young man of Charlotte's dining with them. Surely he wouldn't have left by ten? At any rate, I'll go down with you and see. It takes so long if one "ends a servant first" She put him gently aside, and then paused as a new thought struck her. "Or wait; my maid's in the next room. I'll tell her to go and ask if Margaret will receive me. Yes, that's much the best way."

She turned back and went toward the door that led to her bedroom; but before she could open it she felt Ide's quick touch again.

"I believe, I remember now, Charlotte's young man was suggesting that they should all go out, to a music hall or something of the sort. I'm sure, I'm positively sure that you won't find them."

Her hand dropped from the door, his dropped from her arm, and as they drew back and faced each other she saw the blood rise slowly through his sallow skin, redden his neck and ears, encroach upon the edges of his beard, and settle in dull patches under his kind troubled eyes. She had seen the same blush on another face, and the same impulse of compassion she had then felt made her turn her gaze away again.

A knock on the door broke the silence, and a porter put his head' into the room.

"It's only just to know how many pieces there'll be to go down to the steamer in the morning."

With the words she felt that the veil of painted gauze was torn in tatters, and that she was moving again among the grim edges of reality.

"Oh, dear," she exclaimed, "I never can remember! Wait a minute; I shall have to ask my maid."

She opened her bedroom door and called out: "Annette!"

THE LONG RUN

The shade of those our days that had no tongue.

I

It was last winter, after a twelve years' absence from New York, that I saw again, at one of the Jim Cumnors' dinners, my old friend Halston Merrick.

The Cumnors' house is one of the few where, even after such a lapse of time, one can be sure of finding familiar faces and picking up old threads; where for a moment one can abandon one's self to the illusion that New York humanity is a shade less unstable than its bricks and mortar. And that evening in particular I remember feeling that there could be no pleasanter way of re-entering the confused and careless world to which I was returning than through the quiet softly-lit diningroom in which Mrs. Cumnor, with a characteristic sense of my needing to be broken in gradually, had contrived to assemble so many friendly faces.

I was glad to see them all, including the three or four I did not know, or failed to recognize, but had no difficulty in passing as in the tradition and of the group; but I was most of all glad, as I rather wonderingly found, to set eyes again on Halston Merrick.

He and I had been at Harvard together, for one thing, and had shared there curiosities and ardours a little outside the current tendencies: had, on the whole, been more critical than our comrades, and less amenable to the accepted. Then, for the next following years, Merrick had been a vivid and promising figure in young American life. Handsome, careless, and free, he had wandered and tasted and compared. After leaving Harvard he had spent two years at Oxford; then he had accepted a private secretaryship to our Ambassador in England, and had come back from this adventure with a fresh curiosity about public affairs at home, and the conviction that men of his kind should play a larger part in them. This led, first, to his running for a State Senatorship which he failed to get, and ultimately to a few months of intelligent activity in a municipal office. Soon after being deprived of this post by a change of party he had published a small volume of delicate verse, and, a year later, an odd uneven brilliant book on Municipal Government. After that one hardly knew where to look for his next appearance; but chance rather disappointingly solved the problem by killing off his father and placing Halston at the head of the Merrick Iron Foundry at Yonkers.

His friends had gathered that, whenever this regrettable contingency should occur, he meant to dispose of the business and continue his life of free experiment. As often happens in just such cases, however, it was not the moment for a sale, and Merrick had to take over the management of the foundry. Some two years later he had a chance to free himself; but when it came he did not choose to take it. This tame sequel to an inspiriting start was disappointing to some of us, and I was among those disposed to regret Merrick's drop to the level of the prosperous. Then I went away to a big engineering job in China, and from there to Africa, and spent the next twelve years out of sight and sound of New York doings.

During that long interval I heard of no new phase in Merrick's evolution, but this did not surprise me, as I had never expected from him actions resonant enough to cross the globe. All I knew, and this did surprise me, was that he had not married, and that he was still in the iron business. All through those years, however, I never ceased to wish, in certain situations and at certain turns of thought, that Merrick were in reach, that I could tell this or that to Merrick. I had never, in the interval, found any one with just his quickness of perception and just his sureness of response.

After dinner, therefore, we irresistibly drew together. In Mrs. Cumnor's big easy drawing-room cigars were allowed, and there was no break in the communion of the sexes; and, this being the case, I ought to have sought a seat beside one of the ladies among whom we were allowed to remain. But, as had generally happened of old when Merrick was in sight, I found myself steering straight for him past all minor ports of call.

There had been no time, before dinner, for more than the barest expression of satisfaction at meeting, and our seats had been at opposite ends of the longish table, so that we got our first real look at each other in the secluded corner to which Mrs. Cumnor's vigilance now directed us.

Merrick was still handsome in his stooping tawny way: handsomer perhaps, with thinnish hair and more lines in his face, than in the young excess of his good looks. He was very glad to see me and conveyed his gladness by the same charming smile; but as soon as we began to talk I felt a change. It was not merely the change that years and experience and altered values bring. There was something more fundamental the matter with Merrick, something dreadful, unforeseen, unaccountable: Merrick had grown conventional and dull.

In the glow of his frank pleasure in seeing me I was ashamed to analyze the nature of the change; but presently our talk began to flag, fancy a talk with Merrick flagging!—and self-deception became impossible as I watched myself handing out platitudes with the gesture of the salesman offering something to a purchaser "equally good." The worst of it was that Merrick—Merrick, who had once felt everything!—didn't seem to feel the lack of spontaneity in my remarks, but hung on' them with a harrowing faith in the resuscitating power of our past. It was as if he hugged the empty vessel of our friendship without perceiving that the last drop of its essence was dry.

But after all, I am exaggerating. Through my surprise and disappointment I felt a certain sense of well-being in the mere physical presence of my old friend. I liked looking at the way his dark hair waved away from the forehead, at the tautness of his dry brown cheek, the thoughtful backward tilt of his head, the way his brown eyes mused upon the scene through lowered lids. All the past was in his way of looking and sitting, and I wanted to stay near him, and felt that he wanted me to stay; but the devil of it was that neither of us knew what to talk about.

It was this difficulty which caused me, after a while, since I could not follow Merrick's talk, to follow his eyes in their roaming circuit of the room.

At the moment when our glances joined, his had paused on a lady seated at some distance from our corner. Immersed, at first, in the satisfaction of finding myself again with Merrick, I had been only half aware of this lady, as of one of the few persons present whom I did not know, or had failed to remember. There was nothing in her appearance to challenge my attention or to excite my curiosity, and I don't suppose I should have looked at her again if I had not noticed that my friend was doing so.

She was a woman of about forty-seven, with fair faded hair and a young figure. Her gray dress was handsome but ineffective, and her pale and rather serious face wore a small unvarying smile which might have been pinned on with her ornaments. She was one of the women in whom increasing years show rather what they have taken than what they have bestowed, and only on looking closely did one see that what they had taken must have been good of its kind.

Phil Cumnor and another man were talking to her, and the very intensity of the attention she bestowed on them betrayed the straining of rebellious thoughts. She never let her eyes stray or her smile drop; and at the proper moment I saw she was ready with the proper sentiment.

The party, like most of those that Mrs. Cumnor gathered about her, was not composed of exceptional beings. The people of the old vanished New York set were not exceptional: they were mostly cut on the same convenient and unobtrusive pattern; but they were often exceedingly "nice." And this obsolete quality marked every look and gesture of the lady I was scrutinizing.

While these reflections were passing through my mind I was aware that Merrick's eyes rested still on her. I took a cross-section of his look and found in it neither surprise nor absorption, but only a certain sober pleasure just about at the emotional level of the rest of the room.

If he continued to look at her, his expression seemed to say, it was only because, all things considered, there were fewer reasons for looking at anybody else.

This made me wonder what were the reasons for looking at her; and as a first step toward enlightenment I said:—"I'm sure I've seen the lady over there in gray—"

Merrick detached his eyes and turned them on me with a wondering look.

"Seen her? You know her." He waited. "Don't you know her? It's Mrs. Reardon."

I wondered that he should wonder, for I could not remember, in the Cumnor group or elsewhere, having known any one of the name he mentioned.

"But perhaps," he continued, "you hadn't heard of her marriage? You knew her as Mrs. Trant."

I gave him back his stare. "Not Mrs. Philip Trant?"

"Yes; Mrs. Philip Trant."

"Not Paulina?"

"Yes—Paulina," he said, with a just perceptible delay before the name.

In my surprise I continued to stare at him. He averted his eyes from mine after a moment, and I saw that they had strayed back to her. "You find her so changed?" he asked.

Something in his voice acted as a warning signal, and I tried to reduce my astonishment to less unbecoming proportions. "I don't find that she looks much older."

"No. Only different?" he suggested, as if there were nothing new to him in my perplexity.

"Yes, awfully different."

"I suppose we're all awfully different. To you, I mean—coming from so far?"

"I recognized all the rest of you," I said, hesitating. "And she used to be the one who stood out most."

There was a flash, a wave, a stir of something deep down in his eyes. "Yes," he said. "That's the difference."

"I see it is. She—she looks worn down. Soft but blurred, like the figures in that tapestry behind her."

He glanced at her again, as if to test the exactness of my analogy.

"Life wears everybody down," he said.

"Yes, except those it makes more distinct. They're the rare ones, of course; but she was rare."

He stood up suddenly, looking old and tired. "I believe I'll be off. I wish you'd come down to my place for Sunday.... No, don't shake hands, I want to slide away unawares."

He had backed away to the threshold and was turning the noiseless door-knob. Even Mrs. Cumnor's doorknobs had tact and didn't tell.

"Of course I'll come," I promised warmly. In the last ten minutes he had begun to interest me again.

"All right Good-bye." Half through the door he paused to add:—"She remembers you. You ought to speak to her."

"I'm going to. But tell me a little more." I thought I saw a shade of constraint on his face, and did not add, as I had meant to: "Tell me, because she interests me, what wore her down?" Instead, I asked: "How soon after Trant's death did she remarry?"

He seemed to make an effort of memory. "It was seven years ago, I think."

"And is Reardon here to-night?"

"Yes; over there, talking to Mrs. Cumnor."

I looked across the broken groupings and saw a large glossy man with straw-coloured hair and a red face, whose shirt and shoes and complexion seemed all to have received a coat of the same expensive varnish.

As I looked there was a drop in the talk about us, and I heard Mr. Reardon pronounce in a big booming voice: "What I say is: what's the good of disturbing things? Thank the Lord, I'm content with what I've got!"

"Is that her husband? What's he like?"

"Oh, the best fellow in the world," said Merrick, going.

II

Merrick had a little place at Riverdale, where he went occasionally to be near the Iron Works, and where he hid his week-ends when the world was too much with him.

Here, on the following Saturday afternoon I found him awaiting me in a pleasant setting of books and prints and faded parental furniture.

We dined late, and smoked and talked afterward in his book-walled study till the terrier on the hearth-rug stood up and yawned for bed. When we took the hint and moved toward the staircase I felt, not that I had found the old Merrick again, but that I was on his track, had come across traces of his passage here and there in the thick jungle that had grown up between us. But I had a feeling that when I finally came on the man himself he might be dead....

As we started upstairs he turned back with one of his abrupt shy movements, and walked into the study.

"Wait a bit!" he called to me.

I waited, and he came out in a moment carrying a limp folio.

"It's typewritten. Will you take a look at it? I've been trying to get to work again," he explained, thrusting the manuscript into my hand.

"What? Poetry, I hope?" I exclaimed.

He shook his head with a gleam of derision. "No, just general considerations. The fruit of fifty years of inexperience."

He showed me to my room and said good-night.

The following afternoon we took a long walk inland, across the hills, and I said to Merrick what I could of his book. Unluckily there wasn't much to say. The essays were judicious, polished and cultivated; but they lacked the freshness and audacity of his youthful work. I tried to conceal my opinion behind the usual generalisations, but he broke through these feints with a quick thrust to the heart of my meaning.

"It's worn down, blurred? Like the figures in the Cumnors' tapestry?"

I hesitated. "It's a little too damned resigned," I said.

"Ah," he exclaimed, "so am I. Resigned." He switched the bare brambles by the roadside. "A man can't serve two masters."

"You mean business and literature?"

"No; I mean theory and instinct. The gray tree and the green. You've got to choose which fruit you'll try; and you don't know till afterward which of the two has the dead core."

"How can anybody be sure that only one of them has?"

"I'm sure," said Merrick sharply.

We turned back to the subject of his essays, and I was astonished at the detachment with which he criticised and demolished them. Little by little, as we talked, his old perspective, his old standards came back to him; but with the difference that they no longer seemed like functions of his mind but merely like attitudes assumed or dropped at will. He could still, with an effort, put himself at the angle from which he had formerly seen things; but it was with the effort of a man climbing mountains after a sedentary life in the plain.

I tried to cut the talk short, but he kept coming back to it with nervous insistence, forcing me into the last retrenchments of hypocrisy, and anticipating the verdict I held back. I perceived that a great deal, immensely more than I could see a reason for, had hung for him on my opinion of his book.

Then, as suddenly, his insistence dropped and, as if ashamed of having forced, himself so long on my attention, he began to talk rapidly and uninterestingly of other things.

We were alone again that evening, and after dinner, wishing to efface the impression of the afternoon, and above all to show that I wanted him to talk about himself, I reverted to his work. "You must need an outlet of that sort. When a man's once had it in him, as you have, and when other things begin to dwindle—"

He laughed. "Your theory is that a man ought to be able to return to the Muse as he comes back to his wife after he's ceased to interest other women?"

"No; as he comes back to his wife after the day's work is done." A new thought came to me as I looked at him. "You ought to have had one," I added.

He laughed again. "A wife, you mean? So that there'd have been some one waiting for me even if the Muse decamped?" He went on after a pause: "I've a notion that the kind of woman worth coming back to wouldn't be much more patient than the Muse. But as it happens I never tried, because, for fear they'd chuck me, I put them both out of doors together."

He turned his head and looked past me with a queer expression at the low panelled door at my back. "Out of that very door they went, the two of 'em, on a rainy night like this: and one stopped and looked back, to see if I wasn't going to call her, and I didn't, and so they both went...."

III

"The Muse?" (said Merrick, refilling my glass and stooping to pat the terrier as he went back to his chair)—"well, you've met the Muse in the little volume of sonnets you used to like; and you've met the woman too, and you used to like her; though you didn't know her when you saw her the other evening....

"No, I won't ask you how she struck you when you talked to her: I know. She struck you like that stuff I gave you to read last night She's conformed, I've conformed, the mills have caught us and ground us: ground us, oh, exceedingly small!

"But you remember what she was; and that's the reason why I'm telling you this now....

"You may recall that after my father's death I tried to sell the Works. I was impatient to free myself from anything that would keep me tied to New York. I don't dislike my trade, and I've made, in the end, a fairly good thing of it; but industrialism was not, at that time, in the line of my tastes, and I know now that it wasn't what I was meant for. Above all, I wanted to get away, to see new places and rub up against different ideas. I had reached a time of life, the top of the first hill, so to speak, where the distance draws one, and everything in the foreground seems tame and stale. I was sick to death of the particular set of conformities I had grown up among; sick of being a pleasant popular young man with a long line of dinners on my list, and the dead certainty of meeting the same people, or their prototypes, at all of them.

"Well, I failed to sell the Works, and that increased my discontent. I went through moods of cold unsociability, alternating with sudden flushes of curiosity, when I gloated over stray scraps of talk overheard in railway stations and omnibuses, when strange faces that I passed in the street tantalized me with fugitive promises. I wanted to be among things that were unexpected and unknown; and it seemed to me that nobody about me understood in the least what I felt, but that somewhere just out of reach there was some one who did, and whom I must find or despair....

"It was just then that, one evening, I saw Mrs. Trant for the first time.

"Yes: I know, you wonder what I mean. I'd known her, of course, as a girl; I'd met her several times after her marriage; and I'd lately been thrown with her, quite intimately and continuously, during a succession of country-house visits. But I had never, as it happened, really seen her....

"It was at a dinner at the Cumnors'; and there she was, in front of the very tapestry we saw her against the other evening, with people about her, and her face turned from me, and nothing noticeable or different in her dress or manner; and suddenly she stood out for me against the familiar unimportant background, and for the first time I saw a meaning in the stale phrase of a picture's walking out of its frame. For, after all, most people are just that to us: pictures, furniture, the inanimate accessories of our little island-area of sensation. And then sometimes one of these graven images moves and throws out live filaments toward us, and the line they make draws us across the world as the moon-track seems to draw a boat across the water....

"There she stood; and as this queer sensation came over me I felt that she was looking steadily at me, that her eyes were voluntarily, consciously resting on me with the weight of the very question I was asking.

"I went over and joined her, and she turned and walked with me into the music-room. Earlier in the evening someone had been singing, and there were low lights there, and a few couples still sitting in those confidential corners of which Mrs. Cumnor has the art; but we were under no illusion as to the nature of these presences. We knew that they were just painted in, and that the whole of life was in us two, flowing back and forward between us. We talked, of course; we had the attitudes, even the words, of the others: I remember her telling me her plans for the spring and asking me politely about mine! As if there were the least sense in plans, now that this thing had happened!

"When we went back into the drawing-room I had said nothing to her that I might not have said to any other woman of the party; but when we shook hands I knew we should meet the next day, and the next....

"That's the way, I take it, that Nature has arranged the beginning of the great enduring loves; and likewise of the little epidermal flurries. And how is a man to know where he is going?

"From the first my feeling for Paulina Trant seemed to me a grave business; but then the Enemy is given to producing that illusion. Many a man, I'm talking of the kind with imagination—has thought he was seeking a soul when all he wanted was a closer view of its tenement. And I tried, honestly tried, to make myself think I was in the latter case. Because, in the first place, I didn't, just then, want a big disturbing influence in my life; and because I didn't want to be a dupe; and because Paulina Trant was not, according to hearsay, the kind of woman for whom it was worth while to bring up the big batteries....

"But my resistance was only half-hearted. What I really felt, all I really felt, was the flood of joy that comes of heightened emotion. She had given me that, and I wanted her to give it to me again. That's as near as I've ever come to analyzing my state in the beginning.

"I knew her story, as no doubt you know it: the current version, I mean. She had been poor and fond of enjoyment, and she had married that pompous stick Philip Trant because she needed a home, and perhaps also because she wanted a little luxury. Queer how we sneer at women for wanting the thing that gives them half their attraction!

"People shook their heads over the marriage, and divided, prematurely, into Philip's partisans and hers: for no one thought it would work. And they were almost disappointed when, after all, it did. She and her wooden consort seemed to get on well enough. There was a ripple, at one time, over her friendship with young Jim Dalham, who was always with her during a summer at Newport and an autumn in Italy; then the talk died out, and she and Trant were seen together, as before, on terms of apparent good-fellowship.

"This was the more surprising because, from the first, Paulina had never made the least attempt to change her tone or subdue her colours. In the gray Trant atmosphere she flashed with prismatic fires. She smoked, she talked subversively, she did as she liked and went where she chose, and danced over the Trant prejudices and the Trant principles as if they'd been a ball-room floor; and all without apparent offence to her solemn husband and his cloud of cousins. I believe her frankness and directness struck them dumb. She moved like a kind of primitive Una through the virtuous rout, and never got a finger-mark on her freshness.

"One of the finest things about her was the fact that she never, for an instant, used her situation as a means of enhancing her attraction. With a husband like Trant it would have been so easy! He was a man who always saw the small sides of big things. He thought most of life compressible into a set of by-laws and the rest unmentionable; and with his stiff frock-coated and tall-hatted mind, instinctively distrustful of intelligences in another dress, with his arbitrary classification of whatever he didn't understand into 'the kind of thing I don't approve of,' 'the kind of thing that isn't done,' and, deepest depth of all, 'the kind of thing I'd rather not discuss,' he lived in bondage to a shadowy moral etiquette of which the complex rites and awful penalties had cast an abiding gloom upon his manner.

"A woman like his wife couldn't have asked a better foil; yet I'm sure she never consciously used his dullness to relieve her brilliancy. She may have felt that the case spoke for itself. But I believe her reserve was rather due to a lively sense of justice, and to the rare habit (you said she was rare) of looking at facts as they are, without any throwing of sentimental lime-lights. She knew Trant could no more help being Trant than she could help being herself, and there was an end of it. I've never known a woman who 'made up' so little mentally....

"Perhaps her very reserve, the fierceness of her implicit rejection of sympathy, exposed her the more to—well, to what happened when we met. She said afterward that it was like having been shut up for months in the hold of a ship, and coming suddenly on deck on a day that was all flying blue and silver....

"I won't try to tell you what she was. It's easier to tell you what her friendship made of me; and I can do that best by adopting her metaphor of the ship. Haven't you, sometimes, at the moment of starting on a journey, some glorious plunge into the unknown, been tripped up by the thought: 'If only one hadn't to come back'? Well, with her one had the sense that one would never have to come back; that the magic ship, would always carry one farther. And what an air one breathed on it! And, oh, the wind, and the islands, and the sunsets!

"I said just now 'her friendship'; and I used the word advisedly. Love is deeper than friendship, but friendship is a good deal wider. The beauty of our relation was that it included both dimensions. Our thoughts met as naturally as our eyes: it was almost as if we loved each other because we liked each other. The quality of a love may be tested by the amount of friendship it contains, and in our case there was no dividing line between loving and liking, no disproportion between them, no barrier against which desire beat in vain or from which thought fell back unsatisfied. Ours was a robust passion that could give an open-eyed account of itself, and not a beautiful madness shrinking away from the proof....

"For the first months friendship sufficed us, or rather gave us so much by the way that we were in no hurry to reach what we knew it was leading to. But we were moving there nevertheless, and one day we found ourselves on the borders. It came about through a sudden decision of Trant's to start on a long tour with his wife. We had never foreseen that: he seemed rooted in his New York habits and convinced that the whole social and financial machinery of the metropolis would cease to function if he did not keep an eye on it through the columns of his morning paper, and pronounce judgment on it in the afternoon at his club. But something new had happened to him: he caught a cold, which was followed by a touch of pleurisy, and instantly he perceived the intense interest and importance which ill-health may add to life. He took the fullest advantage of it. A discerning doctor recommended travel in a warm climate; and suddenly, the morning paper, the afternoon club, Fifth Avenue, Wall Street, all the complex phenomena of the metropolis, faded into insignificance, and the rest of the terrestrial globe, from being a mere geographical hypothesis, useful in enabling one to determine the latitude of New York, acquired reality and magnitude as a factor in the convalescence of Mr. Philip Trant.

"His wife was absorbed in preparations for the journey. To move him was like mobilizing an army, and weeks before the date set for their departure it was almost as if she were already gone.

"This foretaste of separation showed us what we were to each other. Yet I was letting her go, and there was no help for it, no way of preventing it. Resistance was as useless as the vain struggles in a nightmare. She was Trant's and not mine: part of his luggage when he travelled as she was part of his household furniture when he stayed at home....

"The day she told me that their passages were taken, it was on a November afternoon, in her drawing-room in town, I turned away from her and, going to the window, stood looking out at the torrent of traffic interminably pouring down Fifth Avenue. I watched the senseless machinery of life revolving in the rain and mud, and tried to picture myself performing my small function in it after she had gone from me.

"'It can't be, it can't be!' I exclaimed.

"'What can't be?'

"I came back into the room and sat down by her. 'This, this—' I hadn't any words. 'Two weeks!' I said. 'What's two weeks?"

"She answered, vaguely, something about their thinking of Spain for the spring—

"'Two weeks, two weeks!' I repeated. 'And the months we've lost, the days that belonged to us!'

"'Yes,' she said, 'I'm thankful it's settled.'

"Our words seemed irrelevant, haphazard. It was as if each were answering a secret voice, and not what the other was saying.

"'Don't you feel anything at all?' I remember bursting out at her. As I asked it the tears were streaming down her face. I felt angry with her, and was almost glad to note that her lids were red and that she didn't cry becomingly. I can't express my sensation to you except by saying that she seemed part of life's huge league against me. And suddenly I thought of an afternoon we had spent together in the country, on a ferny hill-side, when we had sat under a beech-tree, and her hand had lain palm upward in the moss, close to mine, and I had watched a little black-and-red beetle creeping over it....

"The bell rang, and we heard the voice of a visitor and the click of an umbrella in the umbrella-stand.

"She rose to go into the inner drawing-room, and I caught her suddenly by the wrist. 'You understand,' I said, 'that we can't go on like this?'

"'I understand,' she answered, and moved away to meet her visitor. As I went out I heard her saying in the other room: 'Yes, we're really off on the twelfth.'"

IV

"I wrote her a long letter that night, and waited two days for a reply.

"On the third day I had a brief line saying that she was going to spend Sunday with some friends who had a place near Riverdale, and that she would arrange to see me while she was there. That was all.

"It was on a Saturday that I received the note and I came out here the same night. The next morning was rainy, and I was in despair, for I had counted on her asking me to take her for a drive or a long walk. It was hopeless to try to say what I had to say to her in the drawing-room of a crowded country-house. And only eleven days were left!

"I stayed indoors all the morning, fearing to go out lest she should telephone me. But no sign came, and I grew more and more restless and anxious. She was too free and frank for coquetry, but her silence and evasiveness made me feel that, for some reason, she did not wish to hear what she knew I meant to say. Could it be that she was, after all, more conventional, less genuine, than I had thought? I went again and again over the whole maddening round of conjecture; but the only conclusion I could rest in was that, if she loved me as I loved her, she would be as determined as I was to let no obstacle come between us during the days that were left.

"The luncheon-hour came and passed, and there was no word from her. I had ordered my trap to be ready, so that I might drive over as soon as she summoned me; but the hours dragged on, the early twilight came, and I sat here in this very chair, or measured up and down, up and down, the length of this very rug, and still there was no message and no letter.

"It had grown quite dark, and I had ordered away, impatiently, the servant who came in with the lamps: I couldn't bear any definite sign that the day was over! And I was standing there on the rug, staring at the door, and noticing a bad crack in its panel, when I heard the sound of wheels on the gravel. A word at last, no doubt—a line to explain.... I didn't seem to care much for her reasons, and I stood where I was and continued to stare at the door. And suddenly it opened and she came in.

"The servant followed her with a light, and then went out and closed the door. Her face looked pale in the lamplight, but her voice was as clear as a bell.

"'Well,' she said, 'you see I've come.'

"I started toward her with hands outstretched. 'You've come, you've come!' I stammered.

"Yes; it was like her to come in that way, without dissimulation or explanation or excuse. It was like her, if she gave at all, to give not furtively or in haste, but openly, deliberately, without stinting the measure or counting the cost. But her quietness and serenity disconcerted me. She did not look like a woman who has yielded impetuously to an uncontrollable impulse. There was something almost solemn in her face.

"The effect of it stole over me as I looked at her, suddenly subduing the huge flush of gratified longing.

"'You're here, here, here!' I kept repeating, like a child singing over a happy word.

"'You said,' she continued, in her grave clear voice, 'that we couldn't go on as we were—'

"'Ah, it's divine of you!' I held out my arms to her.

"She didn't draw back from them, but her faint smile said, 'Wait,' and lifting her hands she took the pins from her hat, and laid the hat on the table.

"As I saw her dear head bare in the lamp-light, with the thick hair waving away from the parting, I forgot everything but the bliss and wonder of her being here—here, in my house, on my hearth—that fourth rose from the corner of the rug is the exact spot where she was standing....

"I drew her to the fire, and made her sit down in the chair you're in, and knelt down by her, and hid my face on her knees. She put her hand on my head, and I was happy to the depths of my soul.

"'Oh, I forgot—' she exclaimed suddenly. I lifted my head and our eyes met. Hers were smiling.

"She reached out her hand, opened the little bag she had tossed down with her hat, and drew a small object from it. 'I left my trunk at the station. Here's the check. Can you send for it?' she asked.

"Her trunk—she wanted me to send for her trunk! Oh, yes—I see your smile, your 'lucky man!' Only, you see, I didn't love her in that way. I knew she couldn't come to my house without running a big risk of discovery, and my tenderness for her, my impulse to shield her, was stronger, even then, than vanity or desire. Judged from the point of view of those emotions I fell terribly short of my part. I hadn't any of the proper feelings. Such an act of romantic folly was so unlike her that it almost irritated me, and I found myself desperately wondering how I could get her to reconsider her plan without—well, without seeming to want her to.

"It's not the way a novel hero feels; it's probably not the way a man in real life ought to have felt. But it's the way I felt—and she saw it.

"She put her hands on my shoulders and looked at me with deep, deep eyes. 'Then you didn't expect me to stay?' she asked.

"I caught her hands and pressed them to me, stammering out that I hadn't dared to dream....

"'You thought I'd come—just for an hour?'

"'How could I dare think more? I adore you, you know, for what you've done! But it would be known if you—if you stayed on. My servants—everybody about here knows you. I've no right to expose you to the risk.' She made no answer, and I went on tenderly: 'Give me, if you will, the next few hours: there's a train that will get you to town by midnight. And then we'll arrange something, in town, where it's safer for you—more easily managed.... It's beautiful, it's heavenly of you to have come; but I love you too much—I must take care of you and think for you—'

"I don't suppose it ever took me so long to say so few words, and though they were profoundly sincere they sounded unutterably shallow, irrelevant and grotesque. She made no effort to help me out, but sat silent, listening, with her meditative smile. 'It's my duty, dearest, as a man,' I rambled on. The more I love you the more I'm bound—'

"'Yes; but you don't understand,' she interrupted.

"She rose as she spoke, and I got up also, and we stood and looked at each other.

"'I haven't come for a night; if you want me I've come for always,' she said.

"Here again, if I give you an honest account of my feelings I shall write myself down as the poor-spirited creature I suppose I am. There wasn't, I swear, at the moment, a grain of selfishness, of personal reluctance, in my feeling. I worshipped every hair of her head—when we were together I was happy, when I was away from her something was gone from every good thing; but I had always looked on our love for each other, our possible relation to each other, as such situations are looked on in what is called society. I had supposed her, for all her freedom and originality, to be just as tacitly subservient to that view as I was: ready to take what she wanted on the terms on which society concedes such taking, and to pay for it by the usual restrictions, concealments and hypocrisies. In short, I supposed that she would 'play the game'—look out for her own safety, and expect me to look out for it. It sounds cheap enough, put that way, but it's the rule we live under, all of us. And the amazement of finding her suddenly outside of it, oblivious of it, unconscious of it, left me, for an awful minute, stammering at her like a graceless dolt.... Perhaps it wasn't even a minute; but in it she had gone the whole round of my thoughts.

"'It's raining,' she said, very low. 'I suppose you can telephone for a trap?'

"There was no irony or resentment in her voice. She walked slowly across the room and paused before the Brangwyn etching over there. 'That's a good impression. Will you telephone, please?' she repeated.

"I found my voice again, and with it the power of movement. I followed her and dropped at her feet. 'You can't go like this!' I cried.

"She looked down on me from heights and heights. 'I can't stay like this,' she answered.

"I stood up and we faced each other like antagonists. 'You don't know,' I accused her passionately, 'in the least what you're asking me to ask of you!'

"'Yes, I do: everything,' she breathed.

"'And it's got to be that or nothing?'

"'Oh, on both sides,' she reminded me.

"'Not on both sides. It's not fair. That's why—'

"'Why you won't?'

"'Why I cannot, may not!'

"'Why you'll take a night and not a life?'

"The taunt, for a woman usually so sure of her aim, fell so short of the mark that its only effect was to increase my conviction of her helplessness. The very intensity of my longing for her made me tremble where she was fearless. I had to protect her first, and think of my own attitude afterward.

"She was too discerning not to see this too. Her face softened, grew inexpressibly appealing, and she dropped again into that chair you're in, leaned forward, and looked up with her grave smile.

"'You think I'm beside myself, raving? (You're not thinking of yourself, I know.) I'm not: I never was saner. Since I've known you I've often thought this might happen. This thing between us isn't an ordinary thing. If it had been we shouldn't, all these months, have drifted. We should have wanted to skip to the last page, and then throw down the book. We shouldn't have felt we could trust the future as we did. We were in no hurry because we knew we shouldn't get tired; and when two people feel that about each other they must live together, or part. I don't see what else they can do. A little trip along the coast won't answer. It's the high seas, or else being tied up to Lethe wharf. And I'm for the high seas, my dear!'

"Think of sitting here, here, in this room, in this chair, and listening to that, and seeing the tight on her hair, and hearing the sound of her voice! I don't suppose there ever was a scene just like it....

"She was astounding, inexhaustible; through all my anguish of resistance I found a kind of fierce joy in following her. It was lucidity at white heat: the last sublimation of passion. She might have been an angel arguing a point in the empyrean if she hadn't been, so completely, a woman pleading for her life....

"Her life: that was the thing at stake! She couldn't do with less of it than she was capable of; and a woman's life is inextricably part of the man's she cares for.

"That was why, she argued, she couldn't accept the usual solution: couldn't enter into the only relation that society tolerates between people situated like ourselves. Yes: she knew all the arguments on that side: didn't I suppose she'd been over them and over them? She knew (for hadn't she often said it of others?) what is said of the woman who, by throwing in her lot with her lover's, binds him to a lifelong duty which has the irksomeness without the dignity of marriage. Oh, she could talk on that side with the best of them: only she asked me to consider the other, the side of the man and woman who love each other deeply and completely enough to want their lives enlarged, and not diminished, by their love. What, in such a case, she reasoned, must be the inevitable effect of concealing, denying, disowning, the central fact, the motive power of one's existence? She asked me to picture the course of such a love: first working as a fever in the blood, distorting and deflecting everything, making all other interests insipid, all other duties irksome, and then, as the acknowledged claims of life regained their hold, gradually dying, the poor starved passion!—for want of the wholesome necessary food of common living and doing, yet leaving life impoverished by the loss of all it might have been.

"'I'm not talking, dear—' I see her now, leaning toward me with shining eyes: 'I'm not talking of the people who haven't enough to fill their days, and to whom a little mystery, a little manoeuvring, gives an illusion of importance that they can't afford to miss; I'm talking of you and me, with all our tastes and curiosities and activities; and I ask you what our love would become if we had to keep it apart from our lives, like a pretty useless animal that we went to peep at and feed with sweetmeats through its cage?'

"I won't, my dear fellow, go into the other side of our strange duel: the arguments I used were those that most men in my situation would have felt bound to use, and that most women in Paulina's accept instinctively, without even formulating them. The exceptionalness, the significance, of the case lay wholly in the fact that she had formulated them all and then rejected them....

"There was one point I didn't, of course, touch on; and that was the popular conviction (which I confess I shared) that when a man and a woman agree to defy the world together the man really sacrifices much more than the woman. I was not even conscious of thinking of this at the time, though it may have lurked somewhere in the shadow of my scruples for her; but she dragged it out into the daylight and held me face to face with it.

"'Remember, I'm not attempting to lay down any general rule,' she insisted; 'I'm not theorizing about Man and Woman, I'm talking about you and me. How do I know what's best for the woman in the next house? Very likely she'll bolt when it would have been better for her to stay at home. And it's the same with the man: he'll probably do the wrong thing. It's generally the weak heads that commit follies, when it's the strong ones that ought to: and my point is that you and I are both strong enough to behave like fools if we want to....

"'Take your own case first, because, in spite of the sentimentalists, it's the man who stands to lose most. You'll have to give up the Iron Works: which you don't much care about, because it won't be particularly agreeable for us to live in New York: which you don't care much about either. But you won't be sacrificing what is called "a career." You made up your mind long ago that your best chance of self-development, and consequently of general usefulness, lay in thinking rather than doing; and, when we first met, you were already planning to sell out your business, and travel and write. Well! Those ambitions are of a kind that won't be harmed by your dropping out of your social setting. On the contrary, such work as you want to do ought to gain by it, because you'll be brought nearer to life-as-it-is, in contrast to life-as-a-visiting-list....'

"She threw back her head with a sudden laugh. 'And the joy of not having any more visits to make! I wonder if you've ever thought of that? Just at first, I mean; for society's getting so deplorably lax that, little by little, it will edge up to us, you'll see! I don't want to idealize the situation, dearest, and I won't conceal from you that in time we shall be called on. But, oh, the fun we shall have had in the interval! And then, for the first time we shall be able to dictate our own terms, one of which will be that no bores need apply. Think of being cured of all one's chronic bores! We shall feel as jolly as people do after a successful operation.'

"I don't know why this nonsense sticks in my mind when some of the graver things we said are less distinct. Perhaps it's because of a certain iridescent quality of feeling that made her gaiety seem like sunshine through a shower....

"'You ask me to think of myself?' she went on. 'But the beauty of our being together will be that, for the first time, I shall dare to! Now I have to think of all the tedious trifles I can pack the days with, because I'm afraid, I'm afraid, to hear the voice of the real me, down below, in the windowless underground hole where I keep her....

"'Remember again, please, it's not Woman, it's Paulina Trant, I'm talking of. The woman in the next house may have all sorts of reasons, honest reasons, for staying there. There may be some one there who needs her badly: for whom the light would go out if she went. Whereas to Philip I've been simply, well, what New York was before he decided to travel: the most important thing in life till he made up his mind to leave it; and now merely the starting-place of several lines of steamers. Oh, I didn't have to love you to know that! I only had to live with him.... If he lost his eye-glasses he'd think it was the fault of the eye-glasses; he'd really feel that the eyeglasses had been careless. And he'd be convinced that no others would suit him quite as well. But at the optician's he'd probably be told that he needed something a little different, and after that he'd feel that the old eye-glasses had never suited him at all, and that that was their fault too....'

"At one moment, but I don't recall when, I remember she stood up with one of her quick movements, and came toward me, holding out her arms. 'Oh, my dear, I'm pleading for my life; do you suppose I shall ever want for arguments?' she cried....

"After that, for a bit, nothing much remains with me except a sense of darkness and of conflict. The one spot of daylight in my whirling brain was the conviction that I couldn't, whatever happened, profit by the sudden impulse she had acted on, and allow her to take, in a moment of passion, a decision that was to shape her whole life. I couldn't so much as lift my little finger to keep her with me then, unless I were prepared to accept for her as well as for myself the full consequences of the future she had planned for us....

"Well, there's the point: I wasn't. I felt in her, poor fatuous idiot that I was!—that lack of objective imagination which had always seemed to me to account, at least in part, for many of the so-called heroic qualities in women. When their feelings are involved they simply can't look ahead. Her unfaltering logic notwithstanding, I felt this about Paulina as I listened. She had a specious air of knowing where she was going, but she didn't. She seemed the genius of logic and understanding, but the demon of illusion spoke through her lips....

"I said just now that I hadn't, at the outset, given my own side of the case a thought. It would have been truer to say that I hadn't given it a separate thought. But I couldn't think of her without seeing myself as a factor, the chief factor, in her problem, and without recognizing that whatever the experiment made of me, that it must fatally, in the end, make of her. If I couldn't carry the thing through she must break down with me: we should have to throw our separate selves into the melting-pot of this mad adventure, and be 'one' in a terrible indissoluble completeness of which marriage is only an imperfect counterpart....

"There could be no better proof of her extraordinary power over me, and of the way she had managed to clear the air of sentimental illusion, than the fact that I presently found myself putting this before her with a merciless precision of touch.

"'If we love each other enough to do a thing like this, we must love each other enough to see just what it is we're going to do.'

"So I invited her to the dissecting-table, and I see now the fearless eye with which she approached the cadaver. 'For that's what it is, you know,' she flashed out at me, at the end of my long demonstration. 'It's a dead body, like all the instances and examples and hypothetical cases that ever were! What do you expect to learn from thai? The first great anatomist was the man who stuck his knife in a heart that was beating; and the only way to find out what doing a thing will be like is to do it!'

"She looked away from me suddenly, as if she were fixing her eyes on some vision on the outer rim of consciousness. 'No: there's one other way,' she exclaimed; 'and that is, not to do it! To abstain and refrain; and then see what we become, or what we don't become, in the long run, and to draw our inferences. That's the game that almost everybody about us is playing, I suppose; there's hardly one of the dull people one meets at dinner who hasn't had, just once, the chance of a berth on a ship that was off for the Happy Isles, and hasn't refused it for fear of sticking on a sand-bank!

"'I'm doing my best, you know,' she continued, 'to see the sequel as you see it, as you believe it's your duty to me to see it. I know the instances you're thinking of: the listless couples wearing out their lives in shabby watering places, and hanging on the favour of hotel acquaintances; or the proud quarrelling wretches shut up alone in a fine house because they're too good for the only society they can get, and trying to cheat their boredom by squabbling with their tradesmen and spying on their servants. No doubt there are such cases; but I don't recognize either of us in those dismal figures. Why, to do it would be to admit that our life, yours and mine, is in the people about us and not in ourselves; that we're parasites and not self-sustaining creatures; and that the lives we're leading now are so brilliant, full and satisfying that what we should have to give up would surpass even the blessedness of being together!'

"At that stage, I confess, the solid ground of my resistance began to give way under me. It was not that my convictions were shaken, but that she had swept me into a world whose laws were different, where one could reach out in directions that the slave of gravity hasn't pictured. But at the same time my opposition hardened from reason into instinct. I knew it was her voice, and not her logic, that was unsettling me. I knew that if she'd written out her thesis and sent it me by post I should have made short work of it; and again the part of me which I called by all the finest names: my chivalry, my unselfishness, my superior masculine experience, cried out with one voice: 'You can't let a woman use her graces to her own undoing, you can't, for her own sake, let her eyes convince you when her reasons don't!'

"And then, abruptly, and for the first time, a doubt entered me: a doubt of her perfect moral honesty. I don't know how else to describe my feeling that she wasn't playing fair, that in coming to my house, in throwing herself at my head (I called things by their names), she had perhaps not so much obeyed an irresistible impulse as deeply, deliberately reckoned on the dissolvent effect of her generosity, her rashness and her beauty....

"From the moment that this mean doubt raised its head in me I was once more the creature of all the conventional scruples: I was repeating, before the looking-glass of my self-consciousness, all the stereotyped gestures of the 'man of honour.'... Oh, the sorry figure I must have cut! You'll understand my dropping the curtain on it as quickly as I can....

"Yet I remember, as I made my point, being struck by its impressiveness. I was suffering and enjoying my own suffering. I told her that, whatever step we decided to take, I owed it to her to insist on its being taken soberly, deliberately—

"('No: it's "advisedly," isn't it? Oh, I was thinking of the Marriage Service,' she interposed with a faint laugh.)

"—that if I accepted, there, on the spot, her headlong beautiful gift of herself, I should feel I had taken an unfair advantage of her, an advantage which she would be justified in reproaching me with afterward; that I was not afraid to tell her this because she was intelligent enough to know that my scruples were the surest proof of the quality of my love; that I refused to owe my happiness to an unconsidered impulse; that we must see each other again, in her own house, in less agitating circumstances, when she had had time to reflect on my words, to study her heart and look into the future....

"The factitious exhilaration produced by uttering these beautiful sentiments did not last very long, as you may imagine. It fell, little by little, under her quiet gaze, a gaze in which there was neither contempt nor irony nor wounded pride, but only a tender wistfulness of interrogation; and I think the acutest point in my suffering was reached when she said, as I ended: 'Oh; yes, of course I understand.'

"'If only you hadn't come to me here!' I blurted out in the torture of my soul.

"She was on the threshold when I said it, and she turned and laid her hand gently on mine. 'There was no other way,' she said; and at the moment it seemed to me like some hackneyed phrase in a novel that she had used without any sense of its meaning.

"I don't remember what I answered or what more we either of us said. At the end a desperate longing to take her in my arms and keep her with me swept aside everything else, and I went up to her, pleading, stammering, urging I don't know what.... But she held me back with a quiet look, and went. I had ordered the carriage, as she asked me to; and my last definite recollection is of watching her drive off in the rain....

"I had her promise that she would see me, two days later, at her house in town, and that we should then have what I called 'a decisive talk'; but I don't think that even at the moment I was the dupe of my phrase. I knew, and she knew, that the end had come...."

"It was about that time (Merrick went on after a long pause) that I definitely decided not to sell the Works, but to stick to my job and conform my life to it.

"I can't describe to you the rage of conformity that possessed me. Poetry, ideas, all the picture-making processes stopped. A kind of dull self-discipline seemed to me the only exercise worthy of a reflecting mind. I had to justify my great refusal, and I tried to do it by plunging myself up to the eyes into the very conditions I had been instinctively struggling to get away from. The only possible consolation would have been to find in a life of business routine and social submission such moral compensations as may reward the citizen if they fail the man; but to attain to these I should have had to accept the old delusion that the social and the individual man are two. Now, on the contrary, I found soon enough that I couldn't get one part of my machinery to work effectively while another wanted feeding: and that in rejecting what had seemed to me a negation of action I had made all my action negative.

"The best solution, of course, would have been to fall in love with another woman; but it was long before I could bring myself to wish that this might happen to me.... Then, at length, I suddenly and violently desired it; and as such impulses are seldom without some kind of imperfect issue I contrived, a year or two later, to work myself up into the wished-for state.... She was a woman in society, and with all the awe of that institution that Paulina lacked. Our relation was consequently one of those unavowed affairs in which triviality is the only alternative to tragedy. Luckily we had, on both sides, risked only as much as prudent people stake in a drawingroom game; and when the match was over I take it that we came out fairly even.

"My gain, at all events, was of an unexpected kind. The adventure had served only to make me understand Paulina's abhorrence of such experiments, and at every turn of the slight intrigue I had felt how exasperating and belittling such a relation was bound to be between two people who, had they been free, would have mated openly. And so from a brief phase of imperfect forgetting I was driven back to a deeper and more understanding remembrance....

"This second incarnation of Paulina was one of the strangest episodes of the whole strange experience. Things she had said during our extraordinary talk, things I had hardly heard at the time, came back to me with singular vividness and a fuller meaning. I hadn't any longer the cold consolation of believing in my own perspicacity: I saw that her insight had been deeper and keener than mine.

"I remember, in particular, starting up in bed one sleepless night as there flashed into my head the meaning of her last words: 'There was no other way'; the phrase I had half-smiled at at the time, as a parrot-like echo of the novel-heroine's stock farewell. I had never, up to that moment, wholly understood why Paulina had come to my house that night. I had never been able to make that particular act, which could hardly, in the light of her subsequent conduct, be dismissed as a blind surge of passion—square with my conception of her character. She was at once the most spontaneous and the steadiest-minded woman I had ever known, and the last to wish to owe any advantage to surprise, to unpreparedness, to any play on the spring of sex. The better I came, retrospectively, to know her, the more sure I was of this, and the less intelligible her act appeared. And then, suddenly, after a night of hungry restless thinking, the flash of enlightenment came. She had come to my house, had brought her trunk with her, had thrown herself at my head with all possible violence and publicity, in order to give me a pretext, a loophole, an honourable excuse, for doing and saying—why, precisely what I had said and done!

"As the idea came to me it was as if some ironic hand had touched an electric button, and all my fatuous phrases had leapt out on me in fire.

"Of course she had known all along just the kind of thing I should say if I didn't at once open my arms to her; and to save my pride, my dignity, my conception of the figure I was cutting in her eyes, she had recklessly and magnificently provided me with the decentest pretext a man could have for doing a pusillanimous thing....

"With that discovery the whole case took a different aspect. It hurt less to think of Paulina, and yet it hurt more. The tinge of bitterness, of doubt, in my thoughts of her had had a tonic quality. It was harder to go on persuading myself that I had done right as, bit by bit, my theories crumbled under the test of time. Yet, after all, as she herself had said, one could judge of results only in the long run....

"The Trants stayed away for two years; and about a year after they got back, you may remember, Trant was killed in a railway accident. You know Fate's way of untying a knot after everybody has given up tugging at it!

"Well, there I was, completely justified: all my weaknesses turned into merits! I had 'saved' a weak woman from herself, I had kept her to the path of duty, I had spared her the humiliation of scandal and the misery of self-reproach; and now I had only to put out my hand and take my reward.

"I had avoided Paulina since her return, and she had made no effort to see me. But after Trant's death I wrote her a few lines, to which she sent a friendly answer; and when a decent interval had elapsed, and I asked if I might call on her, she answered at once that she would see me.

"I went to her house with the fixed intention of asking her to marry me, and I left it without having done so. Why? I don't know that I can tell you. Perhaps you would have had to sit there opposite her, knowing what I did and feeling as I did, to understand why. She was kind, she was compassionate, I could see she didn't want to make it hard for me. Perhaps she even wanted to make it easy. But there, between us, was the memory of the gesture I hadn't made, forever parodying the one I was attempting! There wasn't a word I could think of that hadn't an echo in it of words of hers I had been deaf to; there wasn't an appeal I could make that didn't mock the appeal I had rejected. I sat there and talked of her husband's death, of her plans, of my sympathy; and I knew she understood; and knowing that, in a way, made it harder.... The door-bell rang and the footman came in to ask if she would receive other visitors. She looked at me a moment and said 'Yes,' and I got up and shook hands and went away.

"A few days later she sailed for Europe, and the next time we met she had married Reardon...."

VI

It was long past midnight, and the terrier's hints became imperious.

Merrick rose from his chair, pushed back a fallen log and put up the fender. He walked across the room and stared a moment at the Brangwyn etching before which Paulina Trant had paused at a memorable turn of their talk. Then he came back and laid his hand on my shoulder.

"She summed it all up, you know, when she said that one way of finding out whether a risk is worth taking is not to take it, and then to see what one becomes in the long run, and draw one's inferences. The long run, well, we've run it, she and I. I know what I've become, but that's nothing to the misery of knowing what she's become. She had to have some kind of life, and she married Reardon. Reardon's a very good fellow in his way; but the worst of it is that it's not her way....

"No: the worst of it is that now she and I meet as friends. We dine at the same houses, we talk about the same people, we play bridge together, and I lend her books. And sometimes Reardon slaps me on the back and says: 'Come in and dine with us, old man! What you want is to be cheered up!' And I go and dine with them, and he tells me how jolly comfortable she makes him, and what an ass I am not to marry; and she presses on me a second helping of poulet Maryland, and I smoke one of Reardon's cigars, and at half-past ten I get into my overcoat, and walk back alone to my rooms...."

COMING HOME

I

The young men of our American Relief Corps are beginning to come back from the front with stories.

There was no time to pick them up during the first months, the whole business was too wild and grim. The horror has not decreased, but nerves and sight are beginning to be disciplined to it. In the earlier days, moreover, such fragments of experience as one got were torn from their setting like bits of flesh scattered by shrapnel. Now things that seemed disjointed are beginning to link themselves together, and the broken bones of history are rising from the battle-fields.

I can't say that, in this respect, all the members of the Relief Corps have made the most of their opportunity. Some are unobservant, or perhaps simply inarticulate; others, when going beyond the bald statistics of their job, tend to drop into sentiment and cinema scenes; and none but H. Macy Greer has the gift of making the thing told seem as true as if one had seen it. So it is on H. Macy Greer that I depend, and when his motor dashes him back to Paris for supplies I never fail to hunt him down and coax him to my rooms for dinner and a long cigar.

Greer is a small hard-muscled youth, with pleasant manners, a sallow face, straight hemp-coloured hair and grey eyes of unexpected inwardness. He has a voice like thick soup, and speaks with the slovenly drawl of the new generation of Americans, dragging his words along like reluctant dogs on a string, and depriving his narrative of every shade of expression that intelligent intonation gives. But his eyes see so much that they make one see even what his foggy voice obscures.

Some of his tales are dark and dreadful, some are unutterably sad, and some end in a huge laugh of irony. I am not sure how I ought to classify the one I have written down here.

II

On my first dash to the Northern fighting line, Greer told me the other night, I carried supplies to an ambulance where the surgeon asked me to have a talk with an officer who was badly wounded and fretting for news of his people in the east of France.

He was a young Frenchman, a cavalry lieutenant, trim and slim, with a pleasant smile and obstinate blue eyes that I liked. He looked as if he could hold on tight when it was worth his while. He had had a leg smashed, poor devil, in the first fighting in Flanders, and had been dragging on for weeks in the squalid camp-hospital where I found him. He didn't waste any words on himself, but began at once about his family. They were living, when the war broke out, at their country-place in the Vosges; his father and mother, his sister, just eighteen, and his brother Alain, two years younger. His father, the Comte de Rechamp, had married late in life, and was over seventy: his mother, a good deal younger, was crippled with rheumatism; and there was, besides, to round off the group, a helpless but intensely alive and domineering old grandmother about whom all the others revolved. You know how French families hang together, and throw out branches that make new roots but keep hold of the central trunk, like that tree, what's it called?—that they give pictures of in books about the East.

Jean de Rechamp, that was my lieutenant's name, told me his family was a typical case. "We're very province," he said. "My people live at Rechamp all the year. We have a house at Nancy, rather a fine old hotel, but my parents go there only once in two or three years, for a few weeks. That's our 'season.'...Imagine the point of view! Or rather don't, because you couldn't...." (He had been about the world a good deal, and known something of other angles of vision.)

Well, of this helpless exposed little knot of people he had had no word, simply nothing, since the first of August. He was at home, staying with them at Rechamp, when war broke out. He was mobilised the first day, and had only time to throw his traps into a cart and dash to the station. His depot was on the other side of France, and communications with the East by mail and telegraph were completely interrupted during the first weeks. His regiment was sent at once to the fighting line, and the first news he got came to him in October, from a communique in a Paris paper a month old, saying: "The enemy yesterday retook Rechamp." After that, dead silence: and the poor devil left in the trenches to digest that "retook"!

There are thousands and thousands of just such cases; and men bearing them, and cracking jokes, and hitting out as hard as they can. Jean de Rechamp knew this, and tried to crack jokes too, but he got his leg smashed just afterward, and ever since he'd been lying on a straw pallet under a horse-blanket, saying to himself: "Rechamp retaken."

"Of course," he explained with a weary smile, "as long as you can tot up your daily bag in the trenches it's a sort of satisfaction, though I don't quite know why; anyhow, you're so dead-beat at night that no dreams come. But lying here staring at the ceiling one goes through the whole business once an hour, at the least: the attack, the slaughter, the ruins...and worse.... Haven't I seen and heard things enough on this side to know what's been happening on the other? Don't try to sugar the dose. I like it bitter."

I was three days in the neighbourhood, and I went back every day to see him. He liked to talk to me because he had a faint hope of my getting news of his family when I returned to Paris. I hadn't much myself, but there was no use telling him so. Besides, things change from day to day, and when we parted I promised to get word to him as soon as I could find out anything. We both knew, of course, that that would not be till Rechamp was taken a third time, by his own troops; and perhaps soon after that, I should be able to get there, or near there, and make enquiries myself. To make sure that I should forget nothing, he drew the family photographs from under his pillow, and handed them over: the little witch-grandmother, with a face like a withered walnut, the father, a fine broken-looking old boy with a Roman nose and a weak chin, the mother, in crape, simple, serious and provincial, the little sister ditto, and Alain, the young brother, just the age the brutes have been carrying off to German prisons, an over-grown thread-paper boy with too much forehead and eyes, and not a muscle in his body. A charming-looking family, distinguished and amiable; but all, except the grandmother, rather usual. The kind of people who come in sets.

As I pocketed the photographs I noticed that another lay face down by his pillow. "Is that for me too?" I asked.

He coloured and shook his head, and I felt I had blundered. But after a moment he turned the photograph over and held it out.

"It's the young girl I am engaged to. She was at Rechamp visiting my parents when war was declared; but she was to leave the day after I did...." He hesitated. "There may have been some difficulty about her going.... I should like to be sure she got away.... Her name is Yvonne Malo."

He did not offer me the photograph, and I did not need it. That girl had a face of her own! Dark and keen and splendid: a type so different from the others that I found myself staring. If he had not said "ma fiancee" I should have understood better. After another pause he went on: "I will give you her address in Paris. She has no family: she lives alone, she is a musician. Perhaps you may find her there." His colour deepened again as he added: "But I know nothing, I have had no news of her either."

To ease the silence that followed I suggested: "But if she has no family, wouldn't she have been likely to stay with your people, and wouldn't that be the reason of your not hearing from her?"

"Oh, no, I don't think she stayed." He seemed about to add: "If she could help it," but shut his lips and slid the picture out of sight.

As soon as I got back to Paris I made enquiries, but without result. The Germans had been pushed back from that particular spot after a fortnight's intermittent occupation; but their lines were close by, across the valley, and Rechamp was still in a net of trenches. No one could get to it, and apparently no news could come from it. For the moment, at any rate, I found it impossible to get in touch with the place.

My enquiries about Mlle. Malo were equally unfruitful. I went to the address Rechamp had given me, somewhere off in Passy, among gardens, in what they call a "Square," no doubt because it's oblong: a kind of long narrow court with aesthetic-looking studio buildings round it. Mlle. Malo lived in one of them, on the top floor, the concierge said, and I looked up and saw a big studio window, and a roof-terrace with dead gourds dangling from a pergola. But she wasn't there, she hadn't been there, and they had no news of her. I wrote to Rechamp of my double failure, he sent me back a line of thanks; and after that for a long while I heard no more of him.

By the beginning of November the enemy's hold had begun to loosen in the Argonne and along the Vosges, and one day we were sent off to the East with a couple of ambulances. Of course we had to have military chauffeurs, and the one attached to my ambulance happened to be a fellow I knew. The day before we started, in talking over our route with him, I said: "I suppose we can manage to get to Rechamp now?" He looked puzzled, it was such a little place that he'd forgotten the name. "Why do you want to get there?" he wondered. I told him, and he gave an exclamation. "Good God! Of course, but how extraordinary! Jean de Rechamp's here now, in Paris, too lame for the front, and driving a motor." We stared at each other, and he went on: "He must take my place, he must go with you. I don't know how it can be done; but done it shall be."

Done it was, and the next morning at daylight I found Jean de Rechamp at the wheel of my car. He looked another fellow from the wreck I had left in the Flemish hospital; all made over, and burning with activity, but older, and with lines about his eyes. He had had news from his people in the interval, and had learned that they were still at Rechamp, and well. What was more surprising was that Mlle. Malo was with them, had never left. Alain had been got away to England, where he remained; but none of the others had budged. They had fitted up an ambulance in the chateau, and Mlle. Malo and the little sister were nursing the wounded. There were not many details in the letters, and they had been a long time on the way; but their tone was so reassuring that Jean could give himself up to unclouded anticipation. You may fancy if he was grateful for the chance I was giving him; for of course he couldn't have seen his people in any other way.

Our permits, as you know, don't as a rule let us into the firing-line: we only take supplies to second-line ambulances, and carry back the badly wounded in need of delicate operations. So I wasn't in the least sure we should be allowed to go to Rechamp, though I had made up my mind to get there, anyhow.

We were about a fortnight on the way, coming and going in Champagne and the Argonne, and that gave us time to get to know each other. It was bitter cold, and after our long runs over the lonely frozen hills we used to crawl into the cafe of the inn, if there was one, and talk and talk. We put up in fairly rough places, generally in a farm house or a cottage packed with soldiers; for the villages have all remained empty since the autumn, except when troops are quartered in them. Usually, to keep warm, we had to go up after supper to the room we shared, and get under the blankets with our clothes on. Once some jolly Sisters of Charity took us in at their Hospice, and we slept two nights in an ice-cold whitewashed cell, but what tales we heard around their kitchen-fire! The Sisters had stayed alone to face the Germans, had seen the town burn, and had made the Teutons turn the hose on the singed roof of their Hospice and beat the fire back from it. It's a pity those Sisters of Charity can't marry....

Rechamp told me a lot in those days. I don't believe he was talkative before the war, but his long weeks in hospital, starving for news, had unstrung him. And then he was mad with excitement at getting back to his own place. In the interval he'd heard how other people caught in their country-houses had fared, you know the stories we all refused to believe at first, and that we now prefer not to think about.... Well, he'd been thinking about those stories pretty steadily for some months; and he kept repeating: "My people say they're all right, but they give no details."

"You see," he explained, "there never were such helpless beings. Even if there had been time to leave, they couldn't have done it. My mother had been having one of her worst attacks of rheumatism, she was in bed, helpless, when I left. And my grandmother, who is a demon of activity in the house, won't stir out of it. We haven't been able to coax her into the garden for years. She says it's draughty; and you know how we all feel about draughts! As for my father, he hasn't had to decide anything since the Comte de Chambord refused to adopt the tricolour. My father decided that he was right, and since then there has been nothing particular for him to take a stand about. But I know how he behaved just as well as if I'd been there, he kept saying: 'One must act, one must act!' and sitting in his chair and doing nothing. Oh, I'm not disrespectful: they were like that in his generation! Besides, it's better to laugh at things, isn't it?" And suddenly his face would darken....

On the whole, however, his spirits were good till we began to traverse the line of ruined towns between Sainte Menehould and Bar-le-Duc. "This is the way the devils came," he kept saying to me; and I saw he was hard at work picturing the work they must have done in his own neighbourhood.

"But since your sister writes that your people are safe!"

"They may have made her write that to reassure me. They'd heard I was badly wounded. And, mind you, there's never been a line from my mother."

"But you say your mother's hands are so lame that she can't hold a pen. And wouldn't Mlle. Malo have written you the truth?"

At that his frown would lift. "Oh, yes. She would despise any attempt at concealment."

"Well, then, what the deuce is the matter?"

"It's when I see these devils' traces—" he could only mutter.

One day, when we had passed through a particularly devastated little place, and had got from the cure some more than usually abominable details of things done there, Rechamp broke out to me over the kitchen-fire of our night's lodging. "When I hear things like that I don't believe anybody who tells me my people are all right!"

"But you know well enough," I insisted, "that the Germans are not all alike—that it all depends on the particular officer...."

"Yes, yes, I know," he assented, with a visible effort at impartiality. "Only, you see—as one gets nearer...." He went on to say that, when he had been sent from the ambulance at the front to a hospital at Moulins, he had been for a day or two in a ward next to some wounded German soldiers, bad cases, they were, and had heard them talking. They didn't know he knew German, and he had heard things.... There was one name always coming back in their talk, von Scharlach, Oberst von Scharlach. One of them, a young fellow, said: "I wish now I'd cut my hand off rather than do what he told us to that night.... Every time the fever comes I see it all again. I wish I'd been struck dead first." They all said "Scharlach" with a kind of terror in their voices, as if he might hear them even there, and come down on them horribly. Rechamp had asked where their regiment came from, and had been told: From the Vosges. That had set his brain working, and whenever he saw a ruined village, or heard a tale of savagery, the Scharlach nerve began to quiver. At such times it was no use reminding him that the Germans had had at least three hundred thousand men in the East in August. He simply didn't listen....

III

The day before we started for Rechamp his spirits flew up again, and that night he became confidential. "You've been such a friend to me that there are certain things, seeing what's ahead of us, that I should like to explain"; and, noticing my surprise, he went on: "I mean about my people. The state of mind in my milieu must be so remote from anything you're used to in your happy country.... But perhaps I can make you understand...."

I saw that what he wanted was to talk to me of the girl he was engaged to. Mlle. Malo, left an orphan at ten, had been the ward of a neighbour of the Rechamps', a chap with an old name and a starred chateau, who had lost almost everything else at baccarat before he was forty, and had repented, had the gout and studied agriculture for the rest of his life. The girl's father was a rather brilliant painter, who died young, and her mother, who followed him in a year or two, was a Pole: you may fancy that, with such antecedents, the girl was just the mixture to shake down quietly into French country life with a gouty and repentant guardian. The Marquis de Corvenaire, that was his name, brought her down to his place, got an old maid sister to come and stay, and really, as far as one knows, brought his ward up rather decently.

Now and then she used to be driven over to play with the young Rechamps, and Jean remembered her as an ugly little girl in a plaid frock, who used to invent wonderful games and get tired of playing them just as the other children were beginning to learn how. But her domineering ways and searching questions did not meet with his mother's approval, and her visits were not encouraged. When she was seventeen her guardian died and left her a little money. The maiden sister had gone dotty, there was nobody to look after Yvonne, and she went to Paris, to an aunt, broke loose from the aunt when she came of age, set up her studio, travelled, painted, played the violin, knew lots of people; and never laid eyes on Jean de Rechamp till about a year before the war, when her guardian's place was sold, and she had to go down there to see about her interest in the property.

The old Rechamps heard she was coming, but didn't ask her to stay. Jean drove over to the shut-up chateau, however, and found Mlle. Malo lunching on a corner of the kitchen table. She exclaimed: "My little Jean!" flew to him with a kiss for each cheek, and made him sit down and share her omelet.... The ugly little girl had shed her chrysalis, and you may fancy if he went back once or twice!

Mlle. Malo was staying at the chateau all alone, with the farmer's wife to come in and cook her dinner: not a soul in the house at night but herself and her brindled sheep dog. She had to be there a week, and Jean suggested to his people to ask her to Rechamp. But at Rechamp they hesitated, coughed, looked away, said the sparerooms were all upside down, and the valet-de-chambre laid up with the mumps, and the cook short-handed, till finally the irrepressible grandmother broke out: "A young girl who chooses to live alone, probably prefers to live alone!"

There was a deadly silence, and Jean did not raise the question again; but I can imagine his blue eyes getting obstinate.

Soon after Mlle. Malo's return to Paris he followed her and began to frequent the Passy studio. The life there was unlike anything he had ever seen—or conceived as possible, short of the prairies. He had sampled the usual varieties of French womankind, and explored most of the social layers; but he had missed the newest, that of the artistic-emancipated. I don't know much about that set myself, but from his descriptions I should say they were a good deal like intelligent Americans, except that they don't seem to keep art and life in such water-tight compartments. But his great discovery was the new girl. Apparently he had never before known any but the traditional type, which predominates in the provinces, and still persists, he tells me, in the last fastnesses of the Faubourg St. Germain. The girl who comes and goes as she pleases, reads what she likes, has opinions about what she reads, who talks, looks, behaves with the independence of a married woman, and yet has kept the Diana-freshness, think how she must have shaken up such a man's inherited view of things! Mlle. Malo did far more than make Rechamp fall in love with her: she turned his world topsy-turvey, and prevented his ever again squeezing himself into his little old pigeon-hole of prejudices.

Before long they confessed their love, just like any young couple of Anglo-Saxons, and Jean went down to Rechamp to ask permission to marry her. Neither you nor I can quite enter into the state of mind of a young man of twenty-seven who has knocked about all over the globe, and been in and out of the usual sentimental coils, and who has to ask his parents' leave to get married! Don't let us try: it's no use. We should only end by picturing him as an incorrigible ninny. But there isn't a man in France who wouldn't feel it his duty to take that step, as Jean de Rechamp did. All we can do is to accept the premise and pass on.

Well—Jean went down and asked his father and his mother and his old grandmother if they would permit him to marry Mlle. Malo; and they all with one voice said they wouldn't. There was an uproar, in fact; and the old grandmother contributed the most piercing note to the concert. Marry Mlle. Malo! A young girl who lived alone! Travelled! Spent her time with foreigners—with musicians and painters! A young girl! Of course, if she had been a married woman, that is, a widow, much as they would have preferred a young girl for Jean, or even, if widow it had to be, a widow of another type, still, it was conceivable that, out of affection for him, they might have resigned themselves to his choice. But a young girl, bring such a young girl to Rechamp! Ask them to receive her under the same roof with their little Simone, their innocent Alain....

He had a bad hour of it; but he held his own, keeping silent while they screamed, and stiffening as they began to wobble from exhaustion. Finally he took his mother apart, and tried to reason with her. His arguments were not much use, but his resolution impressed her, and he saw it. As for his father, nobody was afraid of Monsieur de Rechamp. When he said: "Never, never while I live, and there is a roof on Rechamp!" they all knew he had collapsed inside. But the grandmother was terrible. She was terrible because she was so old, and so clever at taking advantage of it. She could bring on a valvular heart attack by just sitting still and holding her breath, as Jean and his mother had long since found out; and she always treated them to one when things weren't going as she liked. Madame de Rechamp promised Jean that she would intercede with her mother-in-law; but she hadn't much faith in the result, and when she came out of the old lady's room she whispered: "She's just sitting there holding her breath."

The next day Jean himself advanced to the attack. His grandmother was the most intelligent member of the family, and she knew he knew it, and liked him for having found it out; so when he had her alone she listened to him without resorting to any valvular tricks. "Of course," he explained, "you're much too clever not to understand that the times have changed, and manners with them, and that what a woman was criticised for doing yesterday she is ridiculed for not doing to-day. Nearly all the old social thou-shalt-nots have gone: intelligent people nowadays don't give a fig for them, and that simple fact has abolished them. They only existed as long as there was some one left for them to scare." His grandmother listened with a sparkle of admiration in her ancient eyes. "And of course," Jean pursued, "that can't be the real reason for your opposing my marriage, a marriage with a young girl you've always known, who has been received here—"

"Ah, that's it—we've always known her!" the old lady snapped him up.

"What of that? I don't see—"

"Of course you don't. You're here so little: you don't hear things...."

"What things?"

"Things in the air... that blow about.... You were doing your military service at the time...."

"At what time?"

She leaned forward and laid a warning hand on his arm. "Why did Corvenaire leave her all that money—why?"

"But why not—why shouldn't he?" Jean stammered, indignant. Then she unpacked her bag—a heap of vague insinuations, baseless conjectures, village tattle, all, at the last analysis, based, as he succeeded in proving, and making her own, on a word launched at random by a discharged maid-servant who had retailed her grievance to the cure's housekeeper. "Oh, she does what she likes with Monsieur le Marquis, the young miss! She knows how...." On that single phrase the neighbourhood had raised a slander built of adamant.

Well, I'll give you an idea of what a determined fellow Rechamp is, when I tell you he pulled it down—or thought he did. He kept his temper, hunted up the servant's record, proved her a liar and dishonest, cast grave doubts on the discretion of the cure's housekeeper, and poured such a flood of ridicule over the whole flimsy fable, and those who had believed in it, that in sheer shamefacedness at having based her objection on such grounds, his grandmother gave way, and brought his parents toppling down with her.

All this happened a few weeks before the war, and soon afterward Mlle. Malo came down to Rechamp. Jean had insisted on her coming: he wanted her presence there, as his betrothed, to be known to the neighbourhood. As for her, she seemed delighted to come. I could see from Rechamp's tone, when he reached this part of his story, that he rather thought I should expect its heroine to have shown a becoming reluctance—to have stood on her dignity. He was distinctly relieved when he found I expected no such thing.

"She's simplicity itself—it's her great quality. Vain complications don't exist for her, because she doesn't see them... that's what my people can't be made to understand...."

I gathered from the last phrase that the visit had not been a complete success, and this explained his having let out, when he first told me of his fears for his family, that he was sure Mlle. Malo would not have remained at Rechamp if she could help it. Oh, no, decidedly, the visit was not a success....

"You see," he explained with a half-embarrassed smile, "it was partly her fault. Other girls as clever, but less—how shall I say?—less proud, would have adapted themselves, arranged things, avoided startling allusions. She wouldn't stoop to that; she talked to my family as naturally as she did to me. You can imagine for instance, the effect of her saying: 'One night, after a supper at Montmartre, I was walking home with two or three pals'—. It was her way of affirming her convictions, and I adored her for it—but I wished she wouldn't!"

And he depicted, to my joy, the neighbours rumbling over to call in heraldic barouches (the mothers alone—with embarrassed excuses for not bringing their daughters), and the agony of not knowing, till they were in the room, if Yvonne would receive them with lowered lids and folded hands, sitting by in a pose de fiancee while the elders talked; or if she would take the opportunity to air her views on the separation of Church and State, or the necessity of making divorce easier. "It's not," he explained, "that she really takes much interest in such questions: she's much more absorbed in her music and painting. But anything her eye lights on sets her mind dancing—as she said to me once: 'It's your mother's friends' bonnets that make me stand up for divorce!'" He broke off abruptly to add: "Good God, how far off all that nonsense seems!"

IV

The next day we started for Rechamp, not sure if we could get through, but bound to, anyhow! It was the coldest day we'd had, the sky steel, the earth iron, and a snow-wind howling down on us from the north. The Vosges are splendid in winter. In summer they are just plump puddings hills; when the wind strips them they turn to mountains. And we seemed to have the whole country to ourselves—the black firs, the blue shadows, the beech-woods cracking and groaning like rigging, the bursts of snowy sunlight from cold clouds. Not a soul in sight except the sentinels guarding the railways, muffled to the eyes, or peering out of their huts of pine-boughs at the cross-roads. Every now and then we passed a long string of seventy-fives, or a train of supply waggons or army ambulances, and at intervals a cavalryman cantered by, his cloak bellied out by the gale; but of ordinary people about the common jobs of life, not a sign.

The sense of loneliness and remoteness that the absence of the civil population produces everywhere in eastern France is increased by the fact that all the names and distances on the mile-stones have been scratched out and the sign-posts at the cross-roads thrown down. It was done, presumably, to throw the enemy off the track in September: and the signs have never been put back. The result is that one is forever losing one's way, for the soldiers quartered in the district know only the names of their particular villages, and those on the march can tell you nothing about the places they are passing through. We had got badly off our road several times during the trip, but on the last day's run Rechamp was in his own country, and knew every yard of the way—or thought he did. We had turned off the main road, and were running along between rather featureless fields and woods, crossed by a good many wood-roads with nothing to distinguish them; but he continued to push ahead, saying:

"We don't turn till we get to a manor-house on a stream, with a big paper-mill across the road." He went on to tell me that the mill-owners lived in the manor, and were old friends of his people: good old local stock, who had lived there for generations and done a lot for the neighbourhood.

"It's queer I don't see their village-steeple from this rise. The village is just beyond the house. How the devil could I have missed the turn?" We ran on a little farther, and suddenly he stopped the motor with a jerk. We were at a cross-road, with a stream running under the bank on our right. The place looked like an abandoned stoneyard. I never saw completer ruin. To the left, a fortified gate gaped on emptiness; to the right, a mill-wheel hung in the stream. Everything else was as flat as your dinner-table.

"Was this what you were trying to see from that rise?" I asked; and I saw a tear or two running down his face.

"They were the kindest people: their only son got himself shot the first month in Champagne—"

He had jumped out of the car and was standing staring at the level waste. "The house was there, there was a splendid lime in the court. I used to sit under it and have a glass of vin cris de Lorraine with the old people.... Over there, where that cinder-heap is, all their children are buried." He walked across to the grave-yard under a blackened wall, a bit of the apse of the vanished church, and sat down on a grave-stone. "If the devils have done this here, so close to us," he burst out, and covered his face.

An old woman walked toward us down the road. Rechamp jumped up and ran to meet her. "Why, Marie Jeanne, what are you doing in these ruins?" The old woman looked at him with unastonished eyes. She seemed incapable of any surprise. "They left my house standing. I'm glad to see Monsieur," she simply said. We followed her to the one house left in the waste of stones. It was a two-roomed cottage, propped against a cow-stable, but fairly decent, with a curtain in the window and a cat on the sill. Rechamp caught me by the arm and pointed to the door-panel. "Oberst von Scharlach" was scrawled on it. He turned as white as your table-cloth, and hung on to me a minute; then he spoke to the old woman. "The officers were quartered here: that was the reason they spared your house?"

She nodded. "Yes: I was lucky. But the gentlemen must come in and have a mouthful."

Rechamp's finger was on the name. "And this one, this was their commanding officer?"

"I suppose so. Is it somebody's name?" She had evidently never speculated on the meaning of the scrawl that had saved her.

"You remember him, their captain? Was his name Scharlach?" Rechamp persisted.

Under its rich weathering the old woman's face grew as pale as his. "Yes, that was his name, I heard it often enough."

"Describe him, then. What was he like? Tall and fair? They're all that, but what else? What in particular?"

She hesitated, and then said: "This one wasn't fair. He was dark, and had a scar that drew up the left corner of his mouth."

Rechamp turned to me. "It's the same. I heard the men describing him at Moulins."

We followed the old woman into the house, and while she gave us some bread and wine she told us about the wrecking of the village and the factory. It was one of the most damnable stories I've heard yet. Put together the worst of the typical horrors and you'll have a fair idea of it. Murder, outrage, torture: Scharlach's programme seemed to be fairly comprehensive. She ended off by saying: "His orderly showed me a silver-mounted flute he always travelled with, and a beautiful paint-box mounted in silver too. Before he left he sat down on my door-step and made a painting of the ruins...."

Soon after leaving this place of death we got to the second lines and our troubles began. We had to do a lot of talking to get through the lines, but what Rechamp had just seen had made him eloquent. Luckily, too, the ambulance doctor, a charming fellow, was short of tetanus-serum, and I had some left; and while I went over with him to the pine-branch hut where he hid his wounded I explained Rechamp's case, and implored him to get us through. Finally it was settled that we should leave the ambulance there, for in the lines the ban against motors is absolute, and drive the remaining twelve miles. A sergeant fished out of a farmhouse a toothless old woman with a furry horse harnessed to a two-wheeled trap, and we started off by round-about wood-tracks. The horse was in no hurry, nor the old lady either; for there were bits of road that were pretty steadily currycombed by shell, and it was to everybody's interest not to cross them before twilight. Jean de Rechamp's excitement seemed to have dropped: he sat beside me dumb as a fish, staring straight ahead of him. I didn't feel talkative either, for a word the doctor had let drop had left me thinking. "That poor old granny mind the shells? Not she!" he had said when our crazy chariot drove up. "She doesn't know them from snow-flakes any more. Nothing matters to her now, except trying to outwit a German. They're all like that where Scharlach's been, you've heard of him? She had only one boy, half-witted: he cocked a broomhandle at them, and they burnt him. Oh, she'll take you to Rechamp safe enough."

"Where Scharlach's been"—so he had been as close as this to Rechamp! I was wondering if Jean knew it, and if that had sealed his lips and given him that flinty profile. The old horse's woolly flanks jogged on under the bare branches and the old woman's bent back jogged in time with it She never once spoke or looked around at us. "It isn't the noise we make that'll give us away," I said at last; and just then the old woman turned her head and pointed silently with the osier-twig she used as a whip. Just ahead of us lay a heap of ruins: the wreck, apparently, of a great chateau and its dependencies. "Lermont!" Rechamp exclaimed, turning white. He made a motion to jump out and then dropped back into the seat. "What's the use?" he muttered. He leaned forward and touched the old woman's shoulder.

"I hadn't heard of this, when did it happen?"

"In September."

"They did it?"

"Yes. Our wounded were there. It's like this everywhere in our country."

I saw Jean stiffening himself for the next question. "At Rechamp, too?"

She relapsed into indifference. "I haven't been as far as Rechamp."

"But you must have seen people who'd been there, you must have heard."

"I've heard the masters were still there, so there must be something standing. Maybe though," she reflected, "they're in the cellars...."

We continued to jog on through the dusk.

V

"There's the steeple!" Rechamp burst out.

Through the dimness I couldn't tell which way to look; but I suppose in the thickest midnight he would have known where he was. He jumped from the trap and took the old horse by the bridle. I made out that he was guiding us into a long village street edged by houses in which every light was extinguished. The snow on the ground sent up a pale reflection, and I began to see the gabled outline of the houses and the steeple at the head of the street. The place seemed as calm and unchanged as if the sound of war had never reached it. In the open space at the end of the village Rechamp checked the horse.

"The elm, there's the old elm in front of the church!" he shouted in a voice like a boy's. He ran back and caught me by both hands. "It was true, then, nothing's touched!" The old woman asked: "Is this Rechamp?" and he went back to the horse's head and turned the trap toward a tall gate between park walls. The gate was barred and padlocked, and not a gleam showed through the shutters of the porter's lodge; but Rechamp, after listening a minute or two, gave a low call twice repeated, and presently the lodge door opened, and an old man peered out. Well, I leave you to brush in the rest. Old family servant, tears and hugs and so on. I know you affect to scorn the cinema, and this was it, tremolo and all. Hang it! This war's going to teach us not to be afraid of the obvious.

We piled into the trap and drove down a long avenue to the house. Black as the grave, of course; but in another minute the door opened, and there, in the hall, was another servant, screening a light, and then more doors opened on another cinema-scene: fine old drawing-room with family portraits, shaded lamp, domestic group about the fire. They evidently thought it was the servant coming to announce dinner, and not a head turned at our approach. I could see them all over Jean's shoulder: a grey-haired lady knitting with stiff fingers, an old gentleman with a high nose and a weak chin sitting in a big carved armchair and looking more like a portrait than the portraits; a pretty girl at his feet, with a dog's head in her lap, and another girl, who had a Red Cross on her sleeve, at the table with a book. She had been reading aloud in a rich veiled voice, and broke off her last phrase to say: "Dinner...." Then she looked up and saw Jean. Her dark face remained perfectly calm, but she lifted her hand in a just perceptible gesture of warning, and instantly understanding he drew back and pushed the servant forward in his place.

"Madame la Comtesse, it is someone outside asking for Mademoiselle."

The dark girl jumped up and ran out into the hall. I remember wondering: "Is it because she wants to have him to herself first, or because she's afraid of their being startled?" I wished myself out of the way, but she took no notice of me, and going straight to Jean flung her arms about him. I was behind him and could see her hands about his neck, and her brown fingers tightly locked. There wasn't much doubt about those two....

The next minute she caught sight of me, and I was being rapidly tested by a pair of the finest eyes I ever saw, I don't apply the term to their setting, though that was fine too, but to the look itself, a look at once warm and resolute, all-promising and all-penetrating. I really can't do with fewer adjectives....

Rechamp explained me, and she was full of thanks and welcome; not excessive, but, well, I don't know, eloquent! She gave every intonation all it could carry, and without the least emphasis: that's the wonder.

She went back to "prepare" the parents, as they say in melodrama; and in a minute or two we followed. What struck me first was that these insignificant and inadequate people had the command of the grand gesture—had la ligne. The mother had laid aside her knitting, not dropped it, and stood waiting with open arms. But even in clasping her son she seemed to include me in her welcome. I don't know how to describe it; but they never let me feel I was in the way. I suppose that's part of what you call distinction; knowing instinctively how to deal with unusual moments.

All the while, I was looking about me at the fine secure old room, in which nothing seemed altered or disturbed, the portraits smiling from the walls, the servants beaming in the doorway, and wondering how such things could have survived in the trail of death and havoc we had been following.

The same thought had evidently struck Jean, for he dropped his sister's hand and turned to gaze about him too.

"Then nothing's touched, nothing? I don't understand," he stammered.

Monsieur de Rechamp raised himself majestically from his chair, crossed the room and lifted Yvonne Malo's hand to his lips. "Nothing is touched, thanks to this hand and this brain."

Madame de Rechamp was shining on her son through tears. "Ah, yes, we owe it all to Yvonne."

"All, all! Grandmamma will tell you!" Simone chimed in; and Yvonne, brushing aside their praise with a half-impatient laugh, said to her betrothed: "But your grandmother! You must go up to her at once."

A wonderful specimen, that grandmother: I was taken to see her after dinner. She sat by the fire in a bare panelled bedroom, bolt upright in an armchair with ears, a knitting-table at her elbow with a shaded candle on it.

She was even more withered and ancient than she looked in her photograph, and I judge she'd never been pretty; but she somehow made me feel as if I'd got through with prettiness. I don't know exactly what she reminded me of: a dried bouquet, or something rich and clovy that had turned brittle through long keeping in a sandal-wood box. I suppose her sandal-wood box had been Good Society. Well, I had a rare evening with her. Jean and his parents were called down to see the cure, who had hurried over to the chateau when he heard of the young man's arrival; and the old lady asked me to stay on and chat with her. She related their experiences with uncanny detachment, seeming chiefly to resent the indignity of having been made to descend into the cellar—"to avoid French shells, if you'll believe it: the Germans had the decency not to bombard us," she observed impartially. I was so struck by the absence of rancour in her tone that finally, out of sheer curiosity, I made an allusion to the horror of having the enemy under one's roof. "Oh, I might almost say I didn't see them," she returned. "I never go downstairs any longer; and they didn't do me the honour of coming beyond my door. A glance sufficed them—an old woman like me!" she added with a phosphorescent gleam of coquetry.

"But they searched the chateau, surely?" "Oh, a mere form; they were very decent—very decent," she almost snapped at me. "There was a first moment, of course, when we feared it might be hard to get Monsieur de Rechamp away with my young grandson; but Mlle. Malo managed that very cleverly. They slipped off while the officers were dining." She looked at me with the smile of some arch old lady in a Louis XV pastel. "My grandson Jean's fiancee is a very clever young woman: in my time no young girl would have been so sure of herself, so cool and quick. After all, there is something to be said for the new way of bringing up girls. My poor daughter-in-law, at Yvonne's age, was a bleating baby: she is so still, at times. The convent doesn't develop character. I'm glad Yvonne was not brought up in a convent." And this champion of tradition smiled on me more intensely.

Little by little I got from her the story of the German approach: the distracted fugitives pouring in from the villages north of Rechamp, the sound of distant cannonading, and suddenly, the next afternoon, after a reassuring lull, the sight of a single spiked helmet at the end of the drive. In a few minutes a dozen followed: mostly officers; then all at once the place hummed with them. There were supply waggons and motors in the court, bundles of hay, stacks of rifles, artillery-men unharnessing and rubbing down their horses. The crowd was hot and thirsty, and in a moment the old lady, to her amazement, saw wine and cider being handed about by the Rechamp servants. "Or so at least I was told," she added, correcting herself, "for it's not my habit to look out of the window. I simply sat here and waited." Her seat, as she spoke, might have been a curule chair.

Downstairs, it appeared, Mlle. Malo had instantly taken her measures. She didn't sit and wait. Surprised in the garden with Simone, she had made the girl walk quietly back to the house and receive the officers with her on the doorstep. The officer in command—captain, or whatever he was—had arrived in a bad temper, cursing and swearing, and growling out menaces about spies. The day was intensely hot, and possibly he had had too much wine. At any rate Mlle. Malo had known how to "put him in his place"; and when he and the other officers entered they found the dining-table set out with refreshing drinks and cigars, melons, strawberries and iced coffee. "The clever creature! She even remembered that they liked whipped cream with their coffee!"

The effect had been miraculous. The captain, what was his name? Yes, Chariot, Chariot, Captain Chariot had been specially complimentary on the subject of the whipped cream and the cigars. Then he asked to see the other members of the family, and Mlle. Malo told him there were only two, "two old women!" He made a face at that, and said all the same he should like to meet them; and she answered: "'One is your hostess, the Comtesse de Rechamp, who is ill in bed', for my poor daughter-in-law was lying in bed paralyzed with rheumatism—'and the other her mother-in-law, a very old lady who never leaves her room.'"

"But aren't there any men in the family?" he had then asked; and she had said: "Oh yes—two. The Comte de Rechamp and his son."

"And where are they?"

"In England. Monsieur de Rechamp went a month ago to take his son on a trip."

The officer said: "I was told they were here to-day"; and Mlle. Malo replied: "You had better have the house searched and satisfy yourself."

He laughed and said: "The idea had occurred to me." She laughed also, and sitting down at the piano struck a few chords. Captain Chariot, who had his foot on the threshold, turned back—Simone had described the scene to her grandmother afterward. "Some of the brutes, it seems, are musical," the old lady explained; "and this was one of them. While he was listening, some soldiers appeared in the court carrying another who seemed to be wounded. It turned out afterward that he'd been climbing a garden wall after fruit, and cut himself on the broken glass at the top; but the blood was enough— they raised the usual dreadful outcry about an ambush, and a lieutenant clattered into the room where Mlle. Malo sat playing Stravinsky." The old lady paused for her effect, and I was conscious of giving her all she wanted.

"Well—?"

"Will you believe it? It seems she looked at her watch-bracelet and said: 'Do you gentlemen dress for dinner? I do, but we've still time for a little Moussorgsky', or whatever wild names they call themselves, 'if you'll make those people outside hold their tongues.' Our captain looked at her again, laughed, gave an order that sent the lieutenant right about, and sat down beside her at the piano. Imagine my stupour, dear sir: the drawing-room is directly under this room, and in a moment I heard two voices coming up to me. Well, I won't conceal from you that his was the finest. But then I always adored a barytone." She folded her shrivelled hands among their laces. "After that, the Germans were tres bien, tres bien. They stayed two days, and there was nothing to complain of. Indeed, when the second detachment came, a week later, they never even entered the gates. Orders had been left that they should be quartered elsewhere. Of course we were lucky in happening on a man of the world like Captain Chariot."

"Yes, very lucky. It's odd, though, his having a French name."

"Very. It probably accounts for his breeding," she answered placidly; and left me marvelling at the happy remoteness of old age.

VI

The next morning early Jean de Rechamp came to my room. I was struck at once by the change in him: he had lost his first glow, and seemed nervous and hesitating. I knew what he had come for: to ask me to postpone our departure for another twenty-four hours. By rights we should have been off that morning; but there had been a sharp brush a few kilometres away, and a couple of poor devils had been brought to the chateau whom it would have been death to carry farther that day and criminal not to hurry to a base hospital the next morning. "We've simply got to stay till to-morrow: you're in luck," I said laughing.

He laughed back, but with a frown that made me feel I had been a brute to speak in that way of a respite due to such a cause.

"The men will pull through, you know—trust Mlle. Malo for that!" I said.

His frown did not lift. He went to the window and drummed on the pane.

"Do you see that breach in the wall, down there behind the trees? It's the only scratch the place has got. And think of Lennont! It's incredible, simply incredible!"

"But it's like that everywhere, isn't it? Everything depends on the officer in command."

"Yes: that's it, I suppose. I haven't had time to get a consecutive account of what happened: they're all too excited. Mlle. Malo is the only person who can tell me exactly how things went." He swung about on me. "Look here, it sounds absurd, what I'm asking; but try to get me an hour alone with her, will you?"

I stared at the request, and he went on, still half-laughing: "You see, they all hang on me; my father and mother, Simone, the cure, the servants. The whole village is coming up presently: they want to stuff their eyes full of me. It's natural enough, after living here all these long months cut off from everything. But the result is I haven't said two words to her yet."

"Well, you shall," I declared; and with an easier smile he turned to hurry down to a mass of thanksgiving which the cure was to celebrate in the private chapel. "My parents wanted it," he explained; "and after that the whole village will be upon us. But later—"

"Later I'll effect a diversion; I swear I will," I assured him.

By daylight, decidedly, Mlle. Malo was less handsome than in the evening. It was my first thought as she came toward me, that afternoon, under the limes. Jean was still indoors, with his people, receiving the village; I rather wondered she hadn't stayed there with him. Theoretically, her place was at his side; but I knew she was a young woman who didn't live by rule, and she had already struck me as having a distaste for superfluous expenditures of feeling.

Yes, she was less effective by day. She looked older for one thing; her face was pinched, and a little sallow and for the first time I noticed that her cheek-bones were too high. Her eyes, too, had lost their velvet depth: fine eyes still, but not unfathomable. But the smile with which she greeted me was charming: it ran over her tired face like a lamp-lighter kindling flames as he runs.

"I was looking for you," she said. "Shall we have a little talk? The reception is sure to last another hour: every one of the villagers is going to tell just what happened to him or her when the Germans came."

"And you've run away from the ceremony?"

"I'm a trifle tired of hearing the same adventures retold," she said, still smiling.

"But I thought there were no adventures, that that was the wonder of it?"

She shrugged. "It makes their stories a little dull, at any rate; we've not a hero or a martyr to show." She had strolled farther from the house as we talked, leading me in the direction of a bare horse-chestnut walk that led toward the park.

"Of course Jean's got to listen to it all, poor boy; but I needn't," she explained.

I didn't know exactly what to answer and we walked on a little way in silence; then she said: "If you'd carried him off this morning he would have escaped all this fuss." After a pause she added slowly: "On the whole, it might have been as well."

"To carry him off?"

"Yes." She stopped and looked at me. "I wish you would."

"Would? Now?"

"Yes, now: as soon as you can. He's really not strong yet, he's drawn and nervous." ("So are you," I thought.) "And the excitement is greater than you can perhaps imagine—"

I gave her back her look. "Why, I think I can imagine...."

She coloured up through her sallow skin and then laughed away her blush. "Oh, I don't mean the excitement of seeing me! But his parents, his grandmother, the cure, all the old associations—"

I considered for a moment; then I said: "As a matter of fact, you're about the only person he hasn't seen."

She checked a quick answer on her lips, and for a moment or two we faced each other silently. A sudden sense of intimacy, of complicity almost, came over me. What was it that the girl's silence was crying out to me?

"If I take him away now he won't have seen you at all," I continued.

She stood under the bare trees, keeping her eyes on me. "Then take him away now!" she retorted; and as she spoke I saw her face change, decompose into deadly apprehension and as quickly regain its usual calm. From where she stood she faced the courtyard, and glancing in the same direction I saw the throng of villagers coming out of the chateau. "Take him away, take him away at once!" she passionately commanded; and the next minute Jean de Rechamp detached himself from the group and began to limp down the walk in our direction.

What was I to do? I can't exaggerate the sense of urgency Mlle. Malo's appeal gave me, or my faith in her sincerity. No one who had seen her meeting with Rechamp the night before could have doubted her feeling for him: if she wanted him away it was not because she did not delight in his presence. Even now, as he approached, I saw her face veiled by a faint mist of emotion: it was like watching a fruit ripen under a midsummer sun. But she turned sharply from the house and began to walk on.

"Can't you give me a hint of your reason?" I suggested as I followed.

"My reason? I've given it!" I suppose I looked incredulous, for she added in a lower voice: "I don't want him to hear—yet—about all the horrors."

"The horrors? I thought there had been none here."

"All around us—" Her voice became a whisper. "Our friends... our neighbours... every one...."

"He can hardly avoid hearing of that, can he? And besides, since you're all safe and happy.... Look here," I broke off, "he's coming after us. Don't we look as if we were running away?"

She turned around, suddenly paler; and in a stride or two Rechamp was at our side. He was pale too; and before I could find a pretext for slipping away he had begun to speak. But I saw at once that he didn't know or care if I was there.

"What was the name of the officer in command who was quartered here?" he asked, looking straight at the girl.

She raised her eye-brows slightly. "Do you mean to say that after listening for three hours to every inhabitant of Bechamp you haven't found that out?"

"They all call him something different. My grandmother says he had a French name: she calls him Chariot."

"Your grandmother was never taught German: his name was the Oberst von Scharlach." She did not remember my presence either: the two were still looking straight in each other's eyes.

Bechamp had grown white to the lips: he was rigid with the effort to control himself.

"Why didn't you tell me it was Scharlach who was here?" he brought out at last in a low voice.

She turned her eyes in my direction. "I was just explaining to Mr. Greer—"

"To Mr. Greer?" He looked at me too, half-angrily.

"I know the stories that are about," she continued quietly; "and I was saying to your friend that, since we had been so happy as to be spared, it seemed useless to dwell on what has happened elsewhere."

"Damn what happened elsewhere! I don't yet know what happened here."

I put a hand on his arm. Mlle. Malo was looking hard at me, but I wouldn't let her see I knew it. "I'm going to leave you to hear the whole story now," I said to Rechamp.

"But there isn't any story for him to hear!" she broke in. She pointed at the serene front of the chateau, looking out across its gardens to the unscarred fields. "We're safe; the place is untouched. Why brood on other horrors, horrors we were powerless to help?"

Rechamp held his ground doggedly. "But the man's name is a curse and an abomination. Wherever he went he spread ruin."

"So they say. Mayn't there be a mistake? Legends grow up so quickly in these dreadful times. Here—" she looked about her again at the peaceful scene—"here he behaved as you see. For heaven's sake be content with that!"

"Content?" He passed his hand across his forehead. "I'm blind with joy...or should be, if only..."

She looked at me entreatingly, almost desperately, and I took hold of Rechamp's arm with a warning pressure.

"My dear fellow, don't you see that Mlle. Malo has been under a great strain? La joie fait peur—that's the trouble with both of you!"

He lowered his head. "Yes, I suppose it is." He took her hand And kissed it. "I beg your pardon. Greer's right: we're both on edge."

"Yes: I'll leave you for a little while, if you and Mr Greer will excuse me." She included us both in a quiet look that seemed to me extremely noble, and walked lowly away toward the chateau. Rechamp stood gazing after her for a moment; then he dropped down on one of benches at the edge of the path. He covered his face with his hands. "Scharlach, Scharlach!" I heard him say.

We sat there side by side for ten minutes or more without speaking. Finally I said: "Look here, Rechamp, she's right and you're wrong. I shall be sorry I brought you here if you don't see it before it's too late."

His face was still hidden; but presently he dropped his hands and answered me. "I do see. She's saved everything for me, my, people and my house, and the ground we're standing on. And I worship it because she walks on it!"

"And so do your people: the war's done that for you, anyhow," I reminded him.

VII

The morning after we were off before dawn. Our time allowance was up, and it was thought advisable, on account of our wounded, to slip across the exposed bit of road in the dark. Mlle. Malo was downstairs when we started, pale in her white dress, but calm and active. We had borrowed a farmer's cart in which our two men could be laid on a mattress, and she had stocked our trap with food and remedies. Nothing seemed to have been forgotten. While I was settling the men I suppose Rechamp turned back into the hall to bid her good-bye; anyhow, when she followed him out a moment later he looked quieter and less strained. He had taken leave of his parents and his sister upstairs, and Yvonne Malo stood alone in the dark driveway, watching us as we drove away.

There was not much talk between us during our slow drive back to the lines. We had to go it a snail's pace, for the roads were rough; and there was time for meditation. I knew well enough what my companion was thinking about and my own thoughts ran on the same lines. Though the story of the German occupation of Rechamp had been retold to us a dozen times the main facts did not vary. There were little discrepancies of detail, and gaps in the narrative here and there; but all the household, from the astute ancestress to the last bewildered pantry-boy, were at one in saying that Mlle. Malo's coolness and courage had saved the chateau and the village. The officer in command had arrived full of threats and insolence: Mlle. Malo had placated and disarmed him, turned his suspicions to ridicule, entertained him and his comrades at dinner, and contrived during that time, or rather while they were making music afterward (which they did for half the night, it seemed)—that Monsieur de Rechamp and Alain should slip out of the cellar in which they had been hidden, gain the end of the gardens through an old hidden passage, and get off in the darkness. Meanwhile Simone had been safe upstairs with her mother and grandmother, and none of the officers lodged in the chateau had, after a first hasty inspection, set foot in any part of the house but the wing assigned to them. On the third morning they had left, and Scharlach, before going, had put in Mlle. Malo's hands a letter requesting whatever officer should follow him to show every consideration to the family of the Comte de Rechamp, and if possible, owing to the grave illness of the Countess, avoid taking up quarters in the chateau: a request which had been scrupulously observed.

Such were the amazing but undisputed facts over which Rechamp and I, in our different ways, were now pondering. He hardly spoke, and when he did it was only to make some casual reference to the road or to our wounded soldiers; but all the while I sat at his side I kept hearing the echo of the question he was inwardly asking himself, and hoping to God he wouldn't put it to me....

It was nearly noon when we finally reached the lines, and the men had to have a rest before we could start again; but a couple of hours later we landed them safely at the base hospital. From there we had intended to go back to Paris; but as we were starting there came an unexpected summons to another point of the front, where there had been a successful night-attack, and a lot of Germans taken in a blown-up trench. The place was fifty miles away, and off my beat, but the number of wounded on both sides was exceptionally heavy, and all the available ambulances had already started. An urgent call had come for more, and there was nothing for it but to go; so we went.

We found things in a bad mess at the second line shanty-hospital where they were dumping the wounded as fast as they could bring them in. At first we were told that none were fit to be carried farther that night; and after we had done what we could we went off to hunt up a shake-down in the village. But a few minutes later an orderly overtook us with a message from the surgeon. There was a German with an abdominal wound who was in a bad way, but might be saved by an operation if he could be got back to the base before midnight.

Would we take him at once and then come back for others?

There is only one answer to such requests, and a few minutes later we were back at the hospital, and the wounded man was being carried out on a stretcher. In the shaky lantern gleam I caught a glimpse of a livid face and a torn uniform, and saw that he was an officer, and nearly done for. Rechamp had climbed to the box, and seemed not to be noticing what was going on at the back of the motor. I understood that he loathed the job, and wanted not to see the face of the man we were carrying; so when we had got him settled I jumped into the ambulance beside him and called out to Bechamp that we were ready. A second later an infirmier ran up with a little packet and pushed it into my hand. "His papers," he explained. I pocketed them and pulled the door shut, and we were off.

The man lay motionless on his back, conscious, but desperately weak. Once I turned my pocket-lamp on him and saw that he was young, about thirty, with damp dark hair and a thin face. He had received a flesh-wound above the eyes, and his forehead was bandaged, but the rest of the face uncovered. As the light fell on him he lifted his eyelids and looked at me: his look was inscrutable.

For half an hour or so I sat there in the dark, the sense of that face pressing close on me. It was a damnable face, meanly handsome, basely proud. In my one glimpse of it I had seen that the man was suffering atrociously, but as we slid along through the night he made no sound. At length the motor stopped with a violent jerk that drew a single moan from him. I turned the light on him, but he lay perfectly still, lips and lids shut, making no sign; and I jumped out and ran round to the front to see what had happened.

The motor had stopped for lack of gasolene and was stock still in the deep mud. Rechamp muttered something about a leak in his tank. As he bent over it, the lantern flame struck up into his face, which was set and businesslike. It struck me vaguely that he showed no particular surprise.

"What's to be done?" I asked.

"I think I can tinker it up; but we've got to have more essence to go on with."

I stared at him in despair: it was a good hour's walk back to the lines, and we weren't so sure of getting any gasolene when we got there! But there was no help for it; and as Rechamp was dead lame, no alternative but for me to go.

I opened the ambulance door, gave another look at the motionless man inside and took out a remedy which I handed over to Rechamp with a word of explanation. "You know how to give a hypo? Keep a close eye on him and pop this in if you see a change, not otherwise."

He nodded. "Do you suppose he'll die?" he asked below his breath.

"No, I don't. If we get him to the hospital before morning I think he'll pull through."

"Oh, all right." He unhooked one of the motor lanterns and handed it over to me. "I'll do my best," he said as I turned away.

Getting back to the lines through that pitch-black forest, and finding somebody to bring the gasolene back for me was about the weariest job I ever tackled. I couldn't imagine why it wasn't daylight when we finally got to the place where I had left the motor. It seemed to me as if I had been gone twelve hours when I finally caught sight of the grey bulk of the car through the thinning darkness.

Rechamp came forward to meet us, and took hold of my arm as I was opening the door of the car. "The man's dead," he said.

I had lifted up my pocket-lamp, and its light fell on Rechamp's face, which was perfectly composed, and seemed less gaunt and drawn than at any time since we had started on our trip.

"Dead? Why, how? What happened? Did you give him the hypodermic?" I stammered, taken aback.

"No time to. He died in a minute."

"How do you know he did? Were you with him?"

"Of course I was with him," Rechamp retorted, with a sudden harshness which made me aware that I had grown harsh myself. But I had been almost sure the man wasn't anywhere near death when I left him. I opened the door of the ambulance and climbed in with my lantern. He didn't appear to have moved, but he was dead sure enough, had been for two or three hours, by the feel of him. It must have happened not long after I left.... Well, I'm not a doctor, anyhow....

I don't think Rechamp and I exchanged a word during the rest of that run. But it was my fault and not his if we didn't. By the mere rub of his sleeve against mine as we sat side by side on the motor I knew he was conscious of no bar between us: he had somehow got back, in the night's interval, to a state of wholesome stolidity, while I, on the contrary, was tingling all over with exposed nerves.

I was glad enough when we got back to the base at last, and the grim load we carried was lifted out and taken into the hospital. Rechamp waited in the courtyard beside his car, lighting a cigarette in the cold early sunlight; but I followed the bearers and the surgeon into the whitewashed room where the dead man was laid out to be undressed. I had a burning spot at the pit of my stomach while his clothes were ripped off him and the bandages undone: I couldn't take my eyes from the surgeon's face. But the surgeon, with a big batch of wounded on his hands, was probably thinking more of the living than the dead; and besides, we were near the front, and the body before him was an enemy's.

He finished his examination and scribbled something in a note-book. "Death must have taken place nearly five hours ago," he merely remarked: it was the conclusion I had already come to myself.

"And how about the papers?" the surgeon continued. "You have them, I suppose? This way, please."

We left the half-stripped body on the blood-stained oil-cloth, and he led me into an office where a functionary sat behind a littered desk.

"The papers? Thank you. You haven't examined them? Let us see, then."

I handed over the leather note-case I had thrust into my pocket the evening before, and saw for the first time its silver-edged corners and the coronet in one of them. The official took out the papers and spread them on the desk between us. I watched him absently while he did so.

Suddenly he uttered an exclamation. "Ah, that's a haul!" he said, and pushed a bit of paper toward me. On it was engraved the name: Oberst Graf Benno von Scharlach....

"A good riddance," said the surgeon over my shoulder.

I went back to the courtyard and saw Rechamp still smoking his cigarette in the cold sunlight. I don't suppose I'd been in the hospital ten minutes; but I felt as old as Methuselah.

My friend greeted me with a smile. "Ready for breakfast?" he said, and a little chill ran down my spine.... But I said: "Oh, all right, come along...."

For, after all, I knew there wasn't a paper of any sort on that man when he was lifted into my ambulance the night before: the French officials attend to their business too carefully for me not to have been sure of that. And there wasn't the least shred of evidence to prove that he hadn't died of his wounds during the unlucky delay in the forest; or that Rechamp had known his tank was leaking when we started out from the lines.

"I could do with a cafe complet, couldn't you?" Rechamp suggested, looking straight at me with his good blue eyes; and arm in arm we started off to hunt for the inn....

THE CHOICE

Stilling, that night after dinner, had surpassed himself. He always did, Wrayford reflected, when the small fry from Highfield came to dine. He, Cobham Stilling, who had to find his bearings and keep to his level in the big heedless ironic world of New York, dilated and grew vast in the congenial medium of Highfield. The Red House was the biggest house of the Highfield summer colony, and Cobham Stilling was its biggest man. No one else within a radius of a hundred miles (on a conservative estimate) had as many horses, as many greenhouses, as many servants, and assuredly no one else had three motors and a motor-boat for the lake.

The motor-boat was Stilling's latest hobby, and he rode, or steered, it in and out of the conversation all the evening, to the obvious edification of every one present save his wife and his visitor, Austin Wrayford. The interest of the latter two who, from opposite ends of the drawing-room, exchanged a fleeting glance when Stilling again launched his craft on the thin current of the talk, the interest of Mrs. Stilling and Wrayford had already lost its edge by protracted contact with the subject.

But the dinner-guests, the Rector, Mr. Swordsley, his wife Mrs. Swordsley, Lucy and Agnes Granger, their brother Addison, and young Jack Emmerton from Harvard, were all, for divers reasons, stirred to the proper pitch of feeling. Mr. Swordsley, no doubt, was saying to himself: "If my good parishioner here can afford to buy a motor-boat, in addition to all the other expenditures which an establishment like this must entail, I certainly need not scruple to appeal to him again for a contribution for our Galahad Club." The Granger girls, meanwhile, were evoking visions of lakeside picnics, not unadorned with the presence of young Mr. Emmerton; while that youth himself speculated as to whether his affable host would let him, when he came back on his next vacation, "learn to run the thing himself"; and Mr. Addison Granger, the elderly bachelor brother of the volatile Lucy and Agnes, mentally formulated the precise phrase in which, in his next letter to his cousin Professor Spildyke of the University of East Latmos, he should allude to "our last delightful trip in my old friend Cobham Stilling's ten-thousand-dollar motor-launch", for East Latmos was still in that primitive stage of culture on which five figures impinge.

Isabel Stilling, sitting beside Mrs. Swordsley, her bead slightly bent above the needlework with which on these occasions it was her old-fashioned habit to employ herself, Isabel also had doubtless her reflections to make. As Wrayford leaned back in his corner and looked at her across the wide flower-filled drawing-room he noted, first of all, for the how many hundredth time?—the play of her hands above the embroidery-frame, the shadow of the thick dark hair on her forehead, the lids over her somewhat full grey eyes. He noted all this with a conscious deliberateness of enjoyment, taking in unconsciously, at the same time, the particular quality in her attitude, in the fall of her dress and the turn of her head, which had set her for him, from the first day, in a separate world; then he said to himself: "She is certainly thinking: 'Where on earth will Cobham get the money to pay for it?'"

Stilling, cigar in mouth and thumbs in his waistcoat pockets, was impressively perorating from his usual dominant position on the hearth-rug.

"I said: 'If I have the thing at all, I want the best that can be got.' That's my way, you know, Swordsley; I suppose I'm what you'd call fastidious. Always was, about everything, from cigars to wom—" his eye met the apprehensive glance of Mrs. Swordsley, who looked like her husband with his clerical coat cut slightly lower—"so I said: 'If I have the thing at all, I want the best that can be got.' Nothing makeshift for me, no second-best. I never cared for the cheap and showy. I always say frankly to a man: 'If you can't give me a first-rate cigar, for the Lord's sake let me smoke my own.'" He paused to do so. "Well, if you have my standards, you can't buy a thing in a minute. You must look round, compare, select. I found there were lots of motor-boats on the market, just as there's lots of stuff called champagne. But I said to myself: 'Ten to one there's only one fit to buy, just as there's only one champagne fit for a gentleman to drink.' Argued like a lawyer, eh, Austin?" He tossed this to Wrayford. "Take me for one of your own trade, wouldn't you? Well, I'm not such a fool as I look. I suppose you fellows who are tied to the treadmill, excuse me, Swordsley, but work's work, isn't it? I suppose you think a man like me has nothing to do but take it easy: loll through life like a woman. By George, sir, I'd like either of you to see the time it takes, I won't say the brain, but just the time it takes to pick out a good motor-boat. Why, I went—"

Mrs. Stilling set her embroidery-frame noiselessly on the table at her side, and turned her head toward Wrayford. "Would you mind ringing for the tray?"

The interruption helped Mrs. Swordsley to waver to her feet. "I'm afraid we ought really to be going; my husband has an early service to-morrow."

Her host intervened with a genial protest. "Going already? Nothing of the sort! Why, the night's still young, as the poet says. Long way from here to the rectory? Nonsense! In our little twenty-horse car we do it in five minutes, don't we, Belle? Ah, you're walking, to be sure—" Stilling's indulgent gesture seemed to concede that, in such a case, allowances must be made, and that he was the last man not to make them. "Well, then, Swordsley—" He held out a thick red hand that seemed to exude beneficence, and the clergyman, pressing it, ventured to murmur a suggestion.

"What, that Galahad Club again? Why, I thought my wife, Isabel, didn't we—No? Well, it must have been my mother, then. Of course, you know, anything my good mother gives is—well—virtually— You haven't asked her? Sure? I could have sworn; I get so many of these appeals. And in these times, you know, we have to go cautiously. I'm sure you recognize that yourself, Swordsley. With my obligations, here now, to show you don't bear malice, have a brandy and soda before you go. Nonsense, man! This brandy isn't liquor; it's liqueur. I picked it up last year in London, last of a famous lot from Lord St. Oswyn's cellar. Laid down here, it stood me at—Eh?" he broke off as his wife moved toward him. "Ah, yes, of course. Miss Lucy, Miss Agnes, a drop of soda-water? Look here, Addison, you won't refuse my tipple, I know. Well, take a cigar, at any rate, Swordsley. And, by the way, I'm afraid you'll have to go round the long way by the avenue to-night. Sorry, Mrs. Swordsley, but I forgot to tell them to leave the gate into the lane unlocked. Well, it's a jolly night, and I daresay you won't mind the extra turn along the lake. And, by Jove! if the moon's out, you'll have a glimpse of the motorboat. She's moored just out beyond our boat-house; and it's a privilege to look at her, I can tell you!"

The dispersal of his guests carried Stilling out into the hall, where his pleasantries reverberated under the oak rafters while the Granger girls were being muffled for the drive and the carriages summoned from the stables.

By a common impulse Mrs. Stilling and Wrayford had moved together toward the fire-place, which was hidden by a tall screen from the door into the hall. Wrayford leaned his elbow against the mantel-piece, and Mrs. Stilling stood beside him, her clasped hands hanging down before her.

"Have you anything more to talk over with him?" she asked.

"No. We wound it all up before dinner. He doesn't want to talk about it any more than he can help."

"It's so bad?"

"No; but this time he's got to pull up."

She stood silent, with lowered lids. He listened a moment, catching Stilling's farewell shout; then he moved a little nearer, and laid his hand on her arm.

"In an hour?"

She made an imperceptible motion of assent.

"I'll tell you about it then. The key's as usual?"

She signed another "Yes" and walked away with her long drifting step as her husband came in from the hall.

He went up to the tray and poured himself out a tall glass of brandy and soda.

"The weather is turning queer, black as pitch. I hope the Swordsleys won't walk into the lake, involuntary immersion, eh? He'd come out a Baptist, I suppose. What'd the Bishop do in such a case? There's a problem for a lawyer, my boy!"

He clapped his hand on Wrayford's thin shoulder and then walked over to his wife, who was gathering up her embroidery silks and dropping them into her work-bag. Stilling took her by the arms and swung her playfully about so that she faced the lamplight.

"What's the matter with you tonight?"

"The matter?" she echoed, colouring a little, and standing very straight in her desire not to appear to shrink from his touch.

"You never opened your lips. Left me the whole job of entertaining those blessed people. Didn't she, Austin?"

Wrayford laughed and lit a cigarette.

"There! You see even Austin noticed it. What's the matter, I say? Aren't they good enough for you? I don't say they're particularly exciting; but, hang it! I like to ask them here, I like to give people pleasure."

"I didn't mean to be dull," said Isabel.

"Well, you must learn to make an effort. Don't treat people as if they weren't in the room just because they don't happen to amuse you. Do you know what they'll think? They'll think it's because you've got a bigger house and more money than they have. Shall I tell you something? My mother said she'd noticed the same thing in you lately. She said she sometimes felt you looked down on her for living in a small house. Oh, she was half joking, of course; but you see you do give people that impression. I can't understand treating any one in that way. The more I have myself, the more I want to make other people happy." Isabel gently freed herself and laid the work-bag on her embroidery-frame. "I have a headache; perhaps that made me stupid. I'm going to bed." She turned toward Wrayford and held out her hand. "Good night."

"Good night," he answered, opening the door for her.

When he turned back into the room, his host was pouring himself a third glass of brandy and soda.

"Here, have a nip, Austin? Gad, I need it badly, after the shaking up you gave me this afternoon." Stilling laughed and carried his glass to the hearth, where he took up his usual commanding position. "Why the deuce don't you drink something? You look as glum as Isabel. One would think you were the chap that had been hit by this business."

Wrayford threw himself into the chair from which Mrs. Stilling had lately risen. It was the one she usually sat in, and to his fancy a faint scent of her clung to it. He leaned back and looked up at Stilling.

"Want a cigar?" the latter continued. "Shall we go into the den and smoke?"

Wrayford hesitated. "If there's anything more you want to ask me about—"

"Gad, no! I had full measure and running over this afternoon. The deuce of it is, I don't see where the money's all gone to. Luckily I've got plenty of nerve; I'm not the kind of man to sit down and snivel because I've been touched in Wall Street."

Wrayford got to his feet again. "Then, if you don't want me, I think I'll go up to my room and put some finishing touches to a brief before I turn in. I must get back to town to-morrow afternoon."

"All right, then." Stilling set down his empty glass, and held out his hand with a tinge of alacrity. "Good night, old man."

They shook hands, and Wrayford moved toward the door.

"I say, Austin, stop a minute!" his host called after him. Wrayford turned, and the two men faced each other across the hearth-rug. Stilling's eyes shifted uneasily.

"There's one thing more you can do for me before you leave. Tell Isabel about that loan; explain to her that she's got to sign a note for it."

Wrayford, in his turn, flushed slightly. "You want me to tell her?"

"Hang it! I'm soft-hearted, that's the worst of me."

Stilling moved toward the tray, and lifted the brandy decanter. "And she'll take it better from you; she'll have to take it from you. She's proud. You can take her out for a row to-morrow morning, look here, take her out in the motor-launch if you like. I meant to have a spin in it myself; but if you'll tell her—"

Wrayford hesitated. "All right, I'll tell her."

"Thanks a lot, my dear fellow. And you'll make her see it wasn't my fault, eh? Women are awfully vague about money, and she'll think it's all right if you back me up."

Wrayford nodded. "As you please."

"And, Austin—there's just one more thing. You needn't say anything to Isabel about the other business—I mean about my mother's securities."

"Ah?" said Wrayford, pausing.

Stilling shifted from one foot to the other. "I'd rather put that to the old lady myself. I can make it clear to her. She idolizes me, you know—and, hang it! I've got a good record. Up to now, I mean. My mother's been in clover since I married; I may say she's been my first thought. And I don't want her to hear of this beastly business from Isabel. Isabel's a little harsh at times—and of course this isn't going to make her any easier to live with."

"Very well," said Wrayford.

Stilling, with a look of relief, walked toward the window which opened on the terrace. "Gad! what a queer night! Hot as the kitchen-range. Shouldn't wonder if we had a squall before morning. I wonder if that infernal skipper took in the launch's awnings before he went home."

Wrayford stopped with his hand on the door. "Yes, I saw him do it. She's shipshape for the night."

"Good! That saves me a run down to the shore."

"Good night, then," said Wrayford.

"Good night, old man. You'll tell her?"

"I'll tell her."

"And mum about my mother!" his host called after him.

II

The darkness had thinned a little when Wrayford scrambled down the steep path to the shore. Though the air was heavy the threat of a storm seemed to have vanished, and now and then the moon's edge showed above a torn slope of cloud.

But in the thick shrubbery about the boat-house the darkness was still dense, and Wrayford had to strike a match before he could find the lock and insert his key. He left the door unlatched, and groped his way in. How often he had crept into this warm pine-scented obscurity, guiding himself by the edge of the bench along the wall, and hearing the soft lap of water through the gaps in the flooring! He knew just where one had to duck one's head to avoid the two canoes swung from the rafters, and just where to put his hand on the latch of the farther door that led to the broad balcony above the lake.

The boat-house represented one of Stilling's abandoned whims. He had built it some seven years before, and for a time it had been the scene of incessant nautical exploits. Stilling had rowed, sailed, paddled indefatigably, and all Highfield had been impressed to bear him company, and to admire his versatility. Then motors had come in, and he had forsaken aquatic sports for the flying chariot. The canoes of birch-bark and canvas had been hoisted to the roof, the sail-boat had rotted at her moorings, and the movable floor of the boat-house, ingeniously contrived to slide back on noiseless runners, had lain undisturbed through several seasons. Even the key of the boat-house had been mislaid—by Isabel's fault, her husband said—and the locksmith had to be called in to make a new one when the purchase of the motor-boat made the lake once more the centre of Stilling's activity.

As Wrayford entered he noticed that a strange oily odor overpowered the usual scent of dry pine-wood; and at the next step his foot struck an object that rolled noisily across the boards. He lighted another match, and found he had overturned a can of grease which the boatman had no doubt been using to oil the runners of the sliding floor.

Wrayford felt his way down the length of the boathouse, and softly opening the balcony door looked out on the lake. A few yards away, he saw the launch lying at anchor in the veiled moonlight; and just below him, on the black water, was the dim outline of the skiff which the boatman kept to paddle out to her. The silence was so intense that Wrayford fancied he heard a faint rustling in the shrubbery on the high bank behind the boat-house, and the crackle of gravel on the path descending to it.

He closed the door again and turned back into the darkness; and as he did so the other door, on the land-side, swung inward, and he saw a figure in the dim opening. Just enough light entered through the round holes above the respective doors to reveal Mrs. Stilling's cloaked outline, and to guide her to him as he advanced. But before they met she stumbled and gave a little cry.

"What is it?" he exclaimed.

"My foot caught; the floor seemed to give way under me. Ah, of course—" she bent down in the darkness—"I saw the men oiling it this morning."

Wrayford caught her by the arm. "Do take care! It might be dangerous if it slid too easily. The water's deep under here."

"Yes; the water's very deep. I sometimes wish—" She leaned against him without finishing her sentence, and he put both arms about her.

"Hush!" he said, his lips on hers.

Suddenly she threw her head back and seemed to listen.

"What's the matter? What do you hear?"

"I don't know." He felt her trembling. "I'm not sure this place is as safe as it used to be—"

Wrayford held her to him reassuringly. "But the boatman sleeps down at the village; and who else should come here at this hour?"

"Cobham might. He thinks of nothing but the launch.'"

"He won't to-night. I told him I'd seen the skipper put her shipshape, and that satisfied him."

"Ah, he did think of coming, then?"

"Only for a minute, when the sky looked so black half an hour ago, and he was afraid of a squall. It's clearing now, and there's no danger."

He drew her down on the bench, and they sat a moment or two in silence, her hands in his. Then she said: "You'd better tell me."

Wrayford gave a faint laugh. "Yes, I suppose I had. In fact, he asked me to."

"He asked you to?"

"Yes."

She uttered an exclamation of contempt. "He's afraid!"

Wrayford made no reply, and she went on: "I'm not. Tell me everything, please."

"Well, he's chucked away a pretty big sum again—"

"How?"

"He says he doesn't know. He's been speculating, I suppose. The madness of making him your trustee!"

She drew her hands away. "You know why I did it. When we married I didn't want to put him in the false position of the man who contributes nothing and accepts everything; I wanted people to think the money was partly his."

"I don't know what you've made people think; but you've been eminently successful in one respect. He thinks it's all his—and he loses it as if it were."

"There are worse things. What was it that he wished you to tell me?"

"That you've got to sign another promissory note, for fifty thousand this time."

"Is that all?"

Wrayford hesitated; then he said: "Yes, for the present."

She sat motionless, her head bent, her hand resting passively in his.

He leaned nearer. "What did you' mean just now, by worse things?"

She hesitated. "Haven't you noticed that he's been drinking a great deal lately?"

"Yes; I've noticed."

They were both silent; then Wrayford broke out, with sudden vehemence: "And yet you won't—"

"Won't?"

"Put an end to it. Good God! Save what's left of your life."

She made no answer, and in the stillness the throb of the water underneath them sounded like the beat of a tormented heart.

"Isabel—" Wrayford murmured. He bent over to kiss her. "Isabel! I can't stand it! listen—"

"No; no. I've thought of everything. There's the boy, the boy's fond of him. He's not a bad father."

"Except in the trifling matter of ruining his son."

"And there's his poor old mother. He's a good son, at any rate; he'd never hurt her. And I know her. If I left him, she'd never take a penny of my money. What she has of her own is not enough to live on; and how could he provide for her? If I put him out of doors, I should be putting his mother out too."

"You could arrange that, there are always ways."

"Not for her! She's proud. And then she believes in him. Lots of people believe in him, you know. It would kill her if she ever found out."

Wrayford made an impatient movement. "It will kill you if you stay with him to prevent her finding out."

She laid her other hand on his. "Not while I have you."

"Have me? In this way?"

"In any way."

"My poor girl, poor child!"

"Unless you grow tired, unless your patience gives out."

He was silent, and she went on insistently: "Don't you suppose I've thought of that too, foreseen it?"

"Well—and then?" he exclaimed.

"I've accepted that too."

He dropped her hands with a despairing gesture. "Then, indeed, I waste my breath!"

She made no answer, and for a time they sat silent again, a little between them. At length he asked: "You're not crying?"

"No."

"I can't see your face, it's grown so dark."

"Yes. The storm must be coming." She made a motion as if to rise.

He drew close and put his arm about her. "Don't leave me yet. You know I must go to-morrow." He broke off with a laugh. "I'm to break the news to you to-morrow morning, by the way; I'm to take you out in the motorlaunch and break it to you." He dropped her hands and stood up. "Good God! How can I go and leave you here with him?"

"You've done it often."

"Yes; but each time it's more damnable. And then I've always had a hope—"

She rose also. "Give it up! Give it up!"

"You've none, then, yourself?"

She was silent, drawing the folds of her cloak about her.

"None, none?" he insisted.

He had to bend his head to hear her answer. "Only one!"

"What, my dearest? What?"

"Don't touch me! That he may die!"

They drew apart again, hearing each other's quick breathing through the darkness.

"You wish that too?" he said.

"I wish it always, every day, every hour, every moment!" She paused, and then let the words break from her. "You'd better know it; you'd better know the worst of me. I'm not the saint you suppose; the duty I do is poisoned by the thoughts I think. Day by day, hour by hour, I wish him dead. When he goes out I pray for something to happen; when he comes back I say to myself: 'Are you here again?' When I hear of people being killed in accidents, I think: 'Why wasn't he there?' When I read the death-notices in the paper I say: 'So-and-so was just his age.' When I see him taking such care of his health and his diet, as he does, you know, except when he gets reckless and begins to drink too much, when I see him exercising and resting, and eating only certain things, and weighing himself, and feeling his muscles, and boasting that he hasn't gained a pound, I think of the men who die from overwork, or who throw their lives away for some great object, and I say to myself: 'What can kill a man who thinks only of himself?' And night after night I keep myself from going to sleep for fear I may dream that he's dead. When I dream that, and wake and find him there it's worse than ever—"

She broke off with a sob, and the loud lapping of the water under the floor was like the beat of a rebellious heart.

"There, you know the truth!" she said.

He answered after a pause: "People do die."

"Do they?" She laughed. "Yes, in happy marriages!"

They were silent again, and Isabel turned, feeling her way toward the door. As she did so, the profound stillness was broken by the sound of a man's voice trolling out unsteadily the refrain of a music-hall song.

The two in the boat-house darted toward each other with a simultaneous movement, clutching hands as they met.

"He's coming!" Isabel said.

Wrayford disengaged his hands.

"He may only be out for a turn before he goes to bed. Wait a minute. I'll see." He felt his way to the bench, scrambled up on it, and stretching his body forward managed to bring his eyes in line with the opening above the door.

"It's as black as pitch. I can't see anything."

The refrain rang out nearer.

"Wait! I saw something twinkle. There it is again. It's his cigar. It's coming this way, down the path."

There was a long rattle of thunder through the stillness.

"It's the storm!" Isabel whispered. "He's coming to see about the launch."

Wrayford dropped noiselessly from the bench and she caught him by the arm.

"Isn't there time to get up the path and slip under the shrubbery?"

"No, he's in the path now. He'll be here in two minutes. He'll find us."

He felt her hand tighten on his arm.

"You must go in the skiff, then. It's the only way."

"And let him find you? And hear my oars? Listen, there's something I must say."

She flung her arms about him and pressed her face to his.

"Isabel, just now I didn't tell you everything. He's ruined his mother, taken everything of hers too. And he's got to tell her; it can't be kept from her."

She uttered an incredulous exclamation and drew back.

"Is this the truth? Why didn't you tell me before?"

"He forbade me. You were not to know."

Close above them, in the shrubbery, Stilling warbled:

"Nita, Juanita,   Ask thy soul if we must part!"

Wrayford held her by both arms. "Understand this, if he comes in, he'll find us. And if there's a row you'll lose your boy."

She seemed not to hear him. "You—you—you—he'll kill you!" she exclaimed.

Wrayford laughed impatiently and released her, and she stood shrinking against the wall, her hands pressed to her breast. Wrayford straightened himself and she felt that he was listening intently.

Then he dropped to his knees and laid his hands against the boards of the sliding floor. It yielded at once, as if with a kind of evil alacrity; and at their feet they saw, under the motionless solid night, another darker night that moved and shimmered. Wrayford threw himself back against the opposite wall, behind the door.

A key rattled in the lock, and after a moment's fumbling the door swung open. Wrayford and Isabel saw a man's black bulk against the obscurity. It moved a step, lurched forward, and vanished out of sight. From the depths beneath them there came a splash and a long cry.

"Go! go!" Wrayford cried out, feeling blindly for Isabel in the blackness.

"Oh—" she cried, wrenching herself away from him.

He stood still a moment, as if dazed; then she saw him suddenly plunge from her side, and heard another splash far down, and a tumult in the beaten water.

In the darkness she cowered close to the opening, pressing her face over the edge, and crying out the name of each of the two men in turn. Suddenly she began to see: the obscurity was less opaque, as if a faint moon-pallor diluted it. Isabel vaguely discerned the two shapes struggling in the black pit below her; once she saw the gleam of a face. She glanced up desperately for some means of rescue, and caught sight of the oars ranged on brackets against the wall. She snatched down the nearest, bent over the opening, and pushed the oar down into the blackness, crying out her husband's name.

The clouds had swallowed the moon again, and she could see nothing below her; but she still heard the tumult in the beaten water.

"Cobham! Cobham!" she screamed.

As if in answer, she felt a mighty clutch on the oar, a clutch that strained her arms to the breaking-point as she tried to brace her knees against the runners of the sliding floor.

"Hold on! Hold on! Hold on!" a voice gasped out from below; and she held on, with racked muscles, with bleeding palms, with eyes straining from their sockets, and a heart that tugged at her as the weight was tugging at the oar.

Suddenly the weight relaxed, and the oar slipped up through her lacerated hands. She felt a wet body scrambling over the edge of the opening, and Stilling's voice, raucous and strange, groaned out, close to her: "God! I thought I was done for."

He staggered to his knees, coughing and sputtering, and the water dripped on her from his streaming clothes.

She flung herself down, again, straining over the pit. Not a sound came up from it.

"Austin! Austin! Quick! Another oar!" she shrieked.

Stilling gave a cry. "My God! Was it Austin? What in hell—Another oar? No, no; untie the skiff, I tell you. But it's no use. Nothing's any use. I felt him lose hold as I came up."

After that she was conscious of nothing till, hours later, as it appeared to her, she became dimly aware of her husband's voice, high, hysterical and important, haranguing a group of scared lantern-struck faces that had sprung up mysteriously about them in the night.

"Poor Austin! Poor Wrayford... terrible loss to me... mysterious dispensation. Yes, I do feel gratitude, miraculous escape, but I wish old Austin could have known that I was saved!"

Edith Wharton – A Short Biography

The extraordinary American writer Edith Wharton was born Edith Newbold Jones on January 24th, 1862 to George Frederic Jones and Lucretia Stevens Rhinelander at their brownstone at 14 West Twenty-third Street in New York City. Her parents already had two older sons, Frederic Rhinelander, and Henry Edward.

Edith was baptized April 20, 1862, Easter Sunday, at Grace Church. To her friends and family she was apparently known as "Pussy Jones".

The 1860's were a time of Civil War in America but by the time Edith was three the war was over and a more normal life among Americans could resume.

From 1866 to 1872, the Jones family visited France, Italy, Germany, and Spain and Edith became fluent in French, German, and Italian. She was taught by a succession of tutors and governesses. Her thirst for learning was apparent at even this early age. So too was a streak of rebelliousness as she pushed back at society's standards of fashion and etiquette that were thought to be needed to help these young women marry well and to be displayed at balls and parties. She thought this superficial and oppressive.

Although he mother forbade her to read novels until she married (Edith it seems complied with that instruction) she read from her father's library and that of friends.

Edith first step to becoming a writer was inventing stories when she was around six. She would walk around the living room holding a book and reciting her story.

In 1872 at age ten, Edith was taken ill with typhoid fever while the family was at a spa in the Black Forest. The family returned to the United States that same year to begin a cycle of winters in New York and their summers in Newport, Rhode Island.

The following year, 1873, Edith wrote a short story and gave it to her mother to read. It was heavily criticised and Edith retreated to writing only poetry. Despite a child's need for a mother's approval and love, it was rare that she received either. This core relationship was indeed a troubled one.

By the time Edith was 15 she had translated a German poem "Was die Steine Erzählen" ("What the Stones Tell") by Heinrich Karl Brugsch, for which she was paid $50.

However her family did not wish to see her name in print (upper class women of the time only appeared in print to announce birth, marriage, and death). Consequently, the poem was published under the name of a friend's father, E. A. Washburn, a cousin of Ralph Waldo Emerson and a supporter of women's education and a great encourager of Edith's talents.

That same year, 1877, Edith had also secretly written a 30,000 word novella "Fast and Loose". Her central themes came from her experiences with her parents. She was very critical of her own work and would even write public reviews criticizing it. The following year, 1878, her father arranged for a collection of two dozen original poems and five translations, Verses, to be privately published.

In 1880 she had five poems published anonymously in the Atlantic Monthly, a much revered literary magazine. Despite these early successes, she was not encouraged to publish by others but did continue to write.

Edith was courted by Henry Stevens from 1880 and after two years they became engaged. A month before their marriage the engagement abruptly ended.

In 1885, at age 23, she married Edward (Teddy) Robbins Wharton, who was 12 years her senior. He was from a well-established Boston family, a sportsman and a gentleman of the same social class and shared her love of travel.

However this desirable match was blighted. From the late 1880s until 1902, he suffered acute depression. At that latter time his depression manifested as a more serious disorder, after which they lived almost exclusively at their estate; The Mount.

In October 1889 her poem "The Last Giustiniani", was published in Scribner's Magazine.

At age 29 Edith finally had her first short story published. "Mrs. Manstey's View." It had very little success, and another year was to elapse until she published again.

She completed "The Fullness of Life" following her annual European trip with Teddy. Burlingame was critical of this story but Wharton did not want to make edits to it. This story, along with many others, speaks about her marriage. She sent Bunner Sisters to Scribner's in 1892. The editor in chief, Edward L Burlingame wrote back that it was too long for Scribner's to publish. This story is believed to be based on an experience she had as a child. It did not see publication until 1916.

After a visit with her friend, Paul Bourget, she wrote "The Good May Come" and "The Lamp of Psyche". "The Lamp of Psyche" was a comical story with verbal wit and sorrow. After "Something Exquisite" was rejected by Burlingame, she lost confidence in herself.

By 1894 she had decided to write about her travels. This allied with her other interests of garden and interior design came to a publishing point in 1897 with a co-authorship on The Decoration of Houses, the first of several design books.

Her thirst for travel and to explore eventually meant some sixty trips across the Atlantic to travel across Europe and even Morocco.

Her husband, Edward, shared this love of travel and for years they would spend four, or more, month abroad until his illness deteriorated their quality of life such that they remained in America.

In 1888, the Wharton's and their friend, James Van Alen, took a cruise through the Aegean islands. Wharton was 26. The trip cost a substantial amount: $10,000 and lasted four months. Edith kept a travel journal during this trip that was later published as The Cruise of the Vanadis, her earliest known travel writing.

In 1901, Wharton wrote a two act play called "Man of Genius". This play was about an English man who was having an affair with his secretary. The play was rehearsed, but was never produced. One of her earliest literary endeavors (1902) was the translation of the play, "Es Lebe das Leben" ("The Joy of Living"), by Hermann Sudermann. "The Joy of Living" was a short lived Broadway production but was, however, a successful book.

She collaborated with Marie Tempest to write another play, but the two only completed four acts before Marie decided she was no longer interested in costume plays.

In 1902, she designed The Mount, her estate in Lenox, Massachusetts. Edith wrote several of her novels there, including The House of Mirth (1905), the first of many chronicles of life in old New York. At The Mount, she entertained the cream of American literary society, including her close friend, novelist Henry James, who described the estate as "a delicate French chateau mirrored in a Massachusetts pond".

Although she spent many months traveling The Mount was her primary residence until 1911.

With her marriage falling apart, due mainly to Edward's illness, she decided to move to Paris, living first at 53 Rue de Varenne, Paris, in an apartment that belonged to George Washington Vanderbilt II.

In 1908 her husband's mental state was determined to be incurable. In the same year, she began an affair with Morton Fullerton, a journalist for The Times, in whom she also found an intellectual partner.

She divorced Edward Wharton in 1913 after 28 years of marriage.

In 1914 Edith was preparing for her summer vacation when World War I broke out. Many fled Paris, but she moved back to her Paris apartment on the Rue de Varenne and for the next four years was a tireless, ardent supporter of the French war effort.

In August 1914 at the onset of War she opened a workroom for unemployed women; here they were fed and paid one franc a day. Thirty women started and this soon doubled to sixty, and their sewing business began to thrive. When the Germans invaded Belgium in the fall of 1914 and Paris was flooded with Belgian refugees, she helped to set up the American Hostels for Refugees, which gave shelter, meals, clothes and then an agency to help them find work. She raised and collected more than $100,000 on their behalf.

In early 1915 she organized the Children of Flanders Rescue Committee, which gave shelter to almost 900 Belgian refugees whose homes had been bombed by the Germans.

Aided by her influential connections in the French government, she and her long-time friend Walter Berry (then president of the American Chamber of Commerce in Paris), were among the few foreigners in France allowed to travel to the front lines. She and Berry made a total of five journeys between February and August 1915, which Edith described in a series of articles that were first published in Scribner's Magazine and later as Fighting France: From Dunkerque to Belfort, which became a bestseller. Travelling by car, they drove through the war zone; one decimated French village after another. She visited the trenches that were within earshot of artillery fire. She wrote, "We woke to a noise of guns closer and more incessant...and when we went out into the streets it seemed as if, overnight, a new army had sprung out of the ground".

During the war years Edith worked tirelessly in charitable efforts for refugees, the injured, the unemployed, and the displaced.

On 18 April 1916, the President of France appointed her Chevalier of the Legion of Honour, the country's highest award, in recognition of her dedication to the war effort.

Edith also kept up her own work during the war, which was now a prodigious output of novels, short stories, and poems, as well as reporting for the New York Times and keeping up her enormous correspondence. She urged Americans to support the war effort and to enter the war with its enormous resources of industry and men. She wrote the popular romantic novel Summer in 1916, the war novella, The Marne, in 1918, and A Son at the Front in 1919, (though not published until 1923).

When the war ended, she watched the Victory Parade from the Champs Elysees' balcony of a friend's apartment. After four years of intense effort, she decided to leave Paris in favor of the peace and quiet of the countryside. She settled a few miles north of Paris in Saint-Brice-sous-Forêt, buying an eighteenth-century house on seven acres of land which she called Pavillon Colombe. Edith would live there in summer and autumn for the rest of her life. She spent winters and springs on the French Riviera at Sainte Claire du Vieux Chateau in Hyeres.

Edith was a committed supporter of French imperialism, describing herself as a "rabid imperialist", and the war solidified her political views. After the war she travelled to Morocco as the guest of Resident General Hubert Lyautey and wrote a book, In Morocco, about her experiences. Wharton's writing on her Moroccan travels is full of praise for the French administration and for Lyautey and his wife in particular.

During the post war years she divided her time between Hyères and Provence, where she finished The Age of Innocence in 1920, which won the 1921 Pulitzer Prize for literature, making Edith the first woman to win the award.

Edith returned to the United States only once after the war, receiving an honorary doctorate degree from Yale University in 1923.

Edith included in her intellectual circle many of the great artists of her day; Henry James, Sinclair Lewis and Jean Cocteau were among her guests at the time. Theodore Roosevelt and Kenneth Clark were also friends. Of particular note was her meeting with F. Scott Fitzgerald, described as "one of the better known failed encounters in the American literary annals".

In 1934 Edith's autobiography A Backward Glance was published. This glossed over much of the problems in her life barely registering the criticism of her mother, her difficulties with Teddy, and her affair with Morton Fullerton.

On June 1, 1937 Wharton was at the French country home of Ogden Codman, working on a revised edition of The Decoration of Houses, when she suffered a heart attack and collapsed.

Edith Wharton died of a stroke some months later on August 11, 1937 at Le Pavillon Colombe, her 18th-century house on Rue de Montmorency in Saint-Brice-sous-Forêt at 5:30 pm. At her bedside was her friend, Mrs. Royal Tyler. The street is today called rue Edith Wharton.

Edith was buried at the Cimetière des Gonards in Versailles, "with all the honors owed a war hero and a chevalier of the Legion of Honor....a group of a hundred friends sang a verse of the hymn "O Paradise"...." She is buried next to her long-time friend, Walter Berry.

Edith Wharton – A Concise Bibliography

BOOKS
The Touchstone, 1900 (novella)
The Valley of Decision, 1902
Sanctuary, 1903 (novella)
The House of Mirth, 1905
Madame de Treymes, 1907 (novella)
The Fruit of the Tree, 1907
Ethan Frome, 1911 (novella)
The Reef, 1912
The Custom of the Country, 1913
Bunner Sisters, 1916 (novella)
Summer, 1917
The Marne, 1918
The Age of Innocence, 1920 (Pulitzer Prize winner)
The Glimpses of the Moon, 1922
A Son at the Front, 1923
Old New York: False Dawn, The Old Maid, The Spark, New Year's Day, 1924 (novellas)
The Mother's Recompense, 1925
Twilight Sleep, 1927
The Children, 1928
Hudson River Bracketed, 1929
The Gods Arrive, 1932
The Buccaneers, 1938 (unfinished)
Fast and Loose: A Novelette, 1938 (written in 1876–1877)

POETRY
Verses, 1878
Artemis to Actaeon & Other Verse, 1909
Twelve Poems, 1926

SHORT STORY COLLECTIONS
The Greater Inclination, 1899
Souls Belated, 1899
Crucial Instances, 1901
The Descent of Man & Other Stories, 1903
The Hermit and the Wild Woman & Other Stories, 1908
Tales of Men & Ghosts, 1910
Xingu & Other Stories, 1916
Old New York, 1924
Here and Beyond, 1926
Certain People, 1930
Human Nature, 1933
The World Over, 1936

Ghosts, 1937

NON-FICTION

The Decoration of Houses, 1897
Italian Villas and Their Gardens, 1904
Italian Backgrounds, 1905
A Motor-Flight Through France, 1908
Fighting France, from Dunkerque to Belfort, 1915
French Ways and Their Meaning, 1919
In Morocco, 1920
The Writing of Fiction, 1925
A Backward Glance, 1934

AS EDITOR

The Book of the Homeless, 1916

CINEMA

The House of Mirth (La Maison du Brouillard), a 1918 silent film adaptation (6 reels).
The Glimpses Of The Moon, a 1923 silent film adaptation (7 reels)
The Age of Innocence, a 1924 silent film adaptation (7 reels) (of the 1920 novel)
The Marriage Playground, a 1929 film adaptation (70 minutes) (of the 1928 novel The Children)
The Age of Innocence, a 1934 film adaptation (9 reels).
Strange Wives, a 1935 film adaptation (8 reels) (of the 1934 short story Bread Upon the Waters)
The Old Maid, a 1939 film adaptation (95 minutes) (of the 1924 short novella)
Ethan Frome (99 minutes) directed by John Madden. 1993,
The Age of Innocence (138 minutes) directed by Martin Scorsese. 1993,
The Reef (88 minutes) directed by Robert Allan Ackerman. 1999.
The House of Mirth (140 minutes) directed by Terence Davies. 2000.

TV

Ethan Frome, a 1960 (CBS) TV US adaptation.
Looking Back, a 1981 TV US adaptation of two biographies of Edith Wharton.
The House of Mirth, a 1981 TV US adaptation.
The Buccaneers, a 1995 BBC mini-series, starring Carla Gugino and Greg Wise.

THEATRE

The Man of Genius in 1901
"Es Lebe das Leben" ("The Joy of Living"), by Hermann Sudermann in 1902 - Translator.
The House of Mirth was adapted as a play in 1906.
The Age of Innocence was adapted as a play in 1928.

www.ingramcontent.com/pod-product-compliance
Lightning Source LLC
Chambersburg PA
CBHW071358170626
46811CB00003B/1171